D1521896

AFSANEH

Afsaneh
A Novel from Iran

BY
Moniru Ravanipur

TRANSLATED FROM PERSIAN
BY
Rebecca Joubin

Ibex Publishers,
Bethesda, Maryland

Afsaneh, A Novel from Iran by Moniru Ravanipur

Translated and Introduced by Rebecca Joubin
Translation Copyright © 2014 Rebecca Joubin

Cover illustration by Saloumeh Kordestani
Courtesy of Shahla and Behrouz Kordestani

Photographs courtesy of Moniru Ravanipur. Four photographs in afterword: in high school, at the tomb of Hafez with friend, passport photo, and in California.

Ibex Publishers strives to create books which are as complete and free of errors as possible. Please help us with future editions by reporting any errors or suggestions for improvement to the address below, or corrections@ibexpub.com

Ibex Publishers, Inc.
Post Office Box 30087
Bethesda, Maryland 20824
Telephone: 301–718–8188
Facsimile: 301–907–8707
www.ibexpublishers.com

Library of Congress Cataloging-in-Publication Data

Ravanipur, Muniru.
[Dil-i fulad. English]
Afsaneh : a novel from Iran / by Moniru Ravanipur ; translated from the Persian by Rebecca Joubin.
pages   cm
ISBN 978-1-58814-095-1
I. Joubin, Rebecca translator. II. Title.
PK6561.R296D5513 2014
891'.5533—dc23   2013038544

— Contents —

— 1 —

She fled along the rooftops, covering her ears. The wind grasped her in a violent embrace, carrying with it the screams of a man in pursuit of his eyes. She yearned to reach a beam of light and slide down into a small Shiraz garden alley to escape the rooftops and the night. The resonance of Father's shouts seared her nerves, "*Khajeh Tabbal ... Khajeh Tabbal.*"

In the howling wind, she saw a face crumpling in pain. The night reflected eyes staring into darkness. She groped the rooftops and railings with her hands, trying desperately to prevent herself from falling into the small cobblestone streets of the city, Shiraz, the month of *Azar*, 1977. The scent of *narenj* blossoms permeated the darkness, floating alongside the shrieks. Bitter orange trees—hunched and shrinking, leaves withered and dark-lined the alleyways. Her eyes burned. She licked her lips, parched and salty, for the bitter orange tree had dried up.

The sound of Father was like fine sand hitting her face. She heard the cries of the man searching for his eyes, "*Khajeh Tabbal ... Khajeh Tabbal.*" She saw those two empty eye sockets—vacant and cold—but not wounded. Perhaps it was his power of deception.

The wind played with her thin, orange nightgown. She fled. Perhaps she fled toward the voice of Father. Perhaps. The city slumbered. The city of Shiraz in the month of *Azar* of 1977.

— 2 —

As she left the publishing house, she noticed the Dictator and the Horseman standing there, seemingly out of place. She forced a smile, despite her exhaustion. Pulling down her headscarf, she held the publication proofs in her hands for them to see. When they smiled back, she breathed a sigh of relief. She set out in the direction of Enghilab Street, staring at all the cars stuck in traffic. As far as her eyes could see, young men were leaving for war in buses.

She stopped on the sidewalk. The distance between being and not being was the knowledge that no matter what she said, even if she screamed, no one would hear her. She would have given anything to be unseen. She stood still, careful not to even blink an eye. If she blinked, this street would no longer exist. There would be only the ground, barren and scorched, scattered with half-burned tanks and torn bodies throughout the South and the West.

What was the distance between being and non-being? Who existed, who did not? She did not blink an eyelid. With one misstep, these young hands would be dragged into the frame of another picture; these eager hands would be separated from his body.

"*Salavat*."

An adolescent boy with a red band on his forehead thrust his arm out of a bus window.

"We're on our way to Karbala."

"No talking allowed," said the Horseman.

The Dictator frowned as usual and pointed his finger at the boy, who paid no attention.

Beneath the red band was a moonlit face and black hair. A few steps closer and she could reach out her arm and clutch his hand. If only he had put his arm out further, if only she had taken a few steps closer, she could have grabbed his hand. But the young man did not move. His hair was not long, and his eyes were tiny and bewildered. He seemed about twenty years old, tall with broad shoulders. If he sat on a horse with a red mane, the horse would neigh three times in the direction of the sun.

She looked up again but could no longer see him. Sitting on the bus, he frowned and did not know where to turn his eyes. What did this woman, with her puzzled face and wrinkled forehead, want from him? What was she searching for?

Lifting his fist and pointing in her direction, he screamed, "*Marg Bar Bad Hejab … Death to the improperly veiled woman!*" The young men in all of the other buses yelled in unison, "*Marg Bar Bad Hejab,*" attempting to divert all attention to the woman on the street. The caravan set out again. She remained motionless. The Horseman was leaving and the Dictator started to laugh.

The Horseman and the bus were no longer in sight … No—there was no resemblance, no resemblance …

᠅ ᠅ ᠅ ᠅

Four months ago, she saw the picture on Manouchehri Street at a peddler's stand—big black eyes with a curious look in them, long hair that hung loose upon his shoulders, and a *kashkool* in his hands. What were his eyes observing?

"How much is this picture?" she had asked the peddler.

"*In Khedmat-e Shoma Begiram*—I'm at your service. This is a picture of a *Dervish,*" he had replied.

"I know, sir. But how much is it?"

It did not really matter to her who it was. A picture can be interpreted myriad ways by each person. To her, it was a picture of the Hero of the Zand Dynasty. She did not care what the peddler said about the picture, or how her old landlady would gape when she saw it.

᠅ ᠅ ᠅ ᠅

She smiled and set out in the direction of the bookstore. The booksellers on Enghilab Square sold any book that one could ever want. As she ambled, her heart lifted—but suddenly froze in recognition of a sound from the past. The smile drained from her lips. The sound of Father pierced the air again. It originated from a very different time when people had poured into the streets.

His eyes were blinded even while his own servants surrounded him …

Sour and biting memories overwhelmed her. He was searching for two big, blinded black eyes. Two eyes, real …

᠅ ᠅ ᠅ ᠅

Still adrift in the past, she entered the bookstore to evade the cries of that man that once hunted for her on the rooftops. Was he still pursuing his eyes? She turned her head quickly and saw the image of her father, playing chess with that man under the bitter orange tree, and his words haunted her still: "Who can write in the presence of eternal fear?"

The truth always loses itself among memories. The truth can be lost as though it never existed. Not on the ground or anywhere else. The difference between a historical event and an insignificant happening in the life of an individual is that the historical event has witnesses who can differentiate the truth from the fiction. Those witnesses crouch fearfully in a corner, peering at their surroundings. Then slowly, across every age, they observe:

Khan Qajar would burst into laughter when the eyes of ...

And what was the Hero of Zand doing? What had occupied his time through all those ages, trapped in the photograph, lost in the distance between being and non-being?

❄ ❄ ❄ ❄

With chains shackling his hands and feet, he refused to bow down. No one could hear his cries of pain, but the sound of his wounds filled his own ears. Sweat covering his forehead, he squeezed his lips tightly together.

❄ ❄ ❄ ❄

"What do you want, *Khanom?*" asked a salesman, bringing her back to the present.

"A book about Lotf-Ali Khan Zand."

The salesman gaped at the woman, who seemed to be out of touch with reality.

"It's called *The History of the Zand Dynasty*—a story about the life of the Hero of Zand."

The man found the book among the shelves and looked questioningly at the woman again.

"No! Don't wrap it up," she said, "I'd like to read it now."

She held the book about the Zands. Fear suddenly overcame her as she turned the pages. What if they had drawn a picture of him, or ...? She became aware of the Horseman standing at the doorstep. He pointed at her.

"In those days, who could take a picture?"

"A painting, then?" she asked.

"It was forbidden."

She felt relieved. She stopped looking at the Horseman and continued to turn the pages. But the Dictator was in front of her, at the salesman's side, giving orders.

"Go home now. Go home."

She fled the bookstore and headed to Farvardin Street. Fragile leaves slowly severed from their branches. Fall was on its way, the fall of 1986.

— 3 —

The old lady gently opened the door. She placed a plate with *loobiya pollo* on the desk and gestured toward it.

"Meat is expensive."

The young woman pulled the plate closer and put out her cigarette.

"So what?"

"For you, nothing ever matters. All you want to do is puff on your cigarette."

Then the old lady smiled. It was clear that she had something to say and until she did, she would not budge. Her domain was a tiny room of an apartment in a ten story building situated at the corner of Khaghani alley, which ran down to Pastor Street. The apartment itself, two rooms joined by a small foyer, was no bigger than sixty square meters. Her room was a tight, dark space with no windows for the blue sky to penetrate. Her wooden bed and numerous books made it seem even smaller.

"You can eat a piece of candy, pay me some money, and have meat in your meals. The good life. So why smoke?"

The old lady speaking was sixty-five years old. She had a white, round face framed by golden hair that she colored regularly, with small, light colored eyes that perpetually sparkled. Her appearance had brought the tenant to the conclusion that even dolls could grow old. She was just like a doll, and she still hung a picture of Bani Sadr on her wall.

"You know he's a fugitive. Aren't you afraid?" the woman asked.

"No, it's just a picture, not a person," the old lady replied.

※ ※ ※ ※

At eight-thirty every evening when the news bell sounded, the old lady would force the woman to leave her room and sit in front of the television. The old lady would groan, "This *Hajj Agha* isn't so bad. Anyway, I was ready …"

Next, she would stand to pray. The woman could hear the sound of her mumbling. Always, when the old doll finished praying, she would open the door and complain, "You know, a widow is so preoccupied with raising her children that when she suddenly stands before the mirror, she's taken aback. She realizes that she needs to buy some hair color and confront something that has lurched into her home through some unknown door. Then the day comes when she understands that the very picture she has hung on her wall won't ever come alive and rescue her. It'll just continue staring at her until she grows older and withers away."

She would let out a sigh and continue, "Last night I wasn't able to fall asleep. These curtains are useless, the way they let so much light pass through."

Finally, the old lady would say what was really on her mind. She would stand with that same white prayer *chador* at the entrance to the woman's room, "Hey, *Koofti*—you little shit—the electricity bill has come. The way you stay up all night, it's four times what it should be."

The old lady would smile with her small doll eyes and close the door.

※ ※ ※ ※

No one said a word, not a single word. They stood quietly. Perhaps for just one careless moment they would shut their eyes. Then another picture, in another frame, would appear—all because of a quick blinking and shutting of the eyelids. No. They must not close. *With all your might, you must force yourself to see. Open your eyes as wide as possible and stare at the incident. Do not shut your eyes until you can remember everything. Those screams …*

※ ※ ※ ※

The woman stopped eating her *loobiya pollo* and sheltered her face with her hands. Her temples throbbed. She gently placed her hands over the eyes of the *Dervish* in the frame. Velvet, black velvet. The sound of tearing velvet echoed in her ears. She got frightened and stood up. There was no window, no opening in the room. She sat at the edge of the bed and closed her eyes. The world's velvet was tearing, and someone, with chains binding his hands and feet, screamed.

He fell at the feet of Khan Qajar, and Khan Bozorg said that two of his servants … him.

Her eyes burned. The walls crumbled from the screams of Khan Qajar. She had to move to another house. The sound of tapping letters from her own typewriter would not leave her alone. Whenever the keys pounded on the paper, she could no longer hear the sound of the wails.

※ ※ ※ ※

If you write, the screams shall end. But what about the noise of the typewriter and the neighbors, the footsteps coming and going until sunrise, the children who stayed up all night long? How could she work, with no window, no sky, and all this noise—the sound of the neighbors' snoring, the sound of men and women breathing? Soon the children would climb up all the windows and walls of the building like snails and turtles.

She stood up and lit a cigarette. Hatred toward everything filled her—the snails and turtles, the screeching laments of women and men who, without reason, attached a *dakhil* to the enshrined corpse of an *imam* and would not loosen their grip until he had bestowed a blessing upon them.

She longed for a place to walk and smoke her cigarettes in peace. She glanced around in confusion at the gray walls of the room, the books, and the low ceiling. Suddenly, she heard the familiar gunshots in the distance. She had first heard the sounds seven years earlier. Perhaps someone was running. Perhaps someone was forcing her to lift her hand in surrender. Perhaps another hand was searching her. Seven years ago, she heard people screaming as the fury of the gunshots rose.

᠀ ᠀ ᠀ ᠀

She opened *The History of the Zand Dynasty* and scanned the pages:
Mirza Mehdi Khan Esterobadi, secretary and advisor to Nader Shah ... The history of Nader's world conquests ... The revival of the name of Shahrokh's grandfather would have given a new splendor to Shahrokh's own crown and throne ... Under Shahrokh's command! On whose payroll? She heard gunshots in the air, saw hands lifted in surrender, and felt yet more hands investigating her body. *"Stop—otherwise I'll shoot!"* How was it possible to see so many people screaming amidst the gunshots? To see, hear, and feel so many things at once?

᠀ ᠀ ᠀ ᠀

She turned the pages:
Without strength or power, the hand of the rider stopped working, the legs of his horse stopped moving ... His eyes were deprived of sight ... On the way, a group of infantry riflemen died because of the intense cold and severity of the snowfall, and lack of organization. Amid one thousand wounds and hardships, they arrived in Shiraz during the month of Jamadi al-aval ...

She hesitated. Put it down. Close the book. You might suddenly hear something you must not; you might see something you must not. But the Dictator perched on the bed and ordered her, "Read."

She held her hands up in surrender, as she did when the guns used to shoot in the still of the night. As she surrendered to the Dictator, satisfaction spread across his lips.

She leafed through the pages:

The entrance of Lotf-Ali Khan and a large crowd on the outskirts of the city caused fear and terror in Haji Ibrahim. Therefore, he announced that if they stopped helping Lotf-Ali Khan enter Shiraz, they would be safe and receive immense favors. Otherwise, it would be the cause of his displeasure and lead to the destruction of their family and relatives. Since the homes and families of most of those men were in Shiraz, they no longer cared whether they appeared cowardly in the eyes of others. On the third day of the said month, all of them deserted Lotf-Ali Khan. And so, aside from a dozen of the emissaries and the grooms and lightly armed horsemen who had no houses or relatives in Shiraz, no one was left by Lotf-Ali Khan's side.

She gazed at the picture of the man who stood all alone with a kashkool in his hands. Where had he gone?

Amidst thousands of hardships, Lotf-Ali Khan finally brought himself to the entrance of the city of Bandar Abu Shahr. However, Sheikh Nasser Khan blocked the paths of agreement and instead opened the doors of opposition and disobedience. Sheikh Nasser Khan treated Lotf-Ali Khan differently than he had before. Since Lotf-Ali Khan was not allowed to enter Bandar Abu Shahr, he went to Bandar Reeg and sought help from Amir Ali Khan, the governor. Then Amir Ali Khan obediently admitted Lotf-Ali Khan to Bandar Reeg and was determined to serve him.

Once more, he sat on the red maned horse. What would he do? What could be done, if anything? She wanted to leaf through the pages, but her hands trembled. She thought, God forbid he be like other conquerors. But how could you assume that all conquerors behave the same way? How do you know that they do not have other ways and manners? Hesitation warred with desire to hold onto the memory. Finally, she bent over the book again, her tired eyes picking out the ancient words:

Lotf-Ali Khan entered Kazaroon and spent a few days taking care of business there. Because of the way they treated him when he was on the run and as he entered the suburb of Kazaroon, Lotf-Ali Khan punished Reza Gholi Khan Kazarooni, Ali Naghi Khan Valid, and Mir Abd al-Ghofar. For these men had snatched away a few of the special horses in his vanguard. And so Lotf-Ali Khan first blinded these men and then bound them in chains.

Frightened, she closed the book. Stretching her arms over her head, she pulled her black *mantow* onto her shoulders because she was cold. What color were their eyes? Black? Hazel? The color of fire? Blinding has always been the preferred form of torture. Then no one sees anything anymore, and the pictures in one picture frame can easily be switched to another. Sometimes you have to remove them from the sockets. Sometimes you have to tear them out of their heads. There were so many mutilated eyes that Dr. Mehrsayi, all alone in the hospital hallway, would scream, "*Khodaya*—Oh, my God, they must all be blinded!"

Sometimes you are forced to blind people. No one has ever gone to a rooftop and yelled out: "*Khajeh Tabbal … Khajeh Tabbal*" without being particularly compelled.

❀ ❀ ❀ ❀

"That's enough now. Let go, let go."

It was the Dictator, who was ordering her to relax.

"Will you become a captive this quickly? A captive of what you're reading? It's all a lie, a lie."

He was right. Why wouldn't the narrator of *The History of the Zand Dynasty* tell a lie? How do you know they did not bribe him—with all those compliments he made to Khan Qajar? She glanced at the picture. The Hero of Zand looked as if he never needed to sleep. Clean and kind, with a *kashkool* in his hand, he just stared through the velvet of his eyes.

No. He could not deprive any man of his eyesight. He could not. It was common knowledge that people trampled his reputation with rumors that they created and circulated among themselves. They fabricated the damning stories of their own accord, or because they were forced. Perhaps the narrator of The *History of the Zand Dynasty* himself suffered from some loss or some disastrous turn of events. Or perhaps the narrator heard the howls of the Hero of Zand when the group of men attacked him. Perhaps he observed Khan Qajar's court firsthand and witnessed how, with a hot rod, they burned the eyes of the Hero. Perhaps he now wished to relieve himself of guilt by concocting fibs to eliminate such strange and sorrowful memories.

"History is all a lie—a worthless lie. It has no power. None."

She stared at the Dictator, who existed for the very purpose of giving orders. He did not even mind the title of dictator. Indeed the word resounded in his head. She saw that he was laughing. He was pulling at the collar of his shirt. The stars on his shoulders jumped up and he patted them down.

He had bestowed these stars upon himself. As he grew older and taller, he gave himself more and more stars. Now he carried so many stars on his shoulders and grew so tall that his head reached the ceiling of life. He knew that history was useless. He read all of Father's history books. Father would subtly glance at him while playing chess with the man who found his eyes. The Dictator realized that moments were as ephemeral as the wind and that with the passage of just one event, the damned were no longer around or had lost their power. He realized that condemnation was meaningless—just a ridiculous game. It was like a yarn that, once woven, sealed up the earth and time. It made a mountain out of hay, and hay out of a mountain. She heard the faraway voice of Father passing through the mountains and the walls of her room.

"The Hero of Zand didn't wish to die. Somehow, they tortured him in such a way that he remained alive—but not without pain. Did you know that they even humiliated him in the presence of his two servants in front of their very eyes?"

※ ※ ※ ※

History is always ugly. Monstrously ugly ... "*I'm at your service. This is a picture of a Dervish ...*" But she did not want to hear anything. She did not want to read about what was or was not. Father had said, "It makes no difference what's going on in their heads. They're strange men. Like the Hero of Zand."

He passed through history, through the hallway of past generations. The offspring of each generation, forming in their mothers' wombs, must learn something from their predecessors. Thousands of exhausted eyes stared at him and thousands of ears still awaited the truth about his story.

※ ※ ※ ※

It was late at night. Who could say where the singing rooster in the big city came from, or how its voice managed to pass through the walls of the room? The rooster sang three times. The woman smiled with exhaustion, "Who is denying something, someplace?"

"Everyone denies everything, everywhere," replied the Dictator.

She got up. If the rooster sang one more time, the old lady would wake up. She would come to the door, throw a tired glance at the picture and murmur, "It'll be morning soon—won't you sleep?"

With reservation, she turned out the light. The Dictator remained in the dark. She could hear the reverberation of his breathing. He breathed as he had on that very day when he came out from under the bitter orange tree and said, "This is the first rule: never say you're a widow."

She acquiesced. Now it was night. She shivered. In the dark, she held out her arms.

"Come sleep with me. Come."

He came and laid beside her. The woman hid herself in his embrace and shuddered. She saw the *Dervish*, chains shackling his hands and feet. Then the laughter of Khan Qajar rose to the heavens, cracking the sky wide open.

— 4 —

In the evenings when she felt cold, she would hunch inside the Dictator's arms. She rose to his voice at six o'clock every morning. Longing to see the sky, she would leave the house and stroll through Pastor Square, down narrow streets, and into Enghilab Square.

At seven o'clock, she would reach the publishing house. It had been one year since Mr. Mohajerani, the director of the company, gave her the keys so that she could come to the office whenever she wished, even on Fridays.

Inside her office there was a large wall map of Iran. Five years ago, when she was first hired, the Dictator stood there before her and pointed at the map. He announced, "One day all the people of this strange country will read your books."

"But I want to write for children."

"It's stupid to write for children who climb up and down walls like sickly snails and ridiculous turtles."

❦ ❦ ❦ ❦

She cracked a smile. The weather was cold, so she could not open the window.

"Take care of yourself. The weather is unpredictable, and if you fall ill, your work and that of the company will come to a halt."

He was stubborn and stood firm, just as he had nine years earlier. He had emerged from under the bitter orange tree visible through a half-closed door. If someone opened the door, he would see a large tree with bitter orange globes hanging from its branches. It would be as if the bitter orange tree were forever glowing in the frame of that half-open door. All trees could be dried up with just one blink of the eye. A living picture exchanged with a dead picture, in another picture frame. *You only had to blink once. You poured a jar of salt water at the foot at the bitter orange tree and blinked. When you opened your eyes, you would find the bitter oranges withered and hollow, hanging from dried branches.*

The Dictator said, "Let go. It has been nine years."

You are right, you are right. Indeed all the bitter orange trees in the world are parched. I do not have anything else to do. How this room is filled with light! If only I could find a home where the sky is visible; a place with windows. Calm and still, so that in the evenings I can concentrate on the story about the alien Horseman. If only that were possible.

She glanced at the cover of the novel *On the Peak of the Whirlwind*, posted on the right side of the wall. Her lips slowly formed a grin. Her first work was serious and long, compared to children's books. Mr. Mohajerani used to ask, "Why don't you write children's stories? Both the writing and the publication are rather easy."

But the one who came out from under the bitter orange tree told her, "None of them are lasting and fundamental. None of them. Now you have the chance to write something meaningful from sunrise to sunset."

He refused to listen to Mr. Mohajerani.

❦ ❦ ❦ ❦

She placed her purse on the table and leaned back in the chair. How quickly time passed by—like the speed of wind or a flash of lightning. You always think that you are prepared, that you completed all of your work and are ready to ascend the bus. The bus moves toward you, finally arriving at the station. Then you blink, and the bus has departed. The bus departs every time, leaving you behind. You have always been left behind. A woman who, because of a bitter orange tree in the frame of a half-opened door, has placed her life, or at least a part of her life, under the wheels of a bus or a train, and suddenly realizes she has nothing. Only empty hands, maddening thoughts, and a dried-up bitter orange tree. The bus has departed and the train has moved on.

❦ ❦ ❦ ❦

She had to work. Not even Father was pleased with her children's stories—Father, who knew nothing of the bitter orange tree. Father, who despite his passion for history, was perplexed by the life of the man who had lost his homeland and now wandered in some faraway place. Bewildered, the exile was spinning around in circles. But what if he could not find his way?

❦ ❦ ❦ ❦

She shivered. She imagined that she was elderly-hair all white with cane in hand—she would ring their doorbell in Shiraz—the doorbell of the little four—walled house where four lucky pregnant virgins lived. The door would swing open and one of the pregnant virgins would greet her, "*Khodat Bedeh Madar*—may God grant you your needs, my dear ..."

The woman, visiting, would shut the door and then hear the voice of Father, who would patter on and on about history and an age when beggars were abundant.

❧ ❧ ❧ ❧

Someone was banging on the door. Frightened, she lifted her head and quickly composed herself. It was her secretary, a permanent smirk plastered on her face.

"What time is it anyway?" the woman asked herself as she secretly peeked at her watch. Ten o'clock.

"Good morning, Ms. Sar-Boland. Here are the printing proofs …"

The woman behind the desk was well-organized and disciplined. If Father were there to observe, she would have been able to converse with him without uttering a sound. But speech without sound was not possible. The sounds of screams and gunshots were everywhere, and Father was not here in this big city. The Dictator's face turned rosy, and the secretary announced, "In ten more days your book will be distributed. How wonderful, Ms. Sar-Boland!"

Ms. Sar-Boland knew that the girl loved to ramble on for hours. Sometimes when she put tea on the table she would stand there, hesitating, thinking of something to say. Ms. Sar-Boland never replied. Why should she talk about that lost night? Those who had searched for it alongside her, hoping to bring it back from the realm of the lost, no longer recognized her. Neither these pregnant weaving girls nor this old father wearing glasses, who had lost himself among the history books, recognized her.

❧ ❧ ❧ ❧

"Let go. You've gone back enough to that cursed tree and those girls."

She let go. In ten more days she would officially become a writer. She would send ten copies of her book to Shiraz so that Father could find a trace of that lost night. What if she were to write about the Hero of Zand, the alien Horseman who Father loved? But how could she write in that tight, dark room, in the presence of that old lady? She had to find a quiet home with windows facing the sun.

She rang the bell on the desk and the girl appeared in the crack of the door, like a bitter orange tree in a half-lit frame.

"Here's the newspaper, Ms. Sar-Boland."

The woman bent over the classified ads. She drew a line under several numbers and jotted them on a separate piece of paper. She lifted the telephone and paused, an image of the doll-like old lady appearing before her, her old doll eyes filling with tears. "Don't smoke. Have some candy instead."

The woman lit a cigarette. She remembered a time when the old lady cleared a way for the ants so that they could easily come and go in the kitchen.

"Poor creatures, please don't crush them," the old lady begged.

Kindness and affection, even coming from an old doll, could catch a person off guard. That old lady and her sarcastic words. Ms. Sar-Boland wished to be the owner of her own home, but the old lady had been so kind to her.

"Let go. Your stay there is ending. The old lady is afraid of loneliness. There's nothing you can do," the Dictator said.

He was absolutely right, and the woman felt embarrassed for hesitating in front of him, who, frowning, commanded her to begin making the phone calls. Besides, the alien Horseman was waiting. As soon as she placed her finger on the first button, however, the Dictator grabbed her hand. Glaring at her, he said, "Only work. Do you understand? This is a place of work, and nothing else. It's the path that you chose for pleasure, and it's for pleasure that you'll continue on this path."

With her voice cracking in her throat, she replied, "Of course. Only work."

She started with the first number. It was busy. Then she dialed another number.

A male voice answered the phone. "Hello, may I ask who is calling?"

"Hi, excuse me, I'm calling about your advertisement."

"The room's no longer for rent."

"So soon?"

He abruptly hung up the phone, and the woman was perplexed. She had to hurry, or it would be impossible to find a home in this huge, man-eating city. She crossed out that number and dialed another. She tried three or four numbers but they were all busy. The fifth number rang, and the woman felt elated. She adjusted her headscarf.

"Uh, sorry, sir ... about that advertisement."

"How many of you are there?"

"One person."

"Are you alone?"

"Yes."

"How is that so? Your voice sounds so young."

"So, how much is the rent, sir?"

A carefully enunciating voice spoke with a certain familiarity, "Why don't you write down the address? And then we'll come to some agreement."

She hung up the phone, crossed out the number and moved on to the next. The low voice of a troubled woman answered, "Yes."

"Oh, yes, *Khanom*, I wanted to ask about the house ..."

"How many people?"

"I'm alone."

To her surprise, the woman with the soft voice screamed into the phone, "Alone?"

"I ... I'm a writer, living on my own, and well, about my age, I'm not young."

"Well, how old are you?"

"Thirty."

"You're still young then!"

She placed calls until noon, exhausting herself with rejection. She now realized that she was guilty because she lived alone. She was a withered bitter orange tree. How did they find out that she had lost that night? She reached for a jar of salt water to dry out all the bitter oranges. If her hand could reach the jar, would she be able to dry up all the world's trees? The people on the other end of the line were afraid of her, and sometimes tipsy or drunk. They wished for her to come closer so that they could whisper in her ear, "There are some trees here that are filled with bitter oranges," they would say, "Come and see for yourself." The drunken men spoke softly, but the women, like all cats in the world, bared their claws at her. They were afraid that she would approach their tree and scratch it. Scratch it, or pour a carafe of salt water at its base and dry everything up.

She tore up the sheet, face wet with sweat and hands trembling. She yearned to take a salt-water shower or to ask the secretary to pour a jar of salt over her. How nice that Father was not here to lift his head up from the history book and say with a smirk, "Everyone knows what happened that night. Everyone!"

❧ ❧ ❧ ❧

She lit a cigarette and crossed the room to the map of Iran. She looked at the book cover, then at the crowded papers on the table. Everything seemed far away and disconnected. Nothing in the room belonged to her. She was only a woman, a woman who was still young. She smoked her cigarette down to the filter, far enough that its warm glow nearly burned her hand. As she put it out, she pulled another from the pack in her purse.

"Let go," the Dictator said.

How could she let go?

※ ※ ※ ※

Salt water gushed from the holes of the telephone receiver, flooding the floor. It rose and reached her desk. *"You're still young!"* The woman's scream swelled in her ears like the sound of rushing water. The water withered and warped the leaves of the trees, and swallowed the papers on her desk. The salt water rose, slapping at her face and burning her eyes.

"They'll pass. These moments will pass like lightning, and you'll wither away. Of your own choice, you'll wither away. So let go ..."

He was right. She should not let herself wither away. An old lady with a cane in hand should not knock on the door of the little four-walled house in the city of Shiraz, where four voices and four pregnant weaving girls would say, *"Khodat Bedeh Madar*—may God grant you your needs, my dear." Father would sit just beyond the door, speaking with an authoritative voice of history about an era when beggars were abundant.

※ ※ ※ ※

The secretary knocked on the door. At the sight of her, the woman, still standing in the middle of the room, tried to control her nerves, to free them from the lapping salt-water waves.

"Ms. Sar-Boland, these have just arrived."

The secretary handed her two packages containing the stories for her to read, to see if they were good enough for publication.

"Ms. Sar-Boland, the literary discussion session will begin at one o'clock."

The secretary closed the door gently. A literary discussion session commenced. The blood began to move through her veins again. She immediately felt reinvigorated, no longer withered and dry. She saw that woman who had screamed into the telephone, her voice filled with salt water, taking a seat in the back of the conference room.

The woman sat behind the table and took out her notes. A strange desire burned in her. The rush of life and existence imbued her. She forgot everything and, with great anticipation, fixed her eyes on the clock. Its hands moved forward slowly. The clock read a quarter after twelve.

— 5 —

This time, the literary discussion session, which took place once every two weeks, was about *The Greedy Inheritors*. A young writer with some experience collaborating with the publishing house wrote the story.

The group sat around a table, and a veil of cigarette smoke quickly wreathed the conference room. The woman tore through the air with authority, interrogating everyone present. Sometimes she would point in the direction of the young man who sat across from her; it was as if she were putting him on trial. Mr. Mohajerani, with his brown hair, full mustache, and eyes that sparkled like Father's, would put his hands together and stare into the eyes of the others who sat listening in silence. Sometimes he would nod his head as a sign of confirmation. It seemed as if the woman had forgotten the world. Skillful and illuminated phrases flew from her mouth. The resounding sound of her voice broke the silence in the room.

"When someone attempts to create a work of art, it means that he knows more than others. He carries a heavier burden. In the face of his fellow humans, he feels a greater responsibility. But you've written a story without any substance, without character development. The people in your story have no clear aspirations. They lack individuality. Girls who are in the emergency wing of a hospital are sitting by the side of their dying father, fighting among themselves. All the girls in your story are the same, black hearted and hungry for money. Why is it important to the story that one is forty and the other is twenty? What distinguishes your characters from one another? What is the position of each? How could they forget the pain and suffering of their father? What was their relationship with one another and with their father before his infirmity? What was the father like before hospitalization? And now, as he lies on his deathbed, what kind of emotions does he show? You can't depict the father, unconscious on his deathbed, and then have another character notice that his eyes are filling with tears. And these tears, can't they say anything? At least have them say something ... Have them show a father who everyone thinks is unconscious but who, through his own grief, partakes in a consciousness well beyond that of the daughters by his side. Have them show how, through this consciousness, he realizes that his daughters have been raised cold and money-hungry ... Give us a reason for the tears, a reason beyond death itself!"

"Ms. Sar-Boland ... I just wanted—"

With a wave of her hand, she quieted the young writer.

"Listen to me! A work of art is like the story of the Golden Rose."

She paused. A pleasant silence filled the room. She saw that all of those faceless people who she talked with earlier that morning on the phone stood behind the chairs. They listened intently to her loud scream. With a glance at Mr. Mohajerani, she smiled and continued.

"Perhaps you've read this story somewhere. Perhaps you haven't. On this dusty globe, some people think that a golden rose brings luck. One day a poor man who wanted to bring luck to his little girl and free her from sorrow went to a gold jewelry shop. For years he had worked there as a cleaner. In the evenings, he'd take the dirt back to his small hut. Right there he'd filter it until all that remained were the golden particles. The cleaner lost his youth during those years. But one day, he saw that he had enough golden particles to build a golden rose. He presented the rose to the girl, who in the meantime had also grown older. She took the golden flower and finally had luck of her own. And so creating a work of art is like building a golden rose ..."

She started to cough. She covered her mouth with her hands. Smiling, Mr. Mohajerani poured a glass of water for her. The woman nodded her head in thanks and sipped the water.

"Years must be spent. Word after word, image after image, should be gathered until one day you can give the story to other people as a gift. By that time, you will have grown old, but you will have built a golden rose."

Silence followed her speech. A curious but agreeable stillness fell on the room, and Mr. Mohajerani smiled with satisfaction. He nodded his head in approval the same way Father used to when she was a little girl and would recite a poem by heart for him. The Dictator moved his hands into and out of his pockets. His face was flushed with excitement; his eyes were shining. Overcome with emotion, the woman smiled and told the young man,

"I don't consent to the publication of this story. It needs more work."

※ ※ ※ ※

Day turned to night. With fall on its way, days were becoming shorter and nights were lengthening. She was in the street. Everyone moved in haste, searching for a taxi, a bus, anything to take them home. Home ... Once she had a home in Shiraz, with brightly colored windows facing a small road. A bitter orange tree stood in the yard. Its leaves climbed the wall and fell into the cobblestone street. When she opened the door and stepped onto the stones, her feet made a thumping sound. A man with silver eyes would stand at the window frame, chuckling and clapping his hands.

⁂ ⁂ ⁂ ⁂

Now she had a different home in this city. Right down the street. She simply had to pass by Pastor Street and turn into Khaghani to get there. The small, windowless room in the old doll's apartment was her home. Because it existed, she had one room in this big city. But what if it did not exist, what if it were not hers? She saw that she was wandering, that she did not know where to go. She searched one street after another. Now, in this slumbering city, she was alone. All of the world's policemen were blowing their whistles, running alongside her. They pointed her out to one another, saying, "She doesn't have a home."

Had she mentioned anything to the old lady? No, she had not said anything yet. Or maybe she had. Perhaps it had slipped out of her mouth ... *You said it, just last night you said it and the old lady cried.* No, she did not cry. She only said, "Aha, so gather up all your furniture." She started to pick up all the woman's belongings in the kitchen and heap them in the building's yard. They would stay there until the load-carrying taxi came and took them away.

"*Koofti*, you little shit, why are you late? The entire day I was cooped up because of your furniture and things. The entire day."

⁂ ⁂ ⁂ ⁂

The world's policemen gathered together. The city was empty. She reached the intersection and the first policeman yelled, "But how can you have no home? It isn't possible—a person who works, who has a father and a mother ..."

"My mother died when I poured salt water under a bitter orange tree. She had a home in one of those bitter oranges. Right there, in her own home, she dried up and withered away. She was exhausted. She was searching along with others for one night—a night that she had lost."

"You should have notified the Bureau of Information. Special agents can find all lost nights."

A second policeman said, "That is, of course, if it had been robbed from her."

And the first policeman, chewing the tip of his mustache, looked at her skeptically, "Of course, if there existed such a night ..."

The second policeman's snicker was ugly. He shook with mirth. Then he asked, "What about your husband? Do you even have one?"

-26-

With his fist her husband had pounded on the wall and shouted, "With all these policemen around, all of these men … who would believe it, and at this time of evening?"

Her legs shook. She was afraid that suddenly a fist would come from far away and hit her under the eyes. How could she go to the university with a black eye? But she went. She went every day and looked until she found him, to tell him that what he assumed was not so. To tell him that she had not uttered a word to the policemen, that she had not seen any of those men before, and that she had not seen anything except for two silver eyes that, however much she looked at them, would not speak.

⁂ ⁂ ⁂ ⁂

"Khajeh Tabbal … Khajeh Tabbal …"

It was the sound of a drum, and the tumult of the people and soldiers who lingered behind the walls of the city of Kerman. When you blink, you see a hill, one solid hill of eyes—black, green, blue—eyes of all colors.

She ran in the streets and heard the policemen blowing their whistles in unison and yelling, "She doesn't have a home! She doesn't have a home!" The Dictator was absent. History and dictators were always worthless. They could do nothing to help, even in the face of all the world's policemen, blowing into their whistles and screaming about the home she did not have.

She was in Enghilab Square and the Tashakkor Store was close by. She turned the corner. The old lady would relent. She was like a child; certainly she would relent. Once again she would pick up all the woman's possessions and say, "Just stop smoking your cigarettes."

The woman entered the bookstore. Several carpet weavers and a pregnant saleswoman stood before her. She circled around one of them. She wanted to ask, "Are you pregnant, *Khanom*? How many months?" Instead she said, "I'd like to buy a gift for my doll. Something very nice."

The saleslady looked at the woman as if she were afraid, perplexed by the strange turn of phrase, and asked, "What type of gift, *Khanom*?"

"Something that children like."

"But you said your doll."

"There's no difference between a doll and an old lady."

The saleslady once again looked at her warily. She stepped back in fright. She took something out and showed it to the woman, who thought that all pregnant women were frightened and that all frightened women were pregnant. Then the woman stretched her hand over her own stomach. She felt nauseous. The Dictator was responsible for this. Every time he let go, she almost threw up and grew subsequently bigger and bigger.

"Will this do?"

It was a beautiful round mirror.

"Yes, yes," answered the woman.

❧ ❧ ❧ ❧

What a silly game it is, the woman thought, *that a bride at her marriage ceremony must be asked three times if she consents, and only after the third time can she finally say yes. How stupid indeed. I said yes right away to what I wanted. Why must I obtain the consent of my father or my brother? I have always known what I desired. The rest is too much. I don't need permission from anyone.*

❧ ❧ ❧ ❧

The man who once had a bitter orange tree in his yard sneered.

The saleswoman wrote up the bill and walked in the direction of the cash box. When she returned, she wrapped the round mirror in paper. The old lady probably would not like this paper. Her belongings would remain in the yard, and throughout the night, she would hear the sound of the policemen whistling. Her head would swell and the Horseman's head would spin. Suddenly, the particles of his brain would scatter in the air, grotesque, and hit the door and wall. Like the time they were pounding some place in the South and the West. The heads of all the horsemen scattered, and the white and gray particles of their brains stuck to the sand or the trunks of the palm trees marked by gunpowder. She started at the saleswoman's eyes, which looked silver.

"Why isn't the wrapping paper colored?"

The saleswoman's eyes glittered; her stomach was bursting.

"Very well then, I'll change it."

"Use this wrapping paper."

The woman pointed to paper with a blue background and different colored circles. The saleslady mumbled something she could not hear. But the woman was thinking about the old lady and the things she collected: dolls, big and small, colored pillows, fake jewelry, tiny pieces of colored fabric …

❧ ❧ ❧ ❧

She took a cab from Enghilab to Pastor Square. All the world's policemen were blowing their whistles behind her. She took out her two keys: one silver, the other gold. She held them both tightly in her hand. She would not stay away, even if the old lady had thrown all her belongings in the yard. When she stepped out of the cab, she saw that no truck had packed up all of her books and shelves and bedding. There was no driver blasting his horn in anticipation of her arrival, a cigarette dangling from his mouth. Perhaps he tarried on the corner of the street and was not even planning to honk. Perhaps he did not even have a horn. Perhaps the horn was broken. Ruined—like her mood. Her knees trembled and a thousand voices swirled in her head ... *She doesn't have a home ... She doesn't have a home.*

❧ ❧ ❧ ❧

At night where would she go? Where would she sleep in a city without garden alleys? She desired a garden alley to walk to and cry in until morning, but there were none. There was no one there who could watch her, who could see her or the thin orange dress that she was wearing. But she wanted to put something over it. A *chador* or a cloth ... *You were not wearing a chador. You never wore a chador. It was only a thin orange nightgown under which the wind blew. You held onto it with your hands so that it would not lift up and reveal your legs.*

❧ ❧ ❧ ❧

The streets were abandoned: no drivers, no possessions, and no people. She felt relieved, happy even. She quickened her pace, treading so fast that she nearly stumbled. She yearned for the old lady, the doll with the golden hair. She laughed to herself. Then, exuberantly, she laughed aloud. Eager, she pushed the key into the lock, but it did not turn. Finally she gave up. Perhaps the old lady had changed the lock on the door so that her former renter could not get back in. Who had already taken her place; where did she come from? And where could the woman go now amid all these sounds? The sounds of the policemen's whistles cut through the whirlwind that was suddenly rising. *She doesn't have a house ...*

But when did she stop having a home? She had always owned at least a room or a dark closet. Distressed, she glanced around her and saw the black garbage bag she had placed by the dry and empty gutter that morning. Her whole face lit up in laughter. The familiar garbage bag-proof that this was still her home. She beamed in confidence and looked again at the key. Her hands still trembled as she tried the lock again. She had been putting the key in upside down.

The door finally opened. When she closed it behind her, there was no sound. No whirlwind. Suddenly she wanted to see the old lady right there in the yard, to squeeze her tightly and kiss her. But the old lady was not there. She was not even home.

❧ ❧ ❧ ❧

The old lady placed a note with unskilled handwriting on the old refrigerator:

They were selling cigarettes. I went to wait in line.
Khodaya, please protect all the world's old ladies for all eternity.

Cheerfully, she danced around and placed the mirror next to the old lady's note. She stepped into the hall and a peaceful, happy warmth flooded her soul—a home, her own home, even if it was only one room. She looked at the flowers in the hall, the dusty leaves ... For no reason at all, she wished to put herself to work. She wished to shine the flowers in all of the old ladies' homes. She wished to buy a round mirror for each and every one of world's old ladies.

❧ ❧ ❧ ❧

She opened the door to her room. There were no longer any policemen blowing their whistles. The picture was in its place, on top of the desk. She sat on a seat, and the trot of the red-maned horse resounded in her mind. The horse moved farther away ... far away, far away. The Dictator now appeared before her. He sat down on the bed, and with a look of mingled regret and bewilderment, said,

"You're still the same person you used to be."

"It's difficult ... so difficult to change." She was tired.

"So what about your father, what will he be told?"

"I'll find a house. A nice one, suitable for work."

She choked, her eyes burned, and the Dictator wrote a big X on the paper that was before him.

"One mark, so that you'll always remember."

He left, running after the Horseman. He yelled a few times into the air, harsh and bubbling words that the woman did not understand. But the Horseman heard. He tugged on the bridle and trotted toward the Dictator. He was full of energy. Would he also leave because of the small round mirror? She smiled faintly and said to the Horseman, "I'll find a house. It's just a bit difficult."

❧ ❧ ❧ ❧

How soon she had forgotten. She could not look at the eyes of the man in the picture. Pictures, like living people, have the ability to read minds. This picture had died, but the man himself had not. One had only to look into a pair of eyes captured by a camera's lens to know whether the subject was still living. How had she come to understand this? They were the eyes of those same people who put their pictures in the streets. She only had to gaze closely at them to know whether their eyes were real. A picture of a living person is different from a picture of a dead person. It is only with the blink of an eye that you see that the eyes of the individual in the picture are not alive. Little by little, they become empty. They die and do not look in any direction and when the person in the picture does not look in any direction; you realize that he has died. The picture's living subject stares constantly at some unknown place.

⁂ ⁂ ⁂ ⁂

If you want to write the story about the Horseman, you have to leave. Find a place that is more spacious and well lit, where at night you can see the sky filled with stars and a moon that lights up the whole world. You shall go there and you shall write so that you can glimpse those eyes in the picture, at all the eyes. How far are you from that night when you stared at that picture of the bride and the groom, and you saw that the silver eyes of the groom were empty? You were sitting some distance from Father. The album lay before you. You looked, and you wanted Father to also see that the two empty pupils remained without light. But Father was reading history. It was 1978. Father said sadly, "Everyone fled to their rooftops and screamed, '*Khajeh Tabbal … Khajeh Tabbal.* There was a dark and bloody hill of eyes, removed from all the people of Kerman."

You asked, "What about Shiraz, Father? Didn't he come to Shiraz?"

Again Father's head was buried in his book. You were not able to show him the picture of the groom who was dressed in blue. His eye sockets were empty and sweets were scattered in his hair. The bride was laughing. Her eyes glowed.

The woman stood up and took the typewriter out from under her bed. She placed it on the table with a smile. As she faced the picture, she flipped open the paper-holder and settled a clean sheet in it. She spun the roller.

"As soon as I start, I'll be able to …"

⁂ ⁂ ⁂ ⁂

Fingers over the lead-blue letters ... the round mirror ... the policemen who were whistling ... home ... home. Suddenly she was frightened, and with a strained voice she said aloud, "I'm just testing it out ..." She halted before she even wrote the first line. She could not think of a single sentence—the surrounding shrills of policemen whistling and men screaming into the telephone filled her mind. She held her head between her hands. The sound of a horse's neigh reached her despite the thickening whirlwind of surrounding noise. Then the horse galloped farther away.

⁂ ⁂ ⁂ ⁂

There was a rider with blood pooling on the flanks of his horse, dripping from under his severed arms. The bones of his shoulders glistened white in the moon, his arms held to them by thin shreds of raw, red skin .... The policemen whistled as they saw her. Her arms ... Her arms. Father screamed, "You can't, you can't—you're a woman, a woman wearing only a thin orange nightgown ...." The Horseman returned, and with those same severed arms he pulled his sword halfway from its hilt. He galloped right up to the policemen. Frightened, they attempted to retreat, but soon their corpses littered the streets. The Horseman placed his sword back in its sheath. The sad stranger stared at her. Father shook his head and smirked. Father would not believe this story.

⁂ ⁂ ⁂ ⁂

She trembled. Suddenly her hands were above the lead-blue letters, typing furiously. Father's eyes were black. He peered at her from behind thick glasses. She felt cold. The Horseman approached calmly. His eyes were full of kindness and warmth.

The old lady opened the crack of the door and said, "At least take off your dress."

The woman looked up and started. It was as if she were seeing the old lady for the first time. The Horseman fled and the old lady quietly entered the room, "The sound of your typing is heard even in the street."

She threw the cigarettes on the table.

"I got four. I stood in line. *Azadi* cigarettes—each one is two *tomans.*'"

The woman did not understand what the old lady was saying, but she saw the cigarettes. Now she had to open her purse and give the old lady money.

"I'm sorry, I don't have any change."

"Don't worry about it."

The old lady made a funny face and left. The woman was confounded. She closed the door of the typewriter. *The sound was heard even in the street.* No. She had to go. Certainly on this dusty globe, there was a place for her and the wounded Horseman to live. She heard the sound of the old lady saying, "Oh, Afsaneh!"

The old lady came and stood at the doorway. Her eyes sparkled. Her doll—like eyes. She held up the mirror. "What's this?"

"It's for you."

"Really!?"

The old lady's hands shook. She did not know how to unwrap the gift in such a way that the paper would not rip. It did rip, and soon the round mirror was in her hands.

"I cooked you dinner."

The woman got up. She wanted to take off her *mantow*.

"Let me wash your *mantow* for you"

"No."

"No. *Koofi*! Your *mantow*'s covered with dust and filth."

No one can happily escape an old lady. Jokingly, the old lady slapped her hard on the shoulder. "You weak little thing, when are you going to start taking care of yourself?"

When they were eating dinner, she saw that the old lady had placed the round mirror on top of the television. Behind the mirror was a vase filled with artificial flowers. Cautiously, the old lady removed the bones of a fish and put them on the side of the tablecloth. The woman did not speak. She sat reflectively in thought. The wrinkles on her forehead multiplied. As always, she ate quickly. The Horseman was chasing after her, along with a thousand other alien horsemen …

The old lady sighed. She lifted up her head. A glance at the mirror, a glance at the woman. "Do you know that today, for the first time, someone called me an old lady? And I was taken aback. On the sidewalk, a young peddler had spread out a stand. I don't even remember what I wanted to buy, but I started to haggle over the price. The peddler said, 'Old lady—where has the faith gone?' First, I yelled at him, saying that an old lady is also a grandmother and an ancestor. But the man laughed aloud sarcastically and I returned home empty handed. I took out some old pictures and stood in front of the mirror. I have grown old. The peddler was absolutely right."

The old lady's face creased into a frown and she pursed her lips tightly. Tears welled up in her eyes, but she was too proud to allow them to run freely down her cheeks. The woman gazed at the old lady, fretting and mournful, like a child.

Under the woman's stare, the old lady pulled herself together and sighed. The woman smiled. She wanted to say, "It doesn't matter." But why didn't it matter? It was as if she had given up. At least the old lady was emerging from her gloomy state. Perhaps she wanted to make an effort to break the heavy silence. She hit the woman's arm.

"I was saying, you're going to get sick. *Koofti*—what's the use? Just keep on nodding your head and staring at me blankly."

The woman rose. She took a cigarette from on top of the table and sat in the foyer. As she flicked it, ashing, smoke circles lurched and floated through the air like prisoners with bound arms and legs. From afar, the woman observed the old lady, who regarded the billowing haze with disgust. "You smoke like a man."

The woman did not respond. She just puffed hard on the cigarette and followed the direction of the circles to where they opened up, like thin spider threads spreading out through the air. The old lady gazed upon the picture of Bani Sadr. She shook her head and sighed.

"It's no use. Even if you hang a thousand pictures on the walls, you'll still grow old."

The woman stood up. If she stayed seated, she would do nothing but think about the Horseman's picture—about his life and his youth. The old lady stared at her in confusion.

"Where are you going?"

"I have work to do. I'm going to do work."

"You won't even speak one word with someone else, then?"

Back in her room, she sat on a chair and puffed rings of smoke into the air, where they drifted apart. When you reach the end of your story, the same thing happens to you. Full of sadness and loneliness, you begin to drift. You yearn to create a thousand irrational reasons for why the story should never end, and when it does conclude a round mirror will make you shed tears. The main point is to finish the story. Most importantly, you have plucked all the bitter oranges one by one. Now, up there, only one remains, and it will soon fall down or wither. With every bitter orange you pluck, you pour one drop of salt water at the foot of the tree. Only one drop, and finally the last bitter orange will dry up. It makes no difference how many bitter oranges you had up there—be it thirty, forty, or eighty.

❧ ❧ ❧ ❧

The door opened, and the old lady entered with a cup of tea.

"I thought you said you had work to do."

"I do—I'm thinking."

The old lady nodded her head and left. The picture hung on the wall. Smoke circles wafted through the air. Circle after circle, with each connected to the next. Perhaps one day they would take the alien Horseman to Tehran ... Tehran ... In those days there was no Tehran, it was called Ray. What difference did it make where they took him? That same place where his story would end ... They took him, so Khan Qajar could end his story. Hands and feet chained with other captives. Sometimes one would fall, and others would run after him. Whips and bullets, like circles of smoke. The first would open, spreading over the ground, and then the others would follow ... Yes, bodies opening like circles of smoke. And his hands, victims of useless swords, were wounded. Those hands ... In the picture, just one hand was holding a *kashkool*. They say that the Hero of Zand had the heart of a woman ....

"Important people cannot let themselves be controlled by stipulations."

It was the voice of the Dictator. Important people do not allow unwanted conditions to govern their lives. They are true to themselves, and no old lady, man, or woman can influence their lives. They would never buy a round mirror, or apologize to an old woman.

He was correct. For important people, all the mirrors and old ladies, all the words and pictures, could only be something confined to the dust of the jewelry shop. What the important people do not realize is that it is possible to pour jewelry shop dust through a filter for years, and in the end to build a golden rose.

She touched the hand of the Dictator. It was warm like the hand of a man. She wanted to lay her head on his shoulder and sleep. It was late at night, and the sound of gunshots filled the air. Somewhere far away, a rooster was singing.

— 6 —

The secretary placed the *Kayhan* newspaper in front of the woman with, as always, an embarrassed smile fixed on her lips. She was young—perhaps seventeen years old. She had big black eyes and hair that she was always pushing away from her face. The woman took out the classified section and looked at the rent ads: Two homes, three homes, full mortgage, student discounts ...

"Do you write all kinds of stories, Ms. Sar-Boland?"

The woman lifted her head from the newspaper, "What?"

The girl remembered her place.

"I asked ... Why do you write stories?"

The girl flashed a hesitant smile. The woman bent over the newspaper columns, and slowly, she thought to herself, *Why do you write stories? Because people believe stories more, and if there were a bitter orange tree in your life and one lost night, you wouldn't be able to tell the truth, either. No one would believe you. Searching day and night, you could try to find the truth somewhere. But what you cannot find does not exist. The story exists, though. Everything's clear, and even if no one has seen the tree, they can smell it. And all this effort is so that with your speechless tongue, without getting accused of being crazy, you can say that there was a bitter orange tree and one lost night.*

But she did not utter a word aloud. She only lifted her head and straightening her glasses on her nose, said, "Well ... Ms. Azari, look at this page. I'm searching for an apartment. One bedroom and cheap. Write down all the phone numbers on one page, leaving a space underneath them for the address and particulars. Call them and tell them my occupation and anything else you know about me. Tell the owner all the details and just keep me posted."

The girl took the classified ads. She hesitated.

"So you're looking for another house?"

"Yes." The woman gathered all the papers on the table and bent over them.

"Is this recent, then?

Without a word, the woman nodded; with a wide smile, the girl left. When the door was closed, the woman pushed her papers aside. One week had passed. Every day she perused the classified section but she never felt like reaching for the phone. As soon as she touched the receiver, sweat would gather on her forehead. She wanted to pour a jug of salt water at her feet and finish the story. But the alien Horseman would not allow her. Yesterday she had an argument with the Dictator. He slammed his fists on the table and left. He still had not returned.

Step by step, the Horseman followed her. She heard the sound of his moans when they reached the real estate office. He groaned so loudly that she quickly ducked into the real-estate office. Then the weeping of the alien Horseman grew fainter. When she came out of the office empty-handed, he nodded his head in satisfaction.

"You know, rent's expensive," the Horseman said.

"I'm exhausted. How long do I have to keep on searching?"

"That's not the point. You adore the old lady."

Perhaps the Horseman was right. She loved that dark, cramped room and that old lady. Lately she would hasten home. She wanted the old lady to peep her head around the door and say, "*Koofti*, I've prepared tea. Would you like some?" Lately she would take the cup, sit in the foyer, and take her time. She wanted the old lady to talk about herself, about her life.

"But this isn't the way to proceed for someone who wants to …"

She recognized his voice. The Dictator had returned. He addressed her, "So just stop right there and calm down, or else …"

Now, once again, she wished to remind the Dictator that you have to tolerate some things and pay such a price for others. She yearned to tell him that you have to seize the right moment, because you may never be able to again and everything will be lost. You will see how many days and nights you have lost in your life, and then no one will believe your stories, with forgotten time stacking up around you like half-written pages.

"Let go, let go!"

❧ ❧ ❧ ❧

She surrendered. Surrendered. She rose from the table and stood before the window. It was the end of the month of *Mehr*. *Mehr* of the Fall of 1986, with its strange winds. The leaves separated from their branches. Slouching strangers strode into the wind. She hated herself, one worthless old lady—one cup of tea in one small, dark house in the morning. Every morning, craving to see the sky, she would go outside. These sounds—the hoarse croaks and the pregnant women—weavers' screams, reminded her that she was still young.

You were scared. You were scared of the sounds. Everything was now an excuse, even the old lady who had upset the alien Horseman. There was only fear, you must believe that. So just continue wandering ... endure more homelessness ...

An abrupt knock at the door interrupted her pondering. The girl with the flushed cheeks and surprised eyes tied to pretend like nothing had happened. She entered the room.

"Gosh, Ms. Sar-Boland, they're all very expensive."

The girl laid the papers on the table. She scratched details down next to some of the numbers and crossed out others with a thick line. The nervous girl shook the hair off her forehead.

"You know, they're either expensive or dodgy. And they don't know you."

The girl was out of breath. The woman lifted her hand to touch the girl's hair, and the secretary's face glowed.

"That's all right."

Afraid that the moment of intimacy would be lost forever, the girl gushed, "But that can't be right ... It's not possible to ... Well, what a shame that a person would write ... for them."

She paused to catch her breath and continued, "Do you ... Do you know, Ms. Sar-Boland, that I've written a story?"

The woman smiled. The girl had finally said what was on her mind. Now she was no longer breathing heavily. Calmly, the woman offered, "How nice—why don't you bring it to me to read?"

The girl was taken aback. She shook her head, and hair fell in her face. She replied, "Oh, no—damn—it's not with me. Why don't I tell you about it?"

"No."

She said it firmly, and the girl became quiet.

"But ... I'll bring it for you ... Okay?"

"Definitely—tomorrow."

This time the secretary hurried out of the room. The girl had lied, and the woman knew it. Bullets set loose in the dark of the night. The woman stood but then quickly sat back down. She felt distressed, and realized that she had forgotten everything. She slid toward the door. Carefully, she peeped her head out. The secretary took the phone receiver and laid it on the table. She calmly chewed the tip of her pen, an assortment of white papers spread before her.

Many times the woman had seen the girl, armed with a thousand excuses, try to involve herself in the literary discussion sessions. Sometimes she brought tea, or delivered folders to the conference room. Sometimes she even snuck behind the door and listened. But today she wished to write a story.

The woman laughed. She walked toward the door and saw that the girl was nervously swallowing saliva as it filled her mouth. Even from a distance, the woman could see the fear in the secretary's eyes.

The girl aspired to emulate Ms. Sar-Boland, to move her hands, speak, sit, hold her pen in just the same way.

The Dictator laughed and pointed to the map of Iran.

"Everyone, soon. Everyone … But only if you obey," he said.

She surrendered, for she knew he was correct. She whirled around the map of Iran. Suddenly her heart warmed with happiness. This girl and all of the girls of the map—what if all of them become pregnant carpet-weavers? Not all of them. Surely many of them would want to know the story of the bitter orange tree.

She heard the sound of the door and the secretary's murmur.

"Yes, come in," the girl said.

Nasrin, an old friend from college, stepped into her office.

"Well—what a surprise!"

The girl slipped out of the room quickly, and the two friends kissed each other.

"I hope this isn't too much of a shock, but searching for your book in the bookstores has exhausted me terribly."

"It'll be out on Saturday."

"*Tabrik*—Congratulations."

"*Mamnoon*—Thanks."

Nasrin sat in the seat beside the table.

"So … How are you?" the woman asked.

"Better … much better."

She was lying. Nasrin was lying. She had but to say a few more words and she would burst into tears. She was fumbling with the straps of her purse, nervously swallowing the saliva accumulating in her mouth. Her lips pursed tightly together.

"Should I get us some tea?" the woman asked.

"No … no, that's not necessary."

The woman looked down, hoping that Nasrin would not cry, but it was too late. She stood up, lit a cigarette, and held a box of tissues in front of her.

"Please, don't act like a child."

"I can't help it! I can't help it at all. I'm still waiting. Do you know that right on time, two people rang the bell? I was cooking and the smells filled the kitchen. And then I looked to see who was arriving … *Aaakh* …"

The woman closed the door firmly so that the sound of Nasrin's sobbing would not reach the secretary's ears.

"I thought that I could ... that with work I'd fill up my life, just like you."

"But I ..." the woman began. She did not continue, but thought: *What about me? What did I want to say—that there is the depression that comes from a confession?* She remained quiet until Nasrin finished crying. Then, drying her eyes, Nasrin finally replied, "You see? All of a sudden you will burst ... And your dear telephone, which I love to death, is always busy."

"It's been like this all day because I gave a long list of phone numbers to the secretary to call. I'm looking for a house."

"What kind of house?"

"A place to write. A calm, well-lit place."

"I know of such a place."

"Really!? Where?"

"The top floor of the building that I lived in that first year with Khosrow."

"But isn't it noisy?"

"No. An old lady and an old man live there."

"But still, this old lady and old man might have many great-grandchildren."

"As far as I know, most of their children have moved abroad or live in the provinces. There's only one son who still lives there, but he may also be leaving for abroad soon."

"I don't know, but if you think it's a good place ..."

"Do you want me to call?"

Abruptly, the Dictator interrupted, "No! No!"

The woman turned to him in astonishment.

"Why not?"

"That man. That young man."

"But he's going abroad soon!"

"It doesn't matter whether he leaves in one day or one year."

The woman screamed at him, close to tears.

"So you also believe that on that night I ... I ... with that gown ... But, I swear, there was no one there—no men, no policemen—the streets were empty. I just went out for a walk."

The street reached a dead end. A dusty wind scattered the dried, yellow leaves on the ground. Obstinate, it twirled them around in the corner. Swooping up the thorns and twigs, the wind hoisted the leaves into fluttering yellow clouds. She stood at the entrance to the alley. She wanted to see what this small, stubborn whirlwind would do with the dry leaves. She knew that they would surrender to its powerful determination; that is what leaves, brittle and fragile, always do in the face of a whirlwind.

The leaves were small—miniscule. What if they did not fall from the branches or did not separate? They would stay together like a large flock. It was autumn. The laws of the Earth seem inescapable, but some of the leaves do not behave as nature dictates. They always stay fresh, always, like powerful leaders.

Nasrin touched her hand.

"I'm late."

Nasrin and the woman went outside. The woman turned around several times and noticed that the dirty wind continued to twirl the tiny leaves. If the whirlwind could not manage to lift them up and carry them away, it meant that the leaves were stronger than the whirlwind. Yes, resistance could come even from a small yellow leaf. Yellow, dry and separated from its branches ... *You must resist with all your strength, resist.*

She was in the middle of a street filled with autumn leaves. She did not have the heart to trample them. She tried to step over each lightly with the tips of her toes, or to pass around them, cautious of their dried blades and browning veins.

※ ※ ※ ※

The small door of faded blue needed a good cleaning and a fresh coat of paint. Blue once again. Then it would return to its former color—or would it? Yes, it would. A door is not a person. Just a door. All the world's blues are the same color.

Nasrin rang the bell. The woman peered upon the end of the street. There he was, the alien Horseman. He seemed reluctant to come any closer, but gained courage when he met her gaze. Pulling tightly at the reigns of his horse, he entered the street and stood a short distance from the two women.

A smile flickered beneath his black mustache; blood trickled in drops from his fingers. Dry leaves fell on his hair and shoulders. The alien Horseman could not lift his hands to brush them off.

The door opened, and a frightened and confused old lady appeared. She stood in the doorframe with her oval face and disheveled white hair. No light reflected from her eyes.

"*Salam*—Hello Mrs. Hamidi."

Nasrin's voice trembled. Lost memories cause quivers in the vocal chords.

The disconcerted old lady stared at the two of them. Little by little, the fear faded. They said hello, or perhaps they did not. The old lady answered, or perhaps she did not. Perhaps both heads moved and smiled politely.

Mrs. Hamidi opened the door. She peered at the end of the street. Did she see the Horseman?

"It's because of him that I want to move to a new house."

"It's not possible to live here with a horse. Besides, isn't this man a stranger?"

"No, his horse …"

The old lady moved her hand impatiently over her tangled tresses.

"*Befarmayid*—Welcome." To Nasrin, "I'd completely forgotten that you called in the morning."

The old lady flicked the light on in the dark hallway. She could hardly move—clutter filled the hallway and disorder obstructed her path. Black stains splattered the walls. A spider in the corner sat entwined in a web that he was spiraling around himself and the house, silk threads extending around everything. Black filth coated the bricks. The hallway ended with a door that opened into a garden. Between two rooms, layer upon layer of junk buried the blackened stairs.

"First let us look at the yard. If that's possible."

The woman wanted to escape the clutter. The garden was large. A rectangular pool full of toxic sewage was at its center, swimming with feeble fish addicted to dirty water and green algae. They sucked their dirty water while she sucked on her cigarettes. In the rear, there were two rooms facing the main building.

"Let's go and see the upper floor."

Straining, the old lady rearranged all the junk that had accumulated on the stairs. A place for a foot here, a place for a foot there, so that they would be able to reach the top floor.

"I'm sorry about the mess," Nasrin apologized.

The old lady did not say a word. She just groaned, located a place for her foot, and moved upward. The woman noticed a bathroom and a kitchen on the bottom floor, and a storage room under the stairs. The bathroom door was wide open—a black object, once a mirror, hung on the wall. Dirt covered the ceilings and walls of the bathroom.

"No one comes here. That's why it's so messy."

When they reached the top floor, the small objects cluttering the stairs beneath their feet became dislodged and tumbled into the hallway.

There were two large rooms connected to each other, with two windows facing the sun. A green tree was visible through the window—a tree whose branches stuck to the panes as though they wished to enter the room, to open the window and come in. Be sensible, be sensible, woman ... it can't come in. It can never come in.

She opened the window and reached out her hand to feel the leaves. Mrs. Hamidi said, "They're green all year round."

So this tree did not have to abide by the natural laws, did not have to yield to the laws of the broken Earth.

She wished that, like this tree, she could shatter the laws of the world. *I'll work here. Here, I'll definitely work.*

"Up here there's always sunlight. All year round. Winter and summer. But the bathroom and the kitchen are downstairs and then there's the shower. It has been broken for such a long time."

What did she care about the bathroom, kitchen, or shower? She cared solely about this tree, herself, and Nasrin ... *Ah—look at how stupefied they are as they gaze upon this home. What are they searching for? You have to make them see ...*

"Nasrin, the upstairs isn't so bad."

Nasrin was taken aback; she stiffened. The woman laughed. Nasrin was afraid of her—how ridiculous. With the two windows open, the sunlight poured in and filled all the rooms.

"I'm happy that ..." Nasrin began.

"But the downstairs is such a mess." The woman said this very quietly so that the old lady would not hear her, and Nasrin laughed.

"You don't have anything to do downstairs, anyway."

Wanting to re-assure the old lady, the woman approached her. How sloppy she was, not at all like her own doll-like old lady.

"I just want a quiet place to write."

The old lady with the strange Persian–Turkish accent said, "Yes. Nasrin *Khanom* told me … Well, it's just me, my husband, and Siyavash, who is leaving for Germany today or tomorrow."

It did not matter when Siyavash left or returned. He was not a child. Perhaps he was a grown man, and the rent, electricity, and water bills here were much more reasonable than at the other place. She expressed her feelings to Nasrin. "You know, I'd like to be a renter—if that's possible."

"Well?" the old lady asked.

"Nasrin speaks on my behalf with regard to all this."

Then the old lady glanced at Nasrin and laughed ironically. *Khoda ra Shokr—Thank God—I've handed you the responsibility of making all the arrangements*, her laugh seemed to say to Nasrin.

"Oh, Afsaneh *Khanom*, I'm also searching for a companion."

The woman hesitated at "companion." What if she was one of these old ladies who chattered a lot, who would come upstairs constantly and grate her nerves? Her own old lady, her own doll-like old lady, was like that in the beginning. She wanted to sit for hours and talk, or try to take her outside.

"You're just sitting there not doing anything," she would say.

"I'm thinking, just thinking."

Once or twice at the beginning, she went with her. And what an effort she had to make for the old lady to see that she had work to do. But the old lady never got the message. Whenever she saw that the woman was sitting alone in her room 'not doing anything,' her eyes would grow large with pity, and she would bring her a cup of tea. "Don't sit alone. The television is on."

"But I have work to do."

"What work?"

"I have to write."

The old lady never let go. Bitterness would swell in the woman's throat. She wanted to cry out, to tell the old lady that she needed solitude to think about the bitter orange tree that could be seen through a half-opened door. Back then, it was always green and fresh.

Just once, she yelled at the old lady and fiercely pounded on the desk, "I'm thinking … thinking … thinking!"

The old lady, lips pouting and eyes full of fear, left, and for a long time did not step into her room again. Why was she thinking now about her own old lady? At least the woman could lock the door here. This was a separate floor. Still, she had to say everything that was on her mind,

"Perhaps I won't really be a good companion for you."

"Afsaneh, Mrs. Hamidi does not mean that she's seeking a companion."
Nasrin said this on purpose so that the colonel's wife would understand.

"*Madar Jan*—My dear, I won't be in your way. I'm just more relaxed knowing that there's someone upstairs ...."

Why was she more relaxed?

Mrs. Hamidi suddenly got upset. She did not finish her sentence. She seemed frightened. What could the colonel's wife be frightened of? What if the house had *jinn* ...? The woman started to laugh. She looked over at the green tree. Perhaps *jinn* that beat kettledrums in the evening filled the house.

Her conversations with Nasrin that day brought her down. When they left the colonel's residence, it was not yet dark. The whirlwind did its work, twisting up to the sky, and the Horseman left for Pastor Square to wait. He would happily lay down in that dark, tight room for the entire evening.

Nasrin said, "I'm not going to go any further than Enghilab Square. It's late."

Both of them were riding Nasrin's green *Jiyan*.

"Come to my house for tea," the woman said.

"No. It's late," Nasrin said again. "And now when I return, all of the windows will be open, and all of the women of the world will glare at me from behind the windows and yell, 'What an age we live in!' "

ꙮ ꙮ ꙮ ꙮ

The woman filled once again with elation. Though she sensed that the Dictator was anxious, she did not feel like thinking of the jugs of salt water or the shriveling orange trees. The Dictator seemed to have something to say, but she was happy. She did not want to hear any objection. In the corner of her eye, his lips moved, "Don't pay attention."

"They force you to."

"But it's not this. It's something else."

"What is it?"

"Now you are also sitting by the window. You're sitting and yelling."

"You can't just kick people."

"But no one can be crushed from just a kick."

"I can't. I'm finished. Finished ... A widow. My head is about to explode. Here in my head they're banging nails night and day."

The Dictator forced her to listen. She wanted to tell him that perhaps his tree had not dried up but she refrained from speaking. She let the Dictator continue. "You mean, you're ready to go back to that house, and that tree?"

"Tree?"

"Ha! Those circumstances."

"Yeah, I have to go back. There's no room for us in the taxi."

The Dictator felt sick. What if he did throw up? No, the damned dictators are always able to maintain their composure. Now he was rambling too much. That's all. He wanted to talk Nasrin's head off, in the same way he did so long ago in a tight, dark room.

꙰ ꙰ ꙰ ꙰

Aha—perhaps you are talking about a cinema seat, bus ticket, or a line for eggs. The taxi did not have room for us. We had to leave. The line was busy, and the men were pushing, and there were not even enough cigarettes for everyone. Cigarettes.

The Dictator took out a cigarette. Nasrin turned the steering wheel. She looked at the woman.

"In those days I didn't know what was going on outside," Nasrin said.

The Dictator lit the cigarette. He laughed.

"What was going on?"

Nasrin pounded her fist violently on the steering wheel.

"They force you. They force you to take the path they show you. And if you don't, then you can only return to where you came from or stand on a street corner. And then they scream with indignation, 'Oh, people!' You know that in the minds of people, there are no other paths besides these two …"

The abrasive whirlwind twirled again. It carried away all the world's paintbrushes and sketches. Nasrin giggled. She shook her paint-stained hands, and she moved toward another whirlwind. There was a man struggling in a pile of dry plants and yellow leaves.

The Dictator sneered, "Her beloved Khosrow was on the side of traditional women, wasn't he?"

"Perhaps he was, perhaps he was not … Now I'm shattered into pieces. I'm resolved. I don't feel like being drafted into military service. If I continue this way, you'll find me either on the corner of the street or in a psychiatric ward. Fighting isn't easy—fighting tradition. And freedom and struggle are one in the same. Freedom and mutual respect? Nonsense! Here no one can be friends with anyone. You're either beneath or above someone else. A custom two thousand years old."

Nasrin bit her lip, and angrily switched gears.

"Give me a cigarette."

"Aren't you afraid?" the woman asked.

Nasrin turned and stared in silence. Perhaps she had seen the Dictator's sneer. The Dictator, with the excuse of lighting his cigarette, lowered his head and laughed.

"Do you know what I mean?"

The woman wanted to say that she was shattered. Instead, she gave Nasrin a cigarette. She coughed with the first puff.

"No, I won't smoke anymore. I'm afraid ... I'm afraid of everyone. Especially of that old lady who's always stationed at the window, monitoring my comings and goings. Like the most precise calculator, she enters data and controls the world. And if I'm so terrified of this little old lady, then how could I not also fear my husband?"

The woman was not feeling well or she knew that she had surrendered and was searching for her story. The Dictator sat on the *Jiyan*'s dashboard, and from there he stared at her and pointed his index finger. She had no choice but to continue. She spoke, mouthing all the words that the Dictator wanted. He was resting his full weight on the *Jiyan*'s dashboard ... *You're going to crush it* ... But he refused to listen, like all of the presumptuous dictators of the world. At the beginning, he was not like that. He used to be peaceful—he had wanted to start from scratch—but now he was just destroying everything in the middle of the battlefield. When he finished, he would leave. He compelled her to speak, like a wound up clock full of unreleased energy.

She sat up in the seat next to Nasrin and said, "This is really just all talk. You don't give any significance to your work. Work that even the old ladies surrender to. You know, my dear Nasrin, you've become a prisoner, a prisoner of daily routine. When you were a university student, like everyone else, you dreamed of becoming someone important. You'd present poetry ... Freedom ... Freedom ... But you know that one can't simply recite the words of liberty or other notions. A human being isn't a tape recorder, after all. In any era, fighting tradition isn't an easy task."

"Fighting doesn't solve anything. To everyone, I'm still just a woman," Nasrin said.

"But you're also guilty of abiding by the norms. Don't you remember your last sketches? Children, pools, dishes in the kitchen. They all focused on supposedly feminine subjects."

They reached Enghilab Square and she got out. Nasrin smiled bitterly and sighed, "I don't know, perhaps you're right."

The woman turned around so she could not see the man who was now climbing down from the dashboard. "Why aren't you going to Nasrin's house?" the Dictator asked the woman. She wanted to ask Nasrin to take him away with her. But she was afraid of what the old lady would say, that same old lady who would stand at the window and watch Nasrin's comings and goings. The world was now filled with such old ladies. She could not escape the weight of the man who just jumped off from the dashboard and now strolled alongside her.

❦ ❦ ❦ ❦

She traipsed the stretch between Enghilab Square and Pastor Street. The Horseman was not there. There was a woman wearing a green headscarf standing at the corner. Like Nasrin's, her face was thin, her eyes green, with long eyelashes framing them. She was Nasrin's size. A man in a *Renault* turned twice into the square, and suddenly slammed on his brakes in front of her. The woman who resembled Nasrin turned her back. She slowed her pace and lingered. Why was she lingering? She looked at her watch two or three times. A moment later, from the end of Pastor Street, a green *Paykan* turned into the square. It raced toward her but stopped before it reached her. The woman saw the lady's tired smile, a smile that would break anyone's heart. The lady got into the car, took out her purse, and started to apply her lipstick.

Nasrin!? It was her, really her. The woman shivered. The wind whirled; it twirled around her legs—but she was not yet so yellow and dry that it would be able to lift her up and carry her away. She entered Pastor Street and then turned into Khaghani Street. She could not turn the key. Her hands trembled, and she could hardly hear the voice of her old lady calling to her from the baker's shop,

"Why don't you buy a pair of glasses?"

"I wasn't paying attention."

The old lady threw the key at the door.

"I bought you pencils and erasers."

Ah—her own old lady. Not that old lady standing in the doorframe, frightened by everything. The colonel's wife would die beneath her spider webs. Yesterday her own old lady turned the house upside down to find the pencil that she always wrote with. Sadness swelled in her heart. She had to escape this place and get away from this old lady who bought her pencils and erasers.

"Why do you look so suspicious? Come in."

The woman entered, stumbling as she walked. How could she tell the old lady—tell her that at the beginning of the month she would be leaving? The

-48-

old lady opened the door and said, "You're tired. Why don't you take a shower?"

So now her kindness reveals itself...

The voice of the Dictator. He opened the door and sat observing on the bed.

"How many times did she tell you that the water bill had gotten expensive? Don't you remember how when you would be in the bathroom washing your clothes, she would come and turn down the water? Or when you were taking a very long time in the shower, she would knock on the door and say that supper was ready, that dinner had gotten cold? And that night when you were typing, what did she say, eh? Her voice reached the street."

He was right. Now was the time to end this—but how?

"You're late," the old lady said.

Aha—now say it. The time is ripe for you to say it—now, or it will be too late. You blink, and then everything is gone. Everything.

"I went to see a place."

The old lady stood still.

"What kind of place?"

The woman saw her own bitter smile in the mirror that hung in the foyer.

"A home."

The old lady's silence was like a magnet that pulled the words from her tongue.

"I want to write a novel or a short story. But it's too dark here. I need to work in the evenings. I need a place with sunshine. Here there's no sunshine. There's no light, only darkness."

The old woman, silent, remained still. What if she had died? But she was standing up, and no old lady who stood up was dead. What if she had dried up? What if she had dried up just as she was, standing there in her own place? But she moved. She put the pencils and erasers on top of the television. Oh yes—the bread! She took the bread and left. She went into the kitchen.

The woman felt relieved. She entered her room and did not see anyone. The Horseman was not there. She threw herself onto the bed. With the back of her hand on her forehead she stared at the ceiling.

※ ※ ※ ※

The ceiling was gray from the cigarette smoke. Five years had passed, and these walls had grown gray with time. During *Azar* of 1976, she came to Tehran in a cab filled with papers, poetry, and books. She sold all of her belongings and her pockets were filled with seven thousand *tomans*.

"Hey, don't sell my books!" he demanded.

She sold his books only when she reached Amir Kabir Bookstore, across from the university where she waited for Nasrin, so that she would always be able to stay in Tehran. Nasrin joined her on time, like when she would run in Shah-Reza Street and distribute flyers. For hours, the woman would stand at that same corner right in front of the university. It was the time of war. Internal conflicts and civil upheaval surrounded them. She found the old lady through the *Kayhan* newspaper advertising a room for a student.

"I said that dinner's ready."

The old lady's voice was harsh. Tired, the woman got up. She stole a glance through the crack of the door and went into the foyer. The table on the floor was set, and she sat down. Silence. A tormenting silence. Twice she coughed, and the old lady did not consent to say anything. Every now and then, she would stare at the woman. What was the old lady thinking? Finally, she said, "If the rent's too much, we'll reduce it."

The woman was so frustrated that she felt like crying. Her hands trembled. She should act as if she were uncaring and apathetic. She imagined she was in a hospital, and the moonlighters were wearing on her nerves—but she was not in a hospital, she was in her dark, old home across from her sad, old lady.

"It has nothing to do with the rent. It's dark here."

She did not say that she found it impossible to work, because she knew exactly how the old lady would reply. "Put the typewriter on top of my head and type until morning," she would have said in her old doll's voice. She had burned all her bridges. She was a master at burning bridges. She had to go someplace where she would not be tied down to anyone or anything. To be free. Free.

The old lady stayed silent and left the table. She always used to sit patiently and shout at the woman, "You're ruining your stomach with the way you eat. Chew more slowly!" The younger woman was always in a hurry.

Now the old lady wanted to clear the table and push the woman away quickly. The pieces of food got stuck in the woman's throat. She had to leave. She could no longer put up with the old lady. Five years. Five years and it all came down to cigarette smoke and gray walls and the path that she had opened for the ants—the paths that she had tried to open for all creatures, helpless and small.

The woman rose and withdrew to her room. She felt listless and utterly lost. A glance at the books which seemed to jump from the shelves and thump her in the head, a glance at the sofa in the foyer and the refrigerator and all those artificial flowers ... The door opened and the old lady's hand appeared, white with glass bangles, fake and colored. She held out the pencil and eraser toward her. The woman rose without making a sound. They were in her hand, a pencil and an eraser. She closed the door and sat on the chair. The Dervish's picture, the picture of the Hero of Zand, stared back at her, alive and calm. She even imagined that he was laughing. He was moving his *kashkool*, but it was not clear exactly where he was pointing. She knew that it was probably toward Baharestan Square and Gorgan Street, at that other house moldering under spider webs and dust. She said, "Everything's over."

۞ ۞ ۞ ۞

The alien Horseman stopped moving his *kashkool*. The woman said, "What should I do? With all of these books, all of this junk!" A horse had just arrived from the horizon, without a saddle or a rider. In front of them, a Horseman was trotting. On each horse, there was a box of books or something else. With the signaling of the Horseman, they both moved towards Baharestan Square in step. There were a pond and a water fountain in the square. Each horse followed the other, walking in circles around the water fountain, for they had lost their way.

Suddenly the Horseman went toward the sidewalk and asked something of the old lady with golden hair and small, light eyes, whose arms were weighed down with fake bangles. The old lady, her bracelets clacking, pointed him to Jomhoori Street. Across town, the whirlwind suddenly caught the colonel's wife in its grasp. His wife, fragile and as afraid as a fallen yellow leaf, screamed that those streets led to Pastor Square. She took the bridle of the Horseman's steed, showing him instead the way to Gorgan Street. The Horseman signaled with his hands, and all the world's horses trotted alongside him.

The doll-like old lady precipitated toward the colonel's wife. Everyone tried to escape each other. All the world's old ladies ran together in a stampede, crushing the woman under their feet. In all the chaos, her dress ripped off. The horses galloped. Her books fell out of the boxes and flew through the air. An old lady stood by a window. As each book flew up, she jotted something down on a white piece of paper and then nodded her head ...

۞ ۞ ۞ ۞

It was her own old lady once again, bringing her a cup of tea. The woman rose and stood before the door. With an unknown voice, she said, "I don't feel like it right now."

— 8 —

People filled the publisher's conference room. Members of the editorial board, critics ... Mr. Mohajerani was ecstatic. They distributed the book one week ago, and it was selling well. Mr. Mohajerani had discovered a new writer and his eyes were shining; he decided to host a party. Despite his excitement, the woman could feel only sadness. She did not know if Father had read the book or not.

Meanwhile, the Dictator paced from one corner to another listening to conversations. He had grown taller. His hands became so broad and fingers so long that he could gather everyone in the room and squeeze them together and crush them to a pulp, as if he were squeezing a woman's waist. His head smashed through the ceiling and reached the sky. The stars of the faraway heavens hit his head and fell to the ground.

He was not sharing in everyone else's happiness either. She could not understand why Father, with the silver-framed eyeglasses, and the other man, with empty eye sockets, would not let go. Thinking of that house with the big windows of colored glass facing the garden, the dried up bitter orange tree and the cobblestone street, caused a strange sadness to fill her heart. When the book came out, she was tired, very tired. She felt light—headed all day. Now she moved from one corner to another, and she did not know why everyone was laughing. She had jotted down, *Father, write to me. Tell me what you think of my book*; and that very same day, she typed the note. Father could read a book in one day, but she had not yet heard from him. She wanted to know whose strength was greater: that of the woman dressed in orange, or the other one who could write and could ... What could she do? How could she wander through the streets until morning in her thin orange nightgown? There is no street in the entire world that allows a woman with a thin orange nightgown to take shelter, not when there are so many hands and so many men sighing their loneliness into the air of the city. And the man came to Father in the morning, early in the morning, seeking an answer.

"Tell me yourself, sir—tell me if I should put up with this. Tell me if any man should put up with this."

His eyes were silver. He sat chain smoking one cigarette after another. She did not listen to what he was saying. She just looked at his silver eyes, and she knew that no man could live with a woman who, in a city such as Shiraz, with one thin orange nightgown, had lost her night. Father stood up. She squatted in the corner of the room and her throat felt swollen. Father struck her with his belt, screaming, "Where were you … Where?"

Where was she the whole night? Just in the street or someplace like it. What, even with all those hands, all those men, all those policemen and drivers? Yes, but where was the driver? She had to ask everyone, including that old man who knew he was old and was looking at her with astonishment when she stepped out of the taxi. She forced herself to yell, "Taxi, taxi!" on that lost night. After that, she shut up and could not speak for six months. Rumors circulated that she had throat cancer. "The most truthful event must have a witness. All those 'truths' that people believe are no more than lies. He who does not have a witness must flee"—and Father and the pregnant sister carpet-weavers chuckled. "The hell with her," they said. And with that, they discarded the woman like a bag of trash that might bring happiness to a homeless scavenger.

The Dictator stood beside her, taunting, "With your next work, *The Alien Horseman*, you'll be able to make a name for yourself."

"I will?"

"Certainly—you shouldn't distract yourself. Each thought of that night makes you weak, and in your weakness, everyone will mock you. Do you want them to ridicule you? To be pointed out? For them to say, 'Aha—can't you see that we were right?'"

Her blood ran cold. She did not want anyone to deride her: not that man with the empty sockets, or the pregnant carpet-weaving sisters or Father. But Father would not mock her, would he?

"Don't get started again. Look at that man, the young writer, how much he hopes to talk to you. Look."

She rose. The young man stood laughing jovially. She smiled and walked toward him. As she approached, Mr. Mohajerani gave her a cup of tea and slapped her approvingly on the shoulders, just like Father. The young man got up from his chair, and the Dictator once again became talkative. The house with the orange tree disappeared from her thoughts.

"How's your book going—*The Greedy Inheritors*?"

"I'm still working on it."

She took a sugar cube from the table and put it in her cup of tea. The young man asked, "If the story were yours, how would you write it?"

His interest immediately restored her confidence. Now everyone in the salon was watching and the Dictator was laughing.

"If it were me, I'd have given each of those five girls in your book political beliefs, and, well ... before the death of the father, I'd prepare the stage. Each daughter would have her own special interest, and the father wouldn't know how to deal with all of them. In fact, his daughters would feel sorry for him that they had been so hard to take care of, and the irony would be that, through their actions, they would be preparing him for his death."

"But that would be a political story."

"Why not? The father has five daughters and each one of them wants to convince the father that she's the best to bring him to her own side. And then when he dies, they'll fight with each other in front of his body. See the humor of life—after his death, the irony ... Oh, my God, I could describe for you how, when they are carrying his body away during his funeral, they're mourning. A full show. They're fainting, throwing themselves on the body. Why? Because each needs strength for her theatrical performance ... a performance to show off her merits. Perhaps if no one were there, they would ignore the body and just leave. After that, you know what happens. Imagine that every Thursday, armed with an assortment of flowers, these five daughters visit his grave and fight with each other there. The story is no longer about the father or about anyone else; it's about the human condition."

Smiling, Mr. Mohajerani approached them and said, "Ms. Sar-Boland's correct. Dinner's ready."

The secretary entered and exited the dining room a few times. She avoided eye contact with the woman. She was absent the day she was supposed to give the woman her story, and she had not brought it up since; it was as if she had completely forgotten the subject. She was beautiful and could lose many nights in her life. One dark night, the woman fled above the rooftops. Then she came into the streets and did not know where she was or where she wanted to go. A taxi driver let her in and let her descend somewhere, next to a small street beside a garden alley so that she could wander around until morning. Though many years had passed since that night, she was still not able to talk about it, even to herself.

Thin pressed lips filled with sadness—it was uncertain when the secretary would tell the story. It always starts with one lie. A small lie, and then, if you feel like it, you continue. The difference between a liar and an artist is that a liar always makes a false claim and talks on. With one small lie, an artist opens a path for himself and works, and then becomes a writer. Or was she? She still had not gotten a reply from Father. The story of the Horseman was going nowhere, and now the Dictator was standing before her. He always stood in front of her so he could stare directly into her eyes.

"Just one flower doesn't bring the spring season."

"And what if spring never comes?"

"Why not? *The Alien Horseman* will summon spring."

The young writer sat far away from the Dictator. His head hung over his plate in concentration. What was he thinking about? Probably about his wife's cooking, she laughed to herself. His story really was not so bad. In time, it would prove itself. In this country, if you touch anything, it is always this way. Isn't that so? She took her plate and stood up to speak to the young writer again. He said, "It isn't possible. Nothing can compete with the truth. How could such young girls, even if they had the mind for politics, cause so much trouble for their father?"

The woman laughed, "So many black and white pictures have been taken. Black and white. But the world's filled with colors, colors that have no name. So many colors that no one can figure them out. You know, no one here really has much conviction about anything. The people in your story, I mean. They're just like tape recorders—collecting information. You take three of these girls who are between twenty and twenty-two, and you'll see that eight years ago at the time of the revolution they were just little girls. Suddenly, they're prisoners to the revolutionary slogans—the stronger the slogans, the greater their effect. The slogans could make a ten year old girl think she could change the world. But she is just mimicking what she hears—that is all. She realizes that she can't change the world, and then her life loses its natural shape and starts to fall apart. Now these girls are stuck somewhere between a normal, emotional life and a life of revolutionary passion. They are incapable of either extreme."

"If you think that way, everyone's exonerated—even dictators."

"Yes, everyone is absolved. Because if anything happens on this dusty globe today, its roots are from one thousand years ago."

"What do you mean?"

"To find Father's true killer, we have to go back to the year that the Mede Dynasty established itself in Iran."

On Friday, when the old lady left to visit her son, the woman planned to gather her luggage and leave. She told the old lady that she was leaving on Tuesday. The old lady began to balance her accounts from the past few years.

"The first year that you arrived here, the walls were not so gray. You've turned the bathroom faucet on and off so often that it drips. Three years ago, you didn't give me money for three kilos of rice. The electricity and water bill quadrupled because you always stayed up so late and took so many showers."

The old lady looked straight into the woman's eyes. With every bit of money that the woman put before her, the old lady calmed down. She was a gambler, a losing gambler, and an avenger. The old lady would not give up this last chance to make her suffer, to nettle her. The woman remained silent and saw how hatefully the old lady stared at the picture of the Hero of Zand. During the night, the woman had awoken with a start to the sound of coughing and the shouts of the Horseman. The old lady rode the horse but could not hold onto its bridle. Her fake teeth fell out, she started coughing, and suddenly the world was filled with duplicates of her, thousands of toothless old ladies. The Horseman, in the middle of them all, lost his way. The eyes of all the old ladies were light-colored and small. They had golden hair. The woman took the picture and hid it in her purse. It was the middle of the night. No roosters were singing, but there weren't any gunshots in the air either.

ﻙ ﻙ ﻙ ﻙ

"In the old times there were lots of barefoot, hungry people."
Silence!
"In the old times, they'd just put a *dah shahi*, a penny, in their hands."
Silence!
The old lady said, "In two days you'll come back. No one will rent out a home to a single woman. I'm the only one who will put up with this ... all this cigarette smoking!"

The old lady shot bullet after bullet as she entreated her. The woman was slowly raising her hand in surrender when she heard, "Before you leave, find someone else, a woman—a girl—like yourself."

Like yourself. This startled her. Such was the irony of life. She was stunned, and she regretted all those moments when she slowly lifted her hands up in surrender. These gunshots in the air ought to frighten her—"find someone like yourself!" Another person would come into this room, and it would make no difference; everything would remain still, quiet, even the water. It was as if the old lady pounded the woman's face with her fist. This very cursed old woman pummeled her face with a set of papery, soft-veined hands and the Dictator simply laughed.

"Didn't I tell you? Everyone should just take care of their own needs."

⁂ ⁂ ⁂ ⁂

The taxi was stuck at the end of the street—there was a traffic jam. The woman brought down her things with the help of the driver and Nasrin. All the half-closed doors and windows and all the eyes were staring into the street.

The retired colonel Agha Hamidi was tall and thin, with prominent eyes, a small cranberry-colored face, and thick white eyebrows. A large white visor covered his eyes. He brushed his hair carefully, and wore an old wrinkled shirt and pants. He puffed at his cigarette forcefully and blew the smoke into the air. Advancing through the haze, he poked his fingers into the luggage.

"Don't let anything break."

He spoke to the driver, who carried cartons of books on his shoulders. His teeth tightly clenched, the man responded, "They're books—books aren't breakable."

"Awful," the colonel hissed under his breath, "these men are all awful."

The colonel made a path through the furniture and stood above the typewriter, his eyes glowing. He looked reluctantly at his half-finished cigarette and then tossed it into the corner. He pulled the typewriter's paper bar forward. There was already a white sheet in it. Happily, he turned the handle until it came to the beginning of a line. He pulled a box closer to him and placed the typewriter on it. He then cautiously sat on another box and said aloud, "Good for writing a letter."

He put his hands on the big blue keys. Preoccupied with what he was writing, he forgot everything else—the street, the scattered boxes, and the driver who, hunched over from the weight of the refrigerator he carried on his back, glared at him out of the corner of his eye. The colonel impatiently made a cross in the air with his finger. He crossed out what he had typed, turned the handle, and started again:

A line of soldiers, standing in military stance, hands on their foreheads ...

He said aloud, "You write well, very well."

Dummy—hold your rifle correctly ... Yes, this way ... One more time ... You asshole ... Hold your rifle in salute position ...

They unloaded the rest of her things and the cab departed. The colonel continued fiddling with the typewriter, and the woman just stood there not knowing what to say. Nasrin could not speak, because she was doubled over with laughter.

"Mr. Colonel ... If you please, the typewriter?"

"What?" The colonel lifted his head, visibly upset. He rose from the box, turned away, and responded, "Typewriters were much better in the old days."

Before the colonel could change his mind the woman closed the typewriter and, with Nasrin's help, put all of the boxes in the foyer. She saw the old lady lingering with a tray of tea.

"You're tired—here's some tea."

"Not yet, thank you. I'll have some later."

She wanted to clean the house. She completed her work at sunset and organized her books and flowers. She had arranged everything, but still she was not finished. A strange, obsessive meticulousness had come over her. Had it been the doll-like old lady living there, she certainly would have offered her help, but the colonel's wife did not lift a finger; she merely closed the door so that she could not see the filth.

The stairs still needed to be cleaned.

With a bucket of soap-water, she scrubbed and shined the stairs. A few times the colonel, cigarette dangling from his fingers, walked by her. He would raise his eyebrows and whistle, "It can't be erased. The dirt can never be wiped off."

But she wiped it off, and the colonel went into his room. She moved to the bathroom and then shined the window. Finally, she threw down her rag, tired and content. In the meantime, Nasrin had organized her books.

"You deserve it ..." she said.

The woman sat on the bed. She could no longer think.

"What?"

"You deserve success."

"Why do you say that?"

"You never leave anything half-way done. If it had been me, I wouldn't have settled in for six months."

The woman did not feel like saying that she had in fact left many things half-finished. She was so tired that she did not even have the energy to speak.

Nasrin had taken down a book and was staring at it. She lifted her head. *The Song of the Earth*. She rose.

"Put this on the bookcase for poems."

The woman took the book and stood hesitating for a moment. She opened it.

"This is still relevant."

In late afternoon, she thought, exhaustion will come.

Slowly her face became happy again. She looked toward Nasrin and laughed.

By seven o'clock, everything was clean and organized. Nasrin left, and with a bucket of water and a wet cloth, the woman cleaned the leaves of the green tree. The colonel stood next to the pond.

"Leave the tree alone. In two days it will rain. It will wash all the filth away."

She smiled, sprucing all the leaves that her hands could reach. From the outside she cleaned the windows, and then began to brighten them from the inside. She soaked the cloth in the bucket and wrung it out. She started on the upper row, but before she reached the third window she stopped in alarm. There were drops of blood on the windows—blood that was not yet dry. She stared, following the traces of blood. They continued onto the wall and further down; they appeared recent—very recent. She rubbed the cloth over the bloodstains and struggled to wipe them off. They would leave a permanent mark on the wall, unless she applied a fresh coat of blue paint. The entire world's blue can erase all the bloodstains as if they had never been there.

She squeezed the cloth in the water. Black filth leached from her rag, infecting the water. Black water. When blood congeals, it turns black. All blood is black. But here? Certainly someone had been injured. A fight ... A nose bleed? A first, the colonel's fist had hit the old lady's nose. The noses of all the old ladies in the world were bleeding, even the doll-like ones.

She went downstairs and returned with a bucket filled with fresh water. Once again she tried to wipe off all the stains, but she could not. She yearned for blue. She stood between the two rooms—the bed was in the second room, with the desk and typewriter. She needed to buy a curtain rod to divide the two rooms. She wondered who would come here to her gatherings? Obviously, she would come to her own gatherings. The second room was better as an office than as a dining room. She glanced at her flower vases. Their place by the window was perfect, and sunlight reflected off their colored glass surfaces.

"There's always a lot of sunshine. Winter and summer."

She watered the flowers, one glass for each of them—just a glass of water, not salt water. She sat on the sofa, and a feeling of happiness spread over her. The foyer of the doll-like old lady needed this sofa now. The woman could just imagine the current emptiness of her previous foyer ... *Before you leave, find someone who also has a sofa ... No one has a sofa. No one ...*

The sound of someone coming through the door startled her. She thought it was the old lady of Pastor Street, but it was not. It was Mrs. Hamidi, the old lady of Gorgan Street with a tray of tea. The woman was elated to see her.

The old lady stood in the middle of the first room. Her eyes widened with surprise, and her face lit up with happiness. "How nice it looks now. So many books!"

The woman followed the old lady's gaze to the stains of blood at the corner of the wall by the bookshelves. She took a wet cloth.

"I don't know what this is."

Mrs. Hamidi put the tray of tea on the table and approached the stains. "What is it? Is it dirt?"

"No—it's blood. It was also on all the window glass."

Mrs. Hamadi stood rooted to the spot. Her lips trembled, and without looking at the woman, she mumbled, "*Aakh*—was the blood fresh?"

"It was fresh only on the wall right next to the window."

There was panic in the old lady's face. She turned white, faint, aging before the woman's eyes. She bit her fingers anxiously and turned toward the window. She wanted to control herself, but she could not.

"You said the stains were fresh?"

"Yes."

Mrs. Hamidi groaned aloud and tapped her fingers on the wet walls. "It's n—nothing. Perhaps the children wounded some sparrows. Perhaps the windows were open and they flew into the room."

Wounded sparrows. Suddenly, one came in from the window and darted against the wall above the desk, remaining affixed like a picture. The alien Horseman held a *kashkool* in his hands and nodded his head. The picture ... Where was the picture? She remembered it was in her purse by the table. She smiled in relief.

The old lady was surprised by her smile.

"I don't know, perhaps it was something else," she said.

The woman took the tray of tea. She hoped that it was a sparrow, that same sparrow of the wounded Horseman.

"No—it was that very sparrow … the bird."

She was spinning around, like that same homeless sparrow that flew in through the open window and flung itself against the wall. She sat on the sofa, wounded and tired.

"If you hang a curtain here, it will look nice," the old lady said.

"Certainly."

"Siyavash is friends with a curtain seller."

The woman inhabited the world of a Horseman and a bird—of a curtain, an office, and a dining room. The doll-like old lady used to invite herself to sit on the sofa to meditate. Perhaps this old lady would also come and sit across from her, frightened of all the wounded birds. Wasn't she herself wounded? But who, what person can see his own wounds? You always see the wounds of others, but forget your own blood falling softly upon the blue walls of the Earth.

"Mrs. Hamidi, I'll give you money to give to him so that he can buy a curtain and a curtain rod."

The old lady was visibly shaken. The woman gave her a penetrating look, trying to figure out what she was thinking. A few times her lips quivered, but she did not utter a word. It seemed as though she were still ruminating about the bird. All the sparrows of the world were wounded. She did not want to stare at the walls or the windows. Perhaps she recalled that day when the colonel struck her nose with his fist. She escaped from him and came upstairs. Then she had wanted to open the window and throw herself down, but the colonel—sickly, weak—could he have been responsible for all this blood? He could not have done this; his fist did not have enough strength. *It must have been his son's doing*, the woman thought. *What was his name again? Si … Siyavash.*

"Let go. Let go."

You are right—it should not matter to me who did what. And this kid, he can only buy a curtain rod and a curtain … He is friends with the curtain seller and that sparrow! Certainly, it flapped its wings and slammed itself against the walls.

"I told you, let go."

The doorbell rang, and the old lady ran out of the room like a meteor. God willing, she will always run out. Always.

"Oh no, the colonel has been waiting outside the door."

The woman finished her tea. She gazed absently at the typewriter. It was also a calculator. She was organizing her accounts, with herself and with others. With the Horseman she would be able to get rid of everyone—even the pregnant carpet-weaving girls. With everyone gone, Father would most definitely compose his letter to her.

She stood up, opened her purse, and hung the picture of the Horseman on the wall in front of her chair. Had the Horseman seen the bloodstains? It seemed as if he knew everything. The only thing he did not know was whether she knew. She placed her two elbows on the table and stared into his eyes. Then she heard muffled whispers coming from downstairs, the whispers of the colonel and the old lady.

"I told you not to bring ... A hundred times I told you not to bring ..."

Calmly the old lady said something and the colonel yelled, "How many times did I tell you that the general would embarrass us, leave us without pride?"

The woman got up and stood beside the door so she could hear better, but the rest of the words were inaudible. What was the old lady not to bring? A renter? But the colonel consented. It did not matter. She had signed the contract. Who was the general?

"Let go."

She sat down on the chair. The man in the picture frame wore a happy look on his face. Startled, she waved her hands in the air and pulled the typewriter toward her. When she opened the door, the colonel's paper came out and in its place emerged a fresh new sheet.

"I'm going to start. Right now. What time is it?"

The small, red, square-shaped watch lay on the table. It was eight-thirty. She put her fingers on the letters and began.

The sweet melody of tapping keys filled the room, like a thousand wounded sparrows chirping together.

— 10 —

In the morning, she awoke to the flight of dozens of pigeons from the roof across the street. Her bed was next to the window. She rolled over and watched. The colonel stood on the roof in a military salute, monitoring the group formation of the birds. One by one they flew back, settling into their former disarray. The colonel dipped into a bag and threw them a handful of seeds. With each toss, another pigeon perched on the roof. The colonel snickered; he shook his head serenely, and with empty bag in hand he gazed at the throngs of pigeons covering the rooftop.

She turned around and headed toward her desk. It was only five-thirty in the morning. She wrapped herself in a blanket, pulled it up to her neck, and rolled a piece of paper into the typewriter. A satisfied smile spread across her lips. She worked until very late last night, and for the first time in years, she woke up not just in her own room, but in her own home. A lost but familiar sense: two rooms and everything in them belonged to her. She could close the door, leave, and at the end of the day come again. On the way back, she could tell herself that she was returning to her own home.

All of these keys! She was excited. She lived in a place of her own and she had work to do that belonged only to her. During the night, she did not hear the coughing of any old lady, the thud of footsteps in the corridor, or the sound of an insomniac banging dishes against each other in the kitchen. It had been a long time since she had a home to call her own.

There was noise in the garden. She peered out the window. The colonel was climbing down the ladder with the empty bag. At the sound of a new pigeon, the colonel paused. He pointed his index finger at the latecomer. Not paying much attention, the pigeon whirled around and around as if drunk. Then another pigeon rose up from the roof. Passing close to the colonel, it flapped its wings and ascended. Then both the latecomer and the daring one settled back onto the roof's wall. The colonel sighed with grief.

She laughed. She took off the blanket and stood up. It was now six-thirty—she still had time to review last night's work. Once, many years ago, the Dictator had said, "Habit. You can become accustomed to anything, like smoking cigarettes. Once the habit becomes a part of you, quitting is extremely difficult."

For years, she worked as a slave. A slave to habits that were thrust upon her, she merely carried out orders. She had no choice but to obey, for she feared that without this obedience, without this dictated path, she would lose her way.

None of the world's dictators were as bad or ridiculous as the colonel who lived on the bottom floor. Her dictator was a good one. Very good. And she had surrendered in obedience to him—for days, for years.

She worked busily at her desk until seven-thirty. Then, with a smile, she stood up and prepared to leave. Descending the stairs, her eyes fell on a young man still asleep in the room on the left. On his headboard was an ashtray filled with cigarette butts. His blanket had slipped down around him, and the young man's bare shoulder peeked out at her.

"Money for the curtains ..."

Mrs. Hamidi was sitting next to a *samovar* in the room across from the young man. She poured tea. The woman sat down in front of the old lady so that her back faced the room where the young man was sleeping.

What if he catches a cold? the woman wondered.

The Dictator waved his fist in the air and shouted. Frightened, the woman stood up and left her half-drunk tea.

"Here's the money for the curtains and curtain rod."

The old lady, pointing in the direction of the room across, said, "I'll give this to Siyavash."

"*Mamnoon*—Thank you. And here are the keys, so he can put them up himself."

Horrified, the old lady leaned backward.

"Keys!?"

The woman was bewildered.

"Yes—I'll be at work until sunset. He has to take the measurements."

"Why don't we wait until you're also here."

"What does it matter? You're here, aren't you?"

The old lady said no more. She took the keys and looked at them as if they were the tools of a killer.

When the woman left, the young man was still sleeping. Restless, he pulled the covers over himself, and now only his curly black hair showed from under the sheets.

Heavy traffic congested the road from the wooden bridge to Enghilab Square. She arrived late and found the secretary waiting for her. *You need to leave the house earlier—at seven o'clock.*

"Let go. When you start work late, your entire day is ruined. Now you'll see."

She felt guilty. She paced back and forth between the bathroom and her office until she could avoid her secretary no longer.

"I was stuck in rush hour," explained the woman simply.

She looked straight into the girl's eyes and saw that she had still not written that story. It was time for it. It was exactly the time for it. *Anything that you start late will never ever get done, and your future will be black.* It was the voice of the Dictator.

"By the way, what happened to your story?"

Unnerved, the girl stared at her.

"I was sick."

"Yes—you were out for two days."

"I wasn't able to edit the final draft."

"Not able to edit it or not able to write it?"

The girl smiled apologetically. She panicked.

"What do you want from her? This time early in the morning you want a story from her?"

It was her voice. She smiled, and the secretary found the courage to bombard her with words. "Ms. Sar-Boland—I'm not able to, I swear I'm not able to. As long as there's no paper in front of me, I'm able to. Once the paper's in front of me, everything escapes me, everything. But I can talk about it. I wrote it for Reza, my older cousin. Would you like me to read you the letter? Did you know that Reza's on the war front now? When his work's done, he'll come to Tehran and ..."

The girl blushed. The woman realized that if she stayed and listened to the girl until sunset, she would have to wander the war front, apply dressings to the wounds of all the soldiers, give water to the thirsty people, and then see pictures of all of them on the walls.

"So how are sales going?"

"Oh, my God—the printing is almost done. Oh, by the way, Mrs. Mohajerani read your book. She called on Thursday, the same day that you told me not to plug in the telephone. She wanted to speak to you. I told her that you had gone to the printer."

The secretary stared into her eyes and opened the desk's drawers. *On the Peak of the Whirlwind.*

"All right, then ... an autograph."

The girl's eyes widened. She grabbed the book back from the woman's hands. Her cheeks glowed.

"Wow."

The woman retreated to her office. She and the Dictator stood side by side in front of the map of Iran. They already sold five thousand copies, and there were so many more to sell. Now she could work on the story of the Horseman. Six months should be enough time. First, he approached. Then he arrived in Shiraz. The Horseman and his horse stood rooted to their spot amid all the war and fleeing. Despite his bravery, he was just a man. Time and circumstance were to blame for all his misdeeds. If his army took war spoils, if he had to kill, it was only because of the time in which he lived ... Kindness and warmth can change color and complexion—justice and law. Time transforms knowledge into its own color, according to its own wishes ...

※ ※ ※ ※

She remained still. She sided with the Horseman. The Horseman rode toward her but could not reach her. It seemed as if the wind prevented him from hearing her words. The woman tried to yell from the depths of her soul: "If you had co-operated, your eyes –"

The Horseman's big black eyes filled with tears. The woman continued, this time more calmly, "You didn't have a choice. As soon as you turned your head and blinked, someone would come and bomb the walls of the fortress. He'd steal the belongings of the people just so he could take your place. Power ... A war of power. And people would be forced to take someone's side. Wouldn't they?"

The voice of the Horseman drifted toward her in the strange rush of the wind.

"But because of fear, no one took my side ... no one as much as ..."

The Horseman bit his lip and galloped in the garden alleys of Shiraz. She heard the sound of his horse's hooves. He got stuck on the phrase "as much as" and the Dictator shook with laughter. The Horseman slowly trotted away.

She called out to him but he covered his ears and the woman heard his weeping. He wept in the small garden alleys of Shiraz as he fled. Oh, if only he could return to that night in the garden alley and find some wandering woman.

She yelled, "In the evening when you have arrived at the edge of the city, you'll see a small garden alley. You can put a woman on your saddle and leave. If you're embarrassed to look at her in nothing but a thin orange nightgown, cover her shoulders with your jacket. The moments are passing, and now she's growing old."

The Dictator's laughter ceased. He shuddered and went to sit on the table. "Ms. Sar-Boland—telephone."

She picked up the receiver. It was Nasrin saying that she had finished reading the book and cried for two hours.

"Is it based on a true story?"

The woman wanted to say that *everything* was real. In some corner of the world, piece by piece, here and there, everything that happened was patched together so that all of the moments became a quilt, and in the quilt there were images of events. On the dusty quilt of the world, even this story had taken place.

But she did not say this to Nasrin. She muttered out a simple answer, "yes," and listened politely to her compliments. In spite of herself, she began to grow taller and taller. It was like when she was a child and she would show her report card to her father. He would make a bet with all of his friends that one day everyone would be in awe of his daughter.

She sat behind her desk and wrote until the sun began its descent.

After work, she hastened to the flower shop, excited to decorate her new home with bright blossoms. It was always this way: bookstores and flower shops, the unnecessary, frivolous necessities. Those women who, from sunrise to sunset, go from one store to the next to buy balls of thick and thin yarn: are they the pregnant carpet-weaving sisters? That day she went with the old lady of Pastor Street to buy fabric; she panicked and abandoned her in the street. She returned home alone with no fabric. Thank God no old lady became pregnant, not the one on Pastor Street and not this one on Gorgan Street.

The lazy, wafting scent of ripe blossoms permeated the air of the shop. The flowers bowed their heads under the heavy aroma of their own perfume—Shiraz and the heavy scent of *narenj* blossoms. Everyone fell asleep under clouds of this perfume. They slept without ever waking, caught in the eternal opium blossom dream. A woman could easily escape above the rooftops and drop herself into the streets, all because of these vases of *Hosn-e Yusof* flowers.

Three vases were full of *Hosn-e Yusof* and *Kowkab* flowers. The Horseman stretched out his hands to reach for the *Hosn-e Yusof* flowers. She did not let go but waved the *Kowkab* flowers toward him. The Horseman said, "They resemble the old lady on Gorgan Street."

He was right. They were rumpled, fearful, and white, like Mrs. Hamidi's hair. The salesman from the shop brought the flowers to the curb. The woman stepped into a taxi and steadied the vases with her feet, rubbing fallen *Kowkab* petals in her hands.

Kowkab flowers can turn into blood, like the blood that flows from the nose and covers the walls with decadent drops. But if the colonel were to strike someone with his fist ...

❧ ❧ ❧ ❧

Mrs. Hamidi timidly opened the door. It was as if she were expecting someone else. When she saw the woman, her eyes shone with happiness.

"What beautiful flowers!"

The old lady helped carry the vases upstairs. The colonel was sitting in the hallway, a game of backgammon set before him. When he saw the flowers, he stopped playing. He watched with irritation, then shook his head and threw the dice on the board. The woman heard him mumble, "Stupid. Just stupid waste."

In the room, the old lady hesitated, waiting to be invited in. In the meantime, she busied herself placing the *Hosn-e Yusof's* on the second window and arranging the *Kowkab* flowers in the vases.

"*Mamnoon*—Mrs. Hamidi—you shouldn't have."

"You're like my own daughter," the old lady said.

I am only like your daughter now since you are hoping to stay with me in this room ... The woman approached her desk. She made it evident that she had work to do. The old lady stood still and waited. She did not say anything. It was as if no one was in the room. Enveloped in thick silence, the old lady turned to leave. "Let me know if you need anything."

"Okay."

First they say, "if you need anything," and then they persist. She took off her *mantow* and observed the *Kowkab* flowers. They needed water. She took the jug and went downstairs. Mrs. Hamidi was sitting in the room next to the *samovar*.

"Afsaneh *Khanom*, the window rod is ready. I measured it myself and bought it for you."

The woman filled the water jug. Mrs. Hamidi handed her the window rod.

"When Siyavash comes, I'll tell him to hang it up."

"Mrs. Hamidi, I'm busy in the evening. I'll give you the keys; please take care of this during the day when I'm not here."

Again a look of fear rose in the old lady's face. It was as if she had seen bloodstains or a wounded sparrow flapping its wings, but there was nothing before her except the black and dirty tiles. The old lady blushed in embarrassment.

"I mop the floor once a week. On Friday I'll have to remember to clean here," the old lady said.

The woman went upstairs and an astonished Mrs. Hamidi followed her. She entered her room and watered the flowers. The *Kowkab* flowers laughed.

The woman sat behind her desk. If only she could finish her work within six months. Work! The sound of the typewriter danced around the room, bouncing from wall to wall. The Horseman stood in the fortress. Thousands of young and old women waited at the foot of the fortress for the Horseman. All the while, the young man continued sleeping with his bare shoulders revealed. The sun's rays shined through the window onto his skin, illuminating the bright room.

Her fingers suddenly stopped moving. All the young and old women at the foot of the fortress were in the form of Mrs. Hamidi. No other woman could come to her mind. She had even forgotten the faces of the pregnant weaving sisters. Young and old women multiplied, and none of them could hide their fear from the Horseman.

"Let go. Let go."

She worked until her back ached. Someone tapped on the door and, exhausted but happy, she stood up. The old lady slid into the room with a tray of dinner. Her eyes were shining.

"Oh, thank you, you're just like a mother to me."

Mrs. Hamidi carefully put the tray on the table and then stood silently in the door frame.

The woman wondered why the old lady seemed so fearful of her. She smiled and said, "Won't you sit down, my dear mother?"

The old lady, dubious, sat down. Perhaps she misunderstood. The woman was hungry, and she brought the plate closer to herself: hot food, salad, and yogurt—the royal treatment.

"Yum ... How tasty."

"*Noosh-e jan*—enjoy, my dear."

Mrs. Hamidi made herself comfortable on the sofa. The woman drew the glass of water up to her lips. Cold water. It tasted wonderful.

"Have you studied psychology?"

"Yes."

"Is it true that psychologists can save people?"

Her spoon stopped.

"No!"

The old lady was taken aback.

"They themselves are the most pathetic of people."

"How? In what way?"

"They're crazy."

She laughed and the old lady also tried hard to laugh. She inspected the woman from head to toe. "How old are you?"

The woman felt relaxed, no longer hungry now. She wanted to stretch out her legs. One hot cup of tea would hit the spot.

"Thirty years old."

"How nice. You're still young."

She was taken aback. Compared ... It was always this way. She wondered if a string of numbers placed in order filled people's heads. Someone like Nasrin's old lady would sit in a small room and calculate everything.

She turned toward the window rod and remembered that she had to give the old lady the keys.

"Here are the keys. You can give them to him."

"Keep them with you."

The old lady's face changed—her brow furrowed; this obvious anxiety surprised the woman.

"I'm coming home late tomorrow."

"Today you also came home late."

Now that the old lady had gotten it off her chest, she smiled. Yes, she was no different than her own old lady of Pastor Street—the first one, who told her that her hard work would make her age. That was when she was twenty-five years old.

She listened to the eerie sound of the wind blowing against the window and the sweet jangling of the keys. The stress of life and work overwhelmed her. The tapping of the typewriter was lost in the howling of the wind. Invading armies stood at the gates of the city. The Horseman observed them from a tower. The wind tousled the horses' manes.

"We'll attack near sunrise."

It was one-thirty when she rose from her desk, enough time to drink water and sleep. Slowly, she left her room. Everyone was asleep. Darkness had fallen everywhere. In the room downstairs on the left side, there was the glow of a cigarette. She tiptoed into the kitchen and groped for the water faucet in the dark. She drank, and then washed her hands and face. She filled the water carafe and left the door open. On the stairs—the second stair—a hand turned on the lights. Without turning around she whispered, "Thanks."

— 12 —

The old lady threw herself into her work. It was Friday. This morning, like every morning, the woman woke with the flight of the pigeons. She scrutinized the colonel throwing seeds to them. He gave orders to two pigeons that ignored him before he climbed down the ladder. The old lady had been toiling since seven-thirty in the morning, and at eight o'clock, with a bucket of soapy water, she attacked the tiles.

The colonel approached her two or three times, flicking the ashes of his cigarette onto the tiles. "They can't ever be cleaned, ever," he said.

When she had finished, the old lady brought the colonel into the room. She looked elated. She had cleaned the kitchen, previously black with smoke. When Nasrin came at ten o'clock, the black soot and grime covered the old lady, but the kitchen was clean and the tiles were too.

The woman sat with Nasrin in the old lady's room and drank tea. As they walked up the stairs, they could hear the young man coughing. It appeared he had just woken up.

When they reached her room, Nasrin flung herself onto the bed.

"It's so tranquil. I could fall asleep here until tomorrow."

A few moments later, she sat up on the bed. She stared at the woman.

"You know, I can't see how anything could disturb your peace."

The woman was content. From work, from all that had happened early that morning, she was happy.

"I could also have lost my way."

"How?"

She wanted to mention the bitter orange tree, but she did not.

"Well, that is what happens to anyone who exposes themselves to risk."

"Once again, you're being enigmatic. You're always like this when you speak about your life. Have you ever said anything about your life and experiences that we can understand?"

"My life isn't particularly exceptional. Like the lives of most people."

"How did it occur to you to become a writer?"

"It didn't occur to me, it just happened."

"How? You mean the decision wasn't in your own hands?"

The woman was silent. Why did she write? For whom? Was she the one who wanted to or ... or who? It's clear that when you want something, you fix your sights on it and you work. It exists on its own, like a clear day that has no connection to anyone, to any man, old or young.

The Dictator was speaking now. He was always putting words into her mouth. All these years he had spoken for her.

"Yes—it was my own decision."

"So why did you say 'it just happened'?"

"You know, you take the first step. You dry up a tree and then ..."

"What?"

"Forget it. I was just giving an example."

"I don't understand."

"So you haven't dried up a tree yet. It's still wet and fresh."

The Dictator glared at her out of the corner of his eye. He trembled with anger, and she did not feel like disobeying his wishes.

"What are you saying?"

"I'm saying that you're still burdened."

"You're right."

"Do you even know why?"

"No, I still don't know."

"First of all, because that bitter orange tree is fresh and its fruit won't dry up for a while. And secondly, you're afraid of that old lady, of the outside world. But you have to try to get along with your surroundings. You have to force that old lady—who is now sitting down by the window sill and who makes your life so miserable—to just come down and kiss your hands."

"It's hopeless. She won't budge."

"Because you surrendered at the first glance. This is the way it always is—the first person who witnesses something screams and alerts everyone else. Yes, she has surrendered. But the only one you should surrender to is yourself—only yourself."

Mrs. Hamidi brought in a lunch tray. The woman did not say a word until the colonel's wife had left. The smell of home-cooked food and years of loneliness filled the rooms. She forgot everything else. She could no longer remember whether that home with the bitter orange tree in its garden had a kitchen or not. Had she ever seen the bitter orange tree at all?

"So you were saying ...?"

"Let's eat something and then ..."

Together they rose. The woman sat on the sofa and brought her own plate closer.

"Tell me," Nasrin insisted.

The woman forgot who was talking. Was it her voice, or that of the Dictator? She took a piece of meat.

"I said that everything is due to 'habit'—misfortune as well as happiness."

"Habit?"

"Yes—and your problem is that you got used to living with a man in one house for years. Six months have gone by, but it's still not enough time to rid yourself of that habit."

"You think that everyone can change their behavior as if they were one of Pavlov's lab dogs."

"Aren't they? If you lived with an old lady with golden hair, it would also have been like this. You'd also have grown to miss her."

A smile rested on the woman's lips. All the world's old ladies appeared before her, and began to clap and scream for her.

"You're wrong—here you're wrong," Nasrin said. "You're just repeating the principles of psychology that we've read. They're no use at all. Studies are one thing and life is something else."

The Dictator told her not to listen and so she did not. Meanwhile, Nasrin droned on. The sun had set by the time she left. The woman took the lunch plates downstairs and noticed a closed door. She heard the sound of whispering, the familiar voice of the colonel.

"Why won't he leave? Why won't he just get lost?"

The old lady pleaded, "Shsh—be quiet."

With tightly clenched teeth, the colonel replied, "This is even worse. I told you not to bring …"

I told you not to bring … She stood on the steps. She did not have a home. The woman was not concerned; she had signed the contract and had a set of keys. No one could kick her out. How often had she stared at the mouths of homeowners, in this city full of *narenj* blossoms? How frequently had she been afraid of their scowls? The doctor said, "In order for you to get your voice back, you need to leave this house." Father had agreed to let her leave. The doctor said, "She can take care of herself. She got her college degree. What else can a father provide?" She went and sold all her possessions. She was between being and not—being. All of her staring at the eyes of the homeowners had given her a lot to say. One year later, in the fall of '78, she went on the rooftop and yelled like everyone else. And then Tehran, Tehran …

She was sitting in the room when the old lady entered with a plate of grapes. She placed the plate on the table and wiped her hands. She prepared to say something to the woman, but no one who is that frustrated and hopeless can give orders. *No one can kick me out of this house she thought. I have a contract, a contract.*

The old lady asked, "Do you need anything?"

She did not need anything, so with some reluctance the old lady left. It was clear that she hoped to linger but the woman could not let her. Time was flying by. She needed to sit behind the typewriter and not pay attention to anyone—not to the colonel or the colonel's wife, who had caused her to experience this agony. They had made the women in her stories grow old and had forced all the old men to enter Shiraz and lean against the walls and gates. Now these old men would play chess with themselves all alone, constantly watching the pigeons to see when they would fly and when they would perch. There was a young man behind the city walls who would sleep until noon ...

❧ ❧ ❧ ❧

She sat behind her desk and timed herself. She wanted to work faster. To fly and reach Father and ask how the Hero of Zand was. *How is he, Father?*

The door to the garden opened and slammed shut. She walked toward the window. Although it was night, the moonlight illuminated the world. The sublime moon hung in the sky and the blowing wind made the old trees' leaves rustle with a strange noise. A group of dead soldiers fell down behind the city gates—corpses, powerless without horses or their trappings. So many burned tanks and thirsty, wounded bodies.

"I came a few times, but you were working."

She smiled back at Mrs. Hamidi, who stood still with the dinner tray. The woman's laughter made the old lady beam. She ran her hands through her hair and let down her guard. She glanced at the picture and the typewriter. Perhaps it was all because of this ...

Yes, you are right, it is all because of this. What you are observing is that I am similar to the weather in the North; suddenly rainy, suddenly sunny, but brilliant because of the changes. For it is best that you don't know what type of person lives in this room, one who will greet you with either a grimace or hearty laughter.

"I'll come back and gather the plates."

"No, don't bother. I'll bring them myself," the woman said.

How the Dictator frowns when you pound on his chest and don't let him through, and how often he has pounded on your chest so that you will not be able to pass through. Look, he is pouting, and those big blank eyes do not know the meaning of work. They do not know what one jar of salt water can do. If you want to make the tree blossom again, you need much more strength. You must pour clean water and change the dirt.

It was late in the evening when she closed the typewriter. She had worked and had not missed the bus. The Dictator still sat at the window with his figure blocking the entire view. It was as if he wanted to prevent her from seeing the sky and the moon, to ensure that the window would remain closed forever.

He chuckled. He shook his head and made plans. Whenever a new idea occurred to him, he would shake his head and laugh until she said, "Well?"

"You have to write down your daily memoirs, they'll be useful."

"How so?"

"One day they'll be published."

He planned for her death, a book of memoirs. What foresight. He was unlike any other dictator, for he accepted that she would eventually die like everyone else. She could not think of that right now. She was too exhausted.

"I'm tired. The memoirs will begin tomorrow ..."

It seemed as if the moon were calling her from behind the window. She approached the sill, and the Dictator swelled up. Over the top of his shoulders, she could still see one piece of the sky. The voice of the Dictator was choked, "Get back to your writing."

"But it's one-thirty in the morning."

The Dictator did not believe her. He looked at the watch on the table and coughed.

"One o'clock and twenty-five minutes," he rebutted.

"But I'm so tired."

"Time shall pass you by—time and everything else."

She no longer cared about the time. She wanted to sit on the bed near the window and look up at the sky, but if she said that, he would probably sit at the windowsill until morning to block her view. She yawned.

"I want to go to sleep."

He laughed. He wiped his hands together and jumped down from the window. He probably wanted to lie down next to her like every other night when she was exhausted from work. The odor of his breath and those big hairy hands would surround her. She just wanted to sit on the bed and stare at the green leaves of the trees. How could she rid herself of him?

"What's that?"

"It's the same story—*The Alien Horseman.*"

He sat on the bed so that he could watch her. The woman laid down and saw that he was scowling at her. She turned toward the window and pulled up the covers, but not enough to hide her eyes. She saw the majestic moon in a clear blue sky without even the stars for company—just one moon. How many years had it been sitting up there, patient and lonely? No hand could ever reach it. No male hand would ever hold it or caress it—and what tree was that growing on the moon? She saw that a bitter orange tree had taken root on the lunar orb. It grew leaves and branches, and its bitter oranges hung down. If she reached her hand out the window, she would be able to pick a branch with *narenj* blossoms. Silence. What silence? Where had all the pigeons gone? From behind the window, two pigeons flapped their wings, soaring toward the moon; finally, they reached the bitter orange tree. Each took a bitter orange in its mouth then fluttered toward the window, where they both hit the glass.

She rose and opened the window. A gentle wind tossed and scattered the fall leaves. Her vision was clear; even far off objects were visible, like those two pigeons that seemed to drop their bitter oranges into the garden and fly out toward the horizon. She sat by the window, facing the moon with her back to the Dictator. The Dictator yelled at her and pummeled her back with his fists. Once again, she sat alone facing the moon. She placed her hands on the wall, and positioned her whole body in the window frame. There was no more room for anyone else who wanted to push her out and slam shut the window that had been closed for all those years.

Now she grasped both sides of the frame tightly and leaned over the sill. She closed her eyes and the wind passed through the green leaves, and played gently with her hair.

Suddenly someone's voice floated down from the moon. She realized that the song was about *narenj* blossoms, and the smell of the *narenj* blossoms permeated the air. The voice was the voice of a man. A feeling of happiness spread throughout her entire body.

I am the one who was robbed in the desert.
I have lost everything.
Nima Yooshij

She opened her eyes and looked down. The young man was sitting with his back to the wall, smoking a cigarette. Sullen and dazed, he looked up at the moon and pulled at his curly, rumpled hair. Her shoulders hit the window shutter, the shutter hit the wall, and the young man looked up. She saw his eyes. They were shining with pain—or were they reflecting the light of the moon? He wore a strange smile.

— 13 —

In the morning, there were no bitter orange trees in the garden. The colonel climbed down the ladder looking dejected. Bitter oranges exist only in dreams. She felt depressed, and when she was drinking her tea with the old lady, she asked pointedly, "So who's going to hang up the curtain rod?"

In the cab, she regretted this. The Dictator told her that she could also hang it up herself. He looked her in the eye, but she had turned away. At eight o'clock with puffy, sleepy eyes, she reached the publishing house.

By the time Mr. Mohajerani arrived, she was settled behind her desk, working.

"Hello, Ms. Sar-Boland."

She shook his hand and they sat down as usual. Behind the desk, she stretched her legs, rubbing her back with her hands. She did not move from her chair for five hours but still could not bring herself to look into the Dictator's eyes.

"I have some good news for you."

She flashed an inquisitive look at Mr. Mohajerani, whose eyes sparkled.

"Today, I'll deliver your book to the printer."

"Will it also be distributed in Shiraz?"

"Yes."

She looked over at the Dictator, who was laughing.

"So when will the second book be ready?" Mr. Mohajerani asked.

"The second book?" The Dictator asked.

"All the windows must remain closed."

She calculated that if she never opened the window in the evening, and if the moon remained tucked behind the clouds, she'd be able to finish her work in four months.

"Four more months."

"That's great. And the second piece of news is that I want to hire an editor to alleviate some of your burden so you can just focus on writing. And there is something else. My wife wants to see you on Thursday. The second edition is a good excuse for getting together."

"That's fine."

"You can also invite your friends."

The woman waved her hands in a way that indicated there was no one to invite. Mr. Mohajerani shot her a strange look.

"Yes, of course—your relatives are in Shiraz. Oh, by the way, are you comfortable in your new house?"

"Yes."

"You should have told me you were searching and I would have found you a house."

The woman looked at him, and he stopped laughing. He must have found out from the secretary, for she never disclosed anything about her personal life to anyone. When she had first started working at the publishing house, he wanted to protect this single woman who, with each ignorant question, would just stare at him and shift the discussion to her work at the company. In those days, the company monitored telephone calls. Mr. Mohajerani would come into the room unannounced, and would even follow her in the streets to see how she was getting home and with whom she was going.

"With whom, with whom did you go? Where, where were you?"

Father was playing a musical instrument. The pregnant weaving sisters were laughing. A man sat and smoked a cigarette. Mother threw herself on the ground in supplication.

"He'll die. I swear to God, he'll die. Don't let them kill him, don't let them."

The traces of Father's whipping decorated Mother's back—huge ugly welts. She pleaded, "I can, I can. Please believe me, I can."

Mother was crying. Her bruises burned.

"You're a woman—just a woman!"

"But I can—look."

She showed them the Dictator. Mother could not see him. Why couldn't she see him? And Mother's eyes ...?

She flinched at Mr. Mohajerani's intrusion and he became visibly upset. She saw him blush ... *You're thinking about the first day, the day I sat in front of you with a bunch of papers.*

He had moved the first chess piece—attack. She then neutralized it with a counter attack. Perhaps her chapped lips that day tricked him into familiarity.

"Do you also smoke?"

"Yes."

He lit a cigarette and offered her one.

"No, thank you. I smoke only when I work." She emphasized the word 'work.'

He chuckled, "So you must smoke a lot."

She stared at him, which obliged him to collect himself and talk about the company and its programs that day …

"Parvin talked my head off," Mr. Mohajerani said. The woman returned her attention to him again.

Parvin was no longer in danger. Women stand in the first row of the condemned. But then, when they believe you, they become your devoted follower.

"When will you know about the editor?"

"Next week."

"Sounds good."

The woman gathered her papers. Mr. Mohajerani rose, and with his hands in his pockets, he moved toward the door.

"So, is there anything else I can do for you?" he snickered.

When Mr. Mohajerani left, a strange uneasiness filled her soul. *Housewives. As soon as you open your eyes, you see that they've taken all that is in your mind. They are the most masterful interrogators in the world. How easily they force you to speak. And you, without even intending to, reveal everything—and then the depression that comes after confession. When you confess, they are all pleased. Then the whispers begin, and you are broken. You are no longer a person. You are no one. Then they let go of you, but when they do not know anything about you, they surround you.*

Suddenly, at the thought of her new home, she no longer felt exhausted. The curtains—when would the old lady go and buy the curtains? What color would she choose? Perhaps green, perhaps orange. She picked up the telephone and called the colonel's house to ask what happened to the curtains but just as the phone was answered, a shout erupted in the background, "Who were you talking to? Why did you put the phone down as soon as I came in?"

Did he ask who she was talking to? The man who called was bothering them, the voice in the background said accusingly, but he was not. She was the one who was calling him. The city was full of dust, full of yellow dust. She called to confirm that the man had threatened her life. Night and day, he pulled her hair and pounded her head against the wall. They set her on fire under a bitter orange tree and she burned, burned. *You must release me from him …*

Her words were choked with tears. She called the man again, but he said nothing; and she could not break the silence. She could not. The man hung up the phone a few times without saying a word. Finally, when he could speak, what he had to say was even more painful than his silence.

"Why don't you want me to know it's you? Why aren't you speaking? Give me a sign that it's you. I don't even know your name."

The woman enjoyed listening to the sound of his voice. She never heard it in the house.

She put the phone down. She needed to work—to work. *I can, my dear …*

She reached the house at sunset clutching two vases of *sham'dani* flowers—and ran right into Siyavash, who was just leaving the house. She regarded the tall youth in the light of sunset, his strange and beautiful eyes, moonlit skin and black curly hair.

"Let me help you."

He took the keys from the colonel's wife, who smiled when she saw them together. The old lady surveyed her from head to toe. The woman could not explain to herself why she had gotten hot and her face had become red. She hurried up the stairs.

Siyavash stood at the entrance with vases in hand. Amazed by the transformation in the room, he stared around him.

"It looks so different. Now it looks like a house."

She took the flowers and placed them by the window. She saw the wounded sparrow flapping its wings. If it stayed like that in the middle of the room, blood would splatter over every surface.

"Please, have a seat."

It came out of her mouth unintentionally and she realized that she could not take it back. She was dazed and wounded. She saw that she was flapping her wings, too, and blood was splattering onto Siyavash's hands and head. What if the others knew? What if they smelled her bloody wounds and broken wings?

"Did you put up these shelves on your own?"

"Yes. But two of them are loose and it has been one week since the curtain rod has …"

She blamed her wounded wings. The air in the room was hot and filled with the scent of life. The Dictator was sitting on the bed, breathing heavily.

"The door was locked or else I would have hung it," he said.

She gazed at him in surprise.

"But I had given the keys to your mother."

The young man frowned and his lips trembled.

"Old age and forgetfulness."

What sad, dark eyes. And those long eyelashes, those thin and pursed lips—are those black curls and dark, sad eyes real?

"I'm going to grab some tools."

He came back and immediately got to work, tightening the nails on the first shelf. When he put the hammer on the table, he spotted the picture.

"Is it a *Dervish*?"

"No."

"Yes, it's a *Dervish*. I saw one on the front."

"The front?"

"Yes—at the beginning of the war."

The old lady appeared with a plate full of fruit and two cups of tea. It was as if she were throwing a party.

"You're tired—enough work for now."

He was still transfixed by the picture, unable to tear himself away from the image and the bitter memories that it stirred up. He took the curtain rod. What were those sad eyes and drawn face thinking about?

The old lady interrupted his thoughts. "Afsaneh *Khanom*, the tea is getting cold."

She took the cup of tea and sat down so that she could watch the young man, the young man who was now biting his lip and pounding the hammer so hard—as if he were pounding in someone's head.

"You don't get bored being all alone?"

The old lady sipped her tea. With just one word she hoped to unlock the secrets of the woman's life.

The woman glanced at her, but did not answer. All conversations begin with one word. One word. If you refuse to say it, you win.

"Where's your family?" she inquired.

"In Shiraz."

"Ahhh."

The young man brought the hammer down on his hand, and at his yell the woman jumped up from her seat.

The old lady watched both of them and smiled. The woman stood next to the young man and examined his hands.

"I'm so sorry. It's all my fault."

"No, it's not a big deal."

It was not right for her to just stand there in the middle of the room next to a man. And then what? Look at how the colonel's wife was laughing and how her eyes were sparkling.

"Please, have some tea," she said.

Averting his young eyes, he sat on the sofa. He continued to rub his long, thin fingers. She put a cup of tea in front of him. The old lady asked, "How many sisters do you have?"

She did not want to surrender. The colonel's wife was just like Nasrin's old lady.

"Several."

"Have they married?"

"Yes."

Tired, Siyavash said in a hoarse voice, "That's enough, mother."

But the old lady persisted.

"My brides are all about five or six years older than their husbands. They were at the university. They also rented this same place upstairs."

The Dictator screamed. She saw that he wanted to grab the old lady's hair and kick her out, but the old lady would not budge. The young man got up and tested one of the other bookshelves.

"It's loose."

"Be careful it doesn't fall on your head," the woman warned.

"I wish it would."

The young man sighed, and took out a *Zar* cigarette. There was a smirk on his lips ... *Who is it that you are denying?* The old lady looked at the young man and nodded her head in the direction of the woman.

When he finished tightening the screw, he picked up the first volume of Romain Rolland's *Jean-Christophe*.

"Can I borrow this?"

"Of course."

The old lady placed her hands on her knees and stood up. She seemed frightful.

"What do you have there?"

In a mocking tone, the young man said to her, "What do you care?"

The woman quickly explained, "It's the biography of a musician."

The old lady shook her head in envy.

"He also played."

"What?"

"The *tar*."

The melodious tones of the *tar* filled the room. The Horseman doubled over on the floor. With the solemn rhythm of the *tar*, the bitter orange tree blossomed and the hard earth cracked. The Dictator got angry and covered the woman's ears so she could not hear. The woman laughed.

"So why don't you play now?" she asked.

The old lady complained, "He sold it."

"Don't lie," the young man growled.

She saw that his long, thin hands were trembling. His eyes filled with sorrow. He took the book under his arm and went toward the door.

"Afsaneh *Khanom*, do you need anything else?"

A heavy and sorrowful voice—it was as if his voice were clinging to the air—his deep, manly voice. She did not need anything else. Why wouldn't the old lady leave? Why wouldn't she just pick up the empty tray and leave?

"Mama, why don't you also come downstairs? Afsaneh *Khanom* has work to do."

The woman took a long, deep drag of her cigarette and smoked it to the end. She waited impatiently for the old lady to leave so that she would not have to listen to her story. A story. What did she have to tell? And the *tar*. All the world's *tar*s would go on sale. Father claimed that he played the *tar*, and recited poetry. Then there was a hill of eyes—Khan Qajar was responsible. And before that, what? Before or after the alien Horseman had reached the mountaintop and yelled, "Right here we will set up camp"?

In the camp, the *tar*'s tender tones came out from the light, and the alien Horseman beamed rays of sunshine on the young girls' hair. Suddenly a sword had sliced at his hand and the young girls hid their frightened faces behind their fingers …

"Slow down, my dear, slow down; I beg you, please."

The woman opened the door slowly and stood above the stairs. Along with the plea of the old lady, she recognized the voice of the young man and the shouts of the old man. The colonel imitated a forty-star general. Siyavash raised his voice in protest, but the stars darted violently off his shoulders.

"Siyavash is a general. A forty-star general!"

The old lady silenced her.

The old man yelled, "Why won't he leave? I want to know why he won't leave."

And the young man whined, "I'll leave … I swear I'll leave."

"When will you leave, oh forty-star general?"

A forty-star general! Thirty-six of his stars soared away like the pigeons. They had flown away with the fist of the colonel. Who was this fist hitting? And this laughter, this soft feminine laughter, to whom did it belong?

Fall seemed always full of laughter: the laughter of the old woman and the pregnant weaving sisters, the sound of fists and kicks, and the cry of someone who did not want his screams to be heard. There is always someone being crushed under the punch and the kick, someone who does not let himself shout lest the neighbors hear and all the leaves fall from their branches. *Fall struck the leaves, and if you do not follow the rules, you will never get away— never. Now you are just like the one downstairs whom he beat up ...* She wants to go out. No, that is not the way; first, she must wash her face and brush her hair. Then she must go out go out and laugh with the neighbors, joke around with everyone, "What were those strange noises? I heard them too!" ... She walked toward the small garden alleys and went down that same small street, where one night, wearing an orange nightgown, she found shelter. It was as if all the streets had merged, until Father began to whip her again and command, "Speak. Tell the truth!"

The footsteps in the hallway startled her. Under the stairs, she hesitated in front of the mirror. Then she had slammed the door and left. No. She did not slam it shut. She left calmly. She laughed and hoped that no one was there, but the windows were open. Amused, she slowly passed by the small streets. Then she ran as fast as she could. She ran in the small garden alleys of Shiraz ...

Back in the room, the Dictator grew taller once again. His voice was clear. He paced back and forth, nodding his head in affirmation and making plans. "Let go. Let go."

She had to let go or else that old lady with cane in hand would come searching for her. She would knock on the door and the four pregnant weaving girls would open it and say, *"Khodat Bedeh Madar"*—"May God Grant you your wishes, my dear." She heard the voice of Father, who spoke of an age when beggars were abundant.

She sat behind the desk. Why wouldn't they be quiet? The old lady's laughter, elderly and vicious, grew louder. It was as if people were climbing the stairs, standing behind the door, and laughing very lightly, then thumping back down the steps. The doorknob turned. She rose and stood behind the door. What day was it? What if the old lady had become a *jinn* or if this house …? No, this was the sound of a person's footsteps, or perhaps several people. They gathered behind the door, giggling.

She stepped back in fear but she could not just stand there until morning and wait. *Open it! Open …*

She flung the door open. Behind it stood two similar-looking spinsters of the same height, with dresses that were black from top to bottom. At the sight of her, they blinked their bulging eyes. They stuck closely together, biting their fingernails as they giggled.

"*Befarmayid*—Please come in."

She muttered this so quietly that she herself did not hear anything. She was scared that someone downstairs would hear her voice and think that she was talking to herself. And these two would not disappear. There they were there, clinging to one another, chewing their fingernails and giggling.

"*Befarmayid.*"

This time she said it louder and walked several steps forward. Nonetheless, her fear persisted.

"Are you Afsaneh *Khanom*!? They said this in unison then entered the room and went toward the bookshelves.

She relaxed—they were real. They touched the books, picking them up and turning the pages.

"We want a book—a book about a spirit. The spirit of a dead woman."

Their words evoked greater fear in her. Delusions and hallucinations. Together they stepped forward and stood before her. "Tell us, are you able to summon a spirit?"

The first addressed her, "If you can summon the spirit of our mother, we'll sew you a wedding dress."

The second one said, "Just like our dresses—so beautiful! So beautiful!"

And then they giggled. They looked at each other. Clinging to one another, they walked toward the sofa and burst into tears.

"It has been six months since she died. It has been six months since our mother died!"

The second one said, "We used to put our dresses on and walk for her. She laughed so much, so much." And then with her elbow she nudged the first girl in her side.

"Do you remember?"

"I remember. I remember!"

They both continued to cry.

The Horseman had lost his horse's bridle, and the horse was neighing.

The first girl said, "You think she's read everything on the subject?"

"Yes, but I don't see how she could have."

"Why, of course she could have. Nasrin said that she studied psychology."

"You're saying that the glass will crack?"

"Yes, when the spirit leaves the glass, the glass will crack. I read about it."

Suddenly the second girl got up, hit the other girl's shoulder and giggled, "How nice, how nice. We'll put her spirit in the glass and place it right on the chair she used to sit on—just like your chair—and we'll sew right next to it."

"That's it. That's it. We'll sew a wedding dress."

They'll sit here and talk until morning if you let them, the woman thought.

"Ladies!" she said forcefully.

The two of them, clinging to one another, looked at her with their large, bulging eyes.

"Get out! Ladies, get out!"

The spinsters looked at each other and cautiously rose while giggling. They left the room like two specters. Shaken, the woman sat on the chair. Too much work—too many illusions ... But the books were scattered about—there was even one on the table.

She picked up the book and stared at the title: *Memoirs of the House of the Dead.* It was what she expected. She should call the colonel's wife immediately and ask her—but ask her what? And if the colonel's wife came upstairs and then just lingered there? The woman went toward the window. There was no noise. *It's early, so early, and when the garden is lit up by the light of the moon, the pigeons will come. Until then, you have to sit behind the table and then, exhausted, get up and open the window and ...*

She sat behind the table. The women giggled in the hands of the aggressor. They grew old with the sound of their own laughter. Finally, the aggressor released them in the desert halfway to Kerman. The spirits of the two spinsters in wedding dresses, crying night and day, filled the desert.

It was deep into the night when she rose and stood behind the window. A full moon lit up the sky. Slowly she opened the window. There were no sounds. No bitter orange fell on the bed against the wall ...

In the morning, the colonel, climbed down the ladder like a wounded leopard, talking to himself and making threatening signals with his hands. He stuffed his bag with seeds; the sound of pigeons echoed in the room. A few pigeons fluttered above the colonel's head, and when they flew down and he shook his fist at them. Unprovoked by his gesture, the hungry pigeons escaped.

"The *ash* is ready!"

A familiar sound—someone knocked on the door. She sat on the bed.

"You can wait for me downstairs. I'm coming."

She got up and put on her dress. Now everything would become clear.

Everything was real. The old man sat on the only chair in the room with a smirk on his face. He held the bag of seeds on his lap. The colonel's wife and the two spinsters sat on the floor in front of the tablecloth before the *ash*—an *ash* to beat all the *ash*es in the world.

"Sit down here."

The colonel's wife pointed to a chest upon which a *kilim* was spread, and the woman sat down. The two spinsters looked at each other and giggled, and the colonel's wife suppressed her own laughter.

"Afsaneh *Khanom*, Pari and Zari are the colonel's daughters. Their mother recently died."

Zari swallowed her *ash* and clung to Pari, sobbing, "I wish she hadn't died."

The colonel put his bag down on the floor and looked toward the room facing them. "Is that big bum still sleeping?"

Zari and Pari snickered together and devoured their *ash*.

Zari said, "Until now, no spirit has been summoned."

"They can do that abroad. They do everything. If Siyavash goes ..."

The colonel's wife said, "Eat your food, will you!"

The two spinsters clung together. They looked at the woman and continued to giggle.

The colonel yelled at them, "Calm down. What's wrong with you? Have you gone nuts?"

Pari asked, "Again, they haven't come?"

Zari swallowed her food, and said, How many—how many of them haven't come?"

The colonel scrunched up his face, "Just these two … they are pigeons. But what about this lazy bum?"

The old lady said to the woman, "The colonel gives seeds to the pigeons."

The two spinsters giggled and said in unison, "He gives them seeds, he gives them seeds."

The colonel cleared his throat. He waved the bag in the air and replied, "Since I've retired, I've drawn the attention of all the pigeons of this area. Now there are pigeons that even travel a distance to come here. At first there were just a few. It took a while for them to figure out who they were dealing with. But now they all know that if they come five minutes late, there will be no seeds left."

She already knew what he told her. Now he placed the bag on the floor and just stared—that same vicious, mocking stare.

"Every year I spend five thousand *tomans* on seeds. Twice a day—morning and evening—I give them seeds. And if they miss the appointment, they'll be sorry."

The colonel smirked. He raised his fist in the air and waved it.

"Today they all remained hungry. Just because of two."

— 15 —

Due to all the commotion, she did not make it to the publishing house until eight o'clock. As soon as she arrived, she picked up the phone.

Nasrin chuckled with laughter at the other end of the line when the woman recounted her story.

"It's not so bad. You're a writer. Use it for material."

The woman hung up the phone and glanced out the window. It was as if a thousand hungry pigeons were pecking at the glass. She lost herself in the large map. A person will crumble when struck or kicked. The aged souls of the spinster sisters revolved around the young man. They were biting their nails, crying with laughter.

The Dictator shouted, "Youth and incompetence! Why won't you turn and just slap them in the face?"

The Horseman laughed sadly. "He's convicted."

"What's his crime?"

"Youth."

The Dictator pointed his index finger. "In order to avoid accusation, you must convict. Convict so that even if his hands are clean, he can't be exonerated."

The sound of the door prompted her to turn around. The secretary giggled and pointed toward the phone.

"Why wouldn't you answer, Ms. Sar-Boland? It was a man. He said his name was Siyavash Hamidi."

What did he want to tell me, that the girls went to buy the curtain? That they were hanging it up? That he found my book and was reading it? Why are the secretary's eyes shining when she comes into my room, laughing as if she has caught me doing something wrong?

Enraged, the Dictator began to command. "Don't pay any attention to her. Now she'll invite herself in, ramble on about her cousin, and ask you questions about your personal life ..."

She glared at the secretary.

"Get out and don't put through any more calls."

The secretary did not budge. She laughed, though it was not her usual laughter. It seemed to say, "Okay—someday we'll have a talk with each other."

The woman could not work. The whirlwind at the dead end twirled her shredded pieces of paper around—notes and fragments of her books. The old lady wailed. She tore out her hair; she could not stop the two spinsters, who were throwing all the pieces of paper into the street.

Before sunset, the woman picked up the phone a thousand times, and put it down as many. At five-thirty, she left the publishing house. A cab, Gorgan Street, and a dead end. A girl stood at a window.

"Salam, Afsaneh *Khanom*!"

Without thinking, she turned her head and saw that there were no papers in the street. Someone must have closed the window in the upstairs hallway. No doubt the colonel's wife closed it. She rang the bell. Suddenly the sound of an old-fashioned sewing machine stopped. The woman entered the house. Zari and Pari took the curtain in their hands. They unfolded it and danced around each other.

"Come, it's ready."

"We bought the curtain rod."

She frowned and put her foot on the stairs indifferently, saying, "Mrs. Hamidi, I'll be upstairs."

The colonel's wife responded, "Wait a minute—the keys."

Her hands disappeared into the folds of her dress and presented the keys.

"I didn't give them to anyone."

The woman took them and mounted the stairs, unlocking the door to her room. Everything remained in its place, the same way it had been when she left in the morning. She breathed a sigh of relief and fell onto the bed. Tired, she gazed at the desk. Suddenly she lifted herself up onto her elbows. What was this—sprinkles of blood?

She stood up. Near the table on the wall were new splatters of blood. She touched them and the blood lingered on the tips of her fingers. She stood still. The door was locked; she unlocked it. What about the windows? What if the walls themselves became wounded? Walls wounded from standing so long, wounded from thoughts of long ago and events that had transpired between them.

The woman lit a cigarette. She heard the spinsters climbing the stairs and went to lock the door but did not reach it in time. Both girls entered, each with a curtain in her hands. They hung them up quickly, and the old lady entered with four cups of tea and sat down.

Pari said, "Oh, my God, I'm dying of fatigue."

Zari laughed, "Curtains are so difficult to sew!"

They both picked up a cup of tea and settled themselves on the sofa. Pari asked, "Afsaneh *Khanom*, don't you hope to marry one day?"

The woman stood still. The words that flowed from Pari's mouth were like the links of a chain. They spun around the woman, rattling and binding the details of her personal life.

Zari said, "We'll sew one, exactly like our own."

Both of them said together, "So beautiful, so beautiful!"

The woman realized that she would have to say something before she could dismiss them. But what about the walls and these sprinkles of blood?

"Mrs. Hamidi, please come here."

She pulled the curtain aside and took Mrs. Hamidi into the other room, gesturing with her hands.

"These flecks."

The colonel's wife's face grew pale, her lips white—her blank expression reminded the woman of a ghost. The two spinsters followed them, laughing with glee.

"See this? Blood! Blood!"

This delighted Zari and she clapped her hands together. "He has started again."

In panic, Mrs. Hamidi stuttered, "Get out. Get out! Afsaneh *Khanom* has work to do."

The two spinsters exploded in laughter. They bit their nails and stood before the woman.

Zari said, "You really should have a mirror."

Pari elbowed her in the ribs. "A full-size mirror."

The two spinsters looked at each other. They hastened out of the room. Mrs. Hamidi inspected the walls, murmuring to herself, "It's fresh!"

Suddenly she burst into tears. She shook her head and fled from the room. The woman stood rooted to the spot. Drops of blood jumped off of the walls. The Horseman stared into her eyes. She stood in front of the picture. "It's not your doing, is it?"

A knock at the door brought two dancing spinsters in whirling wedding gowns into the room. They twirled around and around, holding onto their veils and laughing with one another. Their dresses were yellow, the fabric moth-eaten. Their spinning suffused the air with a stench of rot and dampness.

They both stared at the wall, chanting, "Again. It has started again."

"She can't get married."

"We can't either."

And they said in unison, "We can't because of our mother, and she can't, either—she can't at all."

She pushed them out forcefully, but the twirling, bubbling spinsters, putrid in their dresses of rotting lace, would not leave. She shouted, and the colonel's wife came and took them downstairs. The woman shut the door.

The typewriter was far away. Far away. Her stories were yellowed. All the musty papers swirled in the air. She had to move. The Dictator's temples throbbed.

Pari had said, "We want to rent this house."

And Zari had laughed, "We want to stay with you so that you won't be alone."

And her doll-like old lady, "In two days, you'll return."

The Horseman was not frowning, nor was he frightened. He remained calmly in the room, unbothered by the ordeal. She stood in front of the picture and arranged the papers into piles. She could—she could work. All she had to do was lock the door from the inside. Then it would be as if she were alone. The bloodstains blossomed, roses browned and rotted against the blue wall.

She locked the door and sat behind her desk. Attackers struck the spinsters. In their yellow stained dresses they ran away through the city streets. They screamed and giggled. She stopped working. There was a sound at the door and she was sure they had returned. She was frightened but could not move from her chair. They were knocking again, though not very loudly. Perhaps it was someone else and not them. She composed herself and got up. Standing behind the door, she asked softly, "Who is it?"

"It's me, Afsaneh *Khanom*!"

It was Siyavash's voice, tired and hoarse.

She opened the door. With a tray in hand, he did not wait for her to invite him in. It was as if someone were following him. He closed the door and put the tray on the table. Without looking at her, he sat down.

"You shouldn't have gone to the trouble," she said.

The young man glanced at the curtain, and a smirk thinned his lips. "They hung up the curtain for you?"

Exhausted, she sat down in front of the young man.

"Yes."

"I'm sure they got on your nerves with all their rambling."

"Yes."

"Mother said that on Fridays you should have lunch with us. Downstairs."

He turned red. He pressed his hands tightly together. The woman noticed his eyes; they looked as if he had been crying.

"I ... I'm reading your book," he confessed.

The woman laughed. He no longer looked agitated. She placed the tray in front of her.

"Won't you join me?"

"No."

"Well, I'm famished."

The Dictator frowned. Attackers surrounded the Horseman, who had just entered the city gates. The city walls were tumbling down. His horse neighed with nowhere to run. The woman screamed, "Come up, come up!"

The Horseman galloped up the stairs—stairs that reached somewhere up high, far above the ground and the rooms. Two rooms. Two open windows facing the sun.

The Dictator yelled, "Shoot at the windows!"

The woman heard the sound of the faraway cannons.

The young man was silent. Head down, he played with his fingernails.

"You said that you were on the front?" she asked.

"Yes. During the first year of the war."

"Where?"

"In the first row of the front ... in the South, then as a prisoner."

"A prisoner?"

※ ※ ※ ※

Father said that he did not surrender; they were not able to capture him either. He galloped to the fortresses close to Kerman, and for a few days he was surrounded. At night there were surprise raids. The Hero of Zand fought until sunrise then escaped—the Horseman and his exhausted hands. How well could he strike with a sword, and with a sword as heavy as that? *You know that shooting an RPG shoulder rocket takes skill, but we only trained for a week and three or four days. They have to lift it onto your shoulder. You must leave a little distance to make sure no one is directly behind you ... The hospital was filled with RPG's, young women, and eyes, eyes.*

※ ※ ※ ※

"Oh, you bum!"

It was the sound of the colonel yelling. The young man was upset at his belligerent tirade. He took out his packet of *Zar* cigarettes and lit one. One greedy puff burned half of it. His hands trembled. Frightened, he glanced at the door but refused to leave.

"Oh."

He rose in a daze. It was as if he wanted to say that the colonel was not talking to him. He turned red; then he let out a strained laugh, *meant to say, It is not I who will be taken down by the strike of a fist or the power of a kick. Saying, Father will not try out all his belts on me, on my shoulders, head, and neck ... You must laugh and be energetic and cheery. For this is the season for crushing the leaves that live according to nature's laws.*

"Sorry. Let me go downstairs to see what's going on."

Then perhaps he will go out, out of the house. No! Don't go. Aren't you afraid that they'll shut the door on you forever? Aren't you afraid that you'll ring the bell and no one will answer? And you'll stay outside the door and the neighbors will peer out at you? The dry fall leaves drift over you and the neighbors come out of their houses and mockingly say, "No, we don't have an extra key, either ... Sometimes this is the way it is. The keys get lost ...

He forgot his *Zar* cigarettes. She picked up the pack and hesitantly rolled it in her hands. What did they taste like? One puff made her cough, so she put out the cigarette. She stood in front of the picture and placed the cigarette pack at its base. The Horseman was on a restless horse, and there was a face in the picture, which was not his. It was someone else's face, which took form in the fog. Whoever was in the picture whipped the horse, and the whips came down on the Horseman's head and chest. It was not clear if the hand that delivered the blows belonged to Father, the colonel, or the Dictator.

"Let go. Don't keep searching for the guilty."

She would not search. Sin makes its home in the soul; if you live by a code, then you must prepare yourself for flagellation. She listened to no one's demands. She took orders—only the Dictator's orders. She could no longer be whipped. Could someone come along with his whip and transform her into a mere point, a final point, a point of death? No—the Dictator's whip was the end of the story, the point, just this. The final point and all points don't always work in the same way. Sometimes it is a point of death. Sometimes it is the starting point as well.

⁂ ⁂ ⁂ ⁂

She felt elated without knowing why. The dark, tarry smoke from a *Zar* cigarette hid the face of a Horseman so that his identity remained a secret. The real Horseman, or maybe an imaginary Horseman, galloped in the distance. Now where was this Horseman going in this salty desert? These bitter orange seeds that sprouted and the smell of the *narenj* blossoms—what were they doing in this desert?

Someone, a neighbor, put the radio on full blast and a group of voices joined in a song: "We're going to Karbala ..." It was the fall of 1986.

— 16 —

It was Thursday and guests filled the publisher's conference room. Mr. Mohajerani's wife would not let go of the woman, which distracted her from thinking about what happened the night before in that large, old house.

Late at night, she had heard a sound coming from downstairs. Someone was struck. The colonel's shouts echoed throughout the house.

"It was new, new!"

The old lady cried, "I'll leave. I'll just leave ..."

Then a door slammed. The woman ran toward the window that looks out onto the street and watched. The colonel's wife, with a *chador* over her head, ran into the street, and the young man pulled at her *chador*.

"Don't leave, mama. Don't leave!"

If she leaves, she'll come back. What about her own mother? Her mother who had dried up with the bitter orange tree?

"Mother ..."

In desperation, she pleaded with her four sisters. Mother sat in front of the hookah, the pipe tube stuck in the corner of her mouth. With dangling hands and crippled fingers, she embraced the neck of the hookah. Facing the horizon with an empty stare, her cheeks were wet with tears. A dry, lifeless body. In her death, the bubbly sound of the hookah continued. One of the sisters said, "She's only just pretending she's dead—the dead don't smoke a hookah."

Another sister knocked over the hookah and their mother fell over onto the ground.

"Don't leave, mama. I'll leave ... I'll ..."

But their mother did not say a word. Where could she go?

The doors and windows open. The neighbors were in the streets, and the colonel was still yelling, "It was new. A brand new suit!"

The woman left the window and paced up and down the room. A new suit. That evening the young man was supposed to come upstairs. He had read the book and wanted to talk about it, but he never came. Instead, he received a blow and a kick downstairs and that was it.

Mrs. Mohajerani said, "You're so simple and naive."

She snapped out of her reverie. Nasrin's words came back to her and she smiled: *They'll force you to behave in the way they want you to.* How often these days had she heard, "You're so simple and naïve"? What had she done to deserve such labels anyway? She had lived through countless afflictions ... *They will build you up whether you want them to or not. They will inflate you so much that you can fill up all the window frames, block the sky, and hide the moon behind your head. The construction of a dictator is no simple act. They'll fill your ears with so much insincere flattery that suddenly you'll look at yourself and see that you're standing in military posture. Yes—you are either a leader or a follower.*

⅔ ⅔ ⅔ ⅔

All dictators are eventually exonerated, every one of them, no matter their crimes. Where was her dictator? The night before, when he learned that the colonel's suit had gone missing, he had snickered. The Horseman's face was changing right before her frightened eyes. The Dictator detached his head and neck from the body and put back the face that had been there before. The process was gruesome, a painful surge of memory. All she wanted to do was sit and listen to his memories of the first year of the war. Father had said, "It makes no difference what heads lie beneath their hats. They're odd people." It was the month of *Mehr* in the year 1980, and the strange men complained, "This is no place for women; this place is covered in blood and barbed with swords."

So in turn, she had gone to the hospital. She worked the night shift amid the shouts of Dr. Mehrsayi: "My God, they'll all have to be blinded—all of them, in order to live."

That same night they got to work. Forty eyes—colored eyes, black eyes, and one set of green, green, green.

"There's no equipment. Either they'll all go blind or they'll die from excessive bleeding."

Dr. Mehrsayi looked desperately at the young commander, who was frantic.

"How can there be no equipment? How?" the commander shouted.

"There's not any equipment! There's not any! I have no help. I'm on my own!"

And the young man said, "Just do something about all this blood."

Dr. Mehrsayi cried aloud. At five o'clock in the morning when all of the roosters were crowing, there was a trash can full of eyes. The black and colored marbles rolled in blood. When she was sure no one was looking, the woman took out her gloves and cleaned the eyes. One set of eyes was green. Green, green, and she held them softly in her palm. She started walking with the green eyes into the hospital hallway. Dr. Mehrsayi, exhausted, followed her.

"Can you hear? They're calling out—they're calling me, these green eyes."

With an agitated voice, the doctor said, "You're tired; you must rest."

"I can't, Doctor. The sound of these eyes won't let me fall asleep. They even know my name. Listen, just bring your ear closer—for a few years have passed since that time, since that period."

Then she brought the green eyes closer to Dr. Mehrsayi. The young commander started to cry and she went to his side. "Are you from Shiraz?" she asked him. "Come, give this to ... No, go yourself to the house that I tell you. There's someone there searching for his eyes. Tell him that I brought these from Kerman."

﷼ ﷼ ﷼ ﷼

She did not want history to repeat itself. She just wanted to hear Siyavash's stories of wartime.

"I'll tell you about them. But don't tell anyone else—even Mama doesn't know."

Mrs. Mohajerani said, "I've intended to come down for some time. Mr. Mohajerani has told me so much about you."

The woman stared at her. She lied, just like all women and all people who, once they've gotten what they want, shut the door on those who helped them get it. They tell lies ... But she would not forget. When one is whipped, one cannot forget the person who delivered the blows.

In those earlier days when the publishing house did not have a secretary and the woman would answer the phone herself, Mrs. Mohajerani, this same arrogant woman who sat in front of her and bombarded her with questions, would want to know when and where Mr. Mohajerani came and went, and with whom.

The woman sighed. Nasrin was right. Women are afraid of other women because of what their husbands might do with them. They were forced to see all other women as their husbands did: as bodies, as compilations of beautiful traits that were detestable to other female eyes. These women did not realize that their husbands like you only for one hour, for one hour only ... All the clocks in the world enraged her. She wanted to crush them with her fists and feet. Instead, she forced herself to laugh. It was too late. The one who figured it out was right after all.

It all came down to power. The Dictator planted his seed in her heart. All the world's dictators frustrated her. She wanted all of them dead; she wanted their heads severed from their bodies. But she wanted the head of her own Dictator to remain intact.

Mr. Mohajerani walked toward them holding a plate filled with fruit. "Out with the old, in with the new."

The woman laughed. Mr. Mohajerani filled both women's plates with grapes, and then he bent his head down and whispered to them, "That writer has finished his story."

"*The Greedy Inheritors?*"

"*Yes.*"

"We must buy the rights to his book."

"How about this: let him go, and write the story yourself. The one that you write will have a political flavor, and it'll be reprinted a hundred times." Sales. The market. Mr. Mohajerani's laughter was ugly. No golden rose, only dirty hands.

Mrs. Mohajerani said, "If the story has something to do with women, then you're qualified. People like you need to bring women's voices to the world."

Nonsense. So that the whole world can hear? The voice will only reach the ears of the market, and what a noise it will make there. Bubbling together with her voice was the sound of her mother's hookah and the sound of the bitter oranges that were separating from their branches and falling to the ground. The sound of the bitter orange hitting the Horseman's head with a dull thud haunted her. Why would he want to wear a brand new suit? It wasn't even his size. Why would he want it when it was certainly old—at least thirty or forty years old? If it was from thirty or forty years ago and fit, perhaps it belonged to one of them—one of those who waited in line until it was his turn, and his eyes ... Ah, the pupils of his eyes and the laughter of Khan Qajar. And this Horseman, indifferent, looked at the man whose eyes had once been green. The Horseman smoked a cigarette, a *Zar* cigarette.

❧ ❧ ❧ ❧

She took the page out of the typewriter and crumpled it. She would start again so that she could take the cigarette out of the Horseman's hands; but as soon as she put in a clean sheet, he would start smoking again.

Now, back turned toward her, the Horseman left on his steed. The woman could tell from the movement of his limp and bloodied hands that he was lighting a cigarette.

On Friday, she wholeheartedly threw herself into the large, run-down garden. Many times she had glimpsed its tangles of foliage from her window. Now she came downstairs, rake in hand. The old lady tried to take it from her, and the old lady's entreaties shook the young man from his sleep. Sleepy-eyed, he picked up the hose and labored beside her. The colonel stood at the entrance of the hallway.

"Ha—the general has thrown himself into work!"

The young man did not even look at him, and the woman pretended that she could not see the colonel or hear his voice. She wished to clean the edge of the pool, which had become black with scum.

She did not have the strength. Siyavash gently took the broom from her.

"Give this to me; this isn't work that you should be doing."

And he set about cleaning the pool. The old lady watched with astonishment and then laughter lit up her face. Suddenly, she kissed Ms. Sar-Boland.

"Perhaps you're God-sent."

The colonel smirked in disbelief. "*Inshahallah* ... God-willing!"

There was an evil smile on the colonel's lips. The woman stood between the young man and his father, blocking their lines of sight. With his vile smirk unseen, the old man finally gave up. He went back into the house, and the woman heard the sound of backgammon pieces hitting the board.

By noon, everything was clean and in order. The pool sparkled like a diamond and the red fish flashed brightly as they swam about in the water. The colonel's wife laid out a brightly colored tablecloth with vegetables, fruit, and salad. She placed heaping plates for the woman and young man next to each other. The two spinsters joined them and ate in silence. Sometimes they would peep at her and the youth and giggle. The young man's hands moved clumsily, as if he were afraid to take a bite surrounded by so many women. He seemed afraid that with any misstep, these visitors and his mother would expel him from the table in his own home's garden. He was like a woman unwanted in her husband's house, who sits at her father's table once again. Everyone watches her, taking note of each bite. They see her hands trembling, food spilling on the table.

One of the pregnant weaving sisters said, "Are you crippled or something?

❧ ❧ ❧ ❧

Always, everywhere, someone will count your bites, since you are a stranger and no longer belong. You overstay your welcome and must leave. She left when all the bitter oranges had dried up and the hookah had fallen. She no longer wanted any bitter orange anywhere to blossom, even in a story.

The colonel observed the young man closely as he ate.

"Mohsen's coming soon!"

The young man swallowed his bite with considerable effort, like a pigeon whose seeds were caught in its throat. He noticed the wicked smile of the colonel.

"My son Mohsen is a great warrior. His chest is big. He leads masses of men. If he hits a wall with his fist, the whole wall tumbles down."

"Afsaneh *Khanom*, you really overexerted yourself today," the old lady said.

The two spinsters stuck close to each other and giggled. They pointed to the young man, whose face hung low and lips said nothing.

"I didn't do anything, your son's the one who did all the work," the woman said.

The colonel smirked. "I hope this is true."

The young man's hands trembled and suddenly he threw down his food and left the room, an unusual action for his generally mild temperament. No one laughed or spoke another word.

The woman was in her room when Pari and Zari came upstairs. Now she was regretful she had forgotten to lock the door.

Zari said, "We're going to a wedding. We thought that perhaps we could borrow blouses from you."

The second sister kneeled down and drew her suitcase out from under the bed. Both of them pulled out all the clothes and scattered them about.

"Gosh, don't you have anything?"

"Books, she only has books."

"Why won't she say anything?"

And together they said, "Say something to us!"

This siege overwhelmed the woman. The two spinster sisters had forgotten themselves and did not seem afraid of anything, or perhaps they did not commit anything to memory so that they would not have to retrieve it and know the meaning of shame. She forced a smiled. Then, bending over the suitcase, she closed it and slid it back under the bed.

"What should I talk about?" she asked.

Perhaps she should just submit and play the game. Nasrin had spoken of situations like this.

They will force you to do the very thing that they want you to do. But who forced her to play the game?

"About the spirit."

They said this together, and Pari nudged Zari in the side with her elbow. "Talk about a dress—about the heavens."

Zari turned around, and with small steps and a great deal of patience, she approached the woman and explained slowly, choosing her words carefully.

"You know, we want to sell our wedding dresses."

The woman struggled to keep herself from laughing.

"What for? Wouldn't that be shameful?"

A gloomy Zari said, "No. Our mother has died. We'll never get married."

Pari grasped the woman's shoulder. "If you can put her spirit in a glass, we can put it on the chair and get to work ..."

"And then we'll sell our wedding dresses and sew new ones."

The two of them stared into each other's eyes, and said, "Mother doesn't agree. She doesn't want us to sew new dresses."

Zari said, "But yes, we'll sew new dresses, we'll sew new dresses."

Pari laughed, "The men will give their consent ... I dreamed it. And now, Afsaneh *Khanom*, please buy this dress from me."

"But I don't need it."

The first one said, "You'll need it."

The second one's eyes fell on the desk drawer. She opened it and her eyes shined.

She took out a small box and put the earrings in her hand. When the woman stretched out her hand, Zari and Pari swatted her arm away. They stood before the window giggling, "*Joon*! How sweet! We'll wear these to the wedding!"

Fingers tapped at the door. It was the young man with a tray of tea. He put it on the table and then his eyes fell on the earrings. He understood the meaning of her absent smile and asked, "Am I interrupting anything, Afsaneh *Khanom*?"

He was not. The two spinsters held the earrings up to their ears and the young man approached the girls. The woman saw the glow in his eyes.

"Give them to us. Let us try them on," they begged.

Instead, she took the earrings and, as if she were talking to children, she said, "These don't belong to you. Now go downstairs. Nahid has come."

When the woman had taken the earrings from them and put them back in the drawer, they said together, "Nahid. Nahid." And, giggling, they disappeared like specters.

"They're not well," said the young man.

He sat down and she faced him.

"They were children when their mother was crippled. She was young and afraid of living alone. She forced them to sew. For thirty-five years she stayed at the sewing machine, and the girls would sew wedding dresses night and day."

"Only wedding dresses?"

"Yes, we have pictures from their childhood. Would you like to see them?"

Without waiting for her reply, the young man dashed out. The sound of whispers drifted toward her from downstairs. She was frightened, but the young man calmly returned with a photo album a moment later. He was jubilant, almost as if no one downstairs had ever hit or kicked him.

A young lady in a wheelchair and two girls beside a sewing machine. A sewing machine and white lace.

"Early on, Father divorced her ... after she became crippled."

❦ ❦ ❦ ❦

The sewing machine mangled the two young girls, left their lives in shreds. First the hem of one girl's dress got caught in the machine. The sewing machine was huge—the size of a huge old house. Then she swallowed the bobbin, a hard object in her soft, long throat—metal against pink flesh. When the second girl took the hand of the first, she got caught and was pulled under the tidal wave of white lace and ribbon. The woman giggled and said, "They're finished, they're finished. There's nothing left of them."

❦ ❦ ❦ ❦

The young man murmured, "For quite some time, you know, they had no contact with others, not even Mohsen."

She was still gazing at the young mother's eyes, which were bright and sharp like a sewing needle. She could thread everyone together and devour them like a spider from her web. The young woman in the wheelchair moved and said, "It took a long time for me to figure it out."

The young mother had lost everything, and she no longer wanted to lose. She had to win. It did not matter at what cost. Two young girls were pulled from beneath the cogs of the sewing machine. Their wedding dresses had become old and musty.

"They once had many suitors."

The girls told the first man, "She isn't feeling well. Wait ... We can't marry yet ..."

The first and then the second and then the third and then nothing. Alone, with dresses that had grown musty and yellow.

"It took quite a long time for her to die. And when she did, marriage was no longer an option for them, because of their age," he explained.

All the world's dictators shall be exonerated and no one will have the right to point their finger and say *Genghis Khan* ... One chair, one wheelchair, is all it takes for you to rule; and once you have ruled, everything must be squashed beneath the wheel of the sewing machine.

❧ ❧ ❧ ❧

The woman heard the unfamiliar voice of a girl downstairs. She listened and the young man told her it was Nahid, the neighbor's daughter. She chewed her lip and grew quiet.

"For a long time they didn't come here. But once again, it has begun."

The young man sat down and did not budge. The woman could hear the sound of a sewing machine and a mother who sat in a wheelchair and laughed. Her eyes glimmered.

"It was Father's fault, really. Otherwise she was a really good woman."

So nothing could be done. He had the upper hand.

"She really helped me."

It should not be said: black pictures, white pictures, it is not just those; there are also gray and other colors.

The young man rested his neck on the sofa familiarly and looked around with envy.

"In my home there was never any quiet, but now ..."

Then he started to play with his fingers. "I have no desire at all to be downstairs. It's different up here."

Now certainly she must pay a compliment, say something. Wasn't that what he wanted?

"You can come up whenever you like. We can talk about the war front."

"But you have work."

"Come at a time I don't have work."

"What about today? Are you free today?"

She remained silent.

"We went to the front. It was our country, after all."

He started to sweat. Then he left without even saying good-bye, visibly agitated, with a lump in his throat.

She sat still, all alone in a room where the air was thick with dust and filth. Where were the small drops of water? Or a moment's peace? She longed to awaken from a night's sleep and find herself blissfully alone, far away from the woman in the wheelchair and the colonel's two daughters.

Outside the bathroom, pictures covered the walls—pictures that did not look anywhere.

She heard the whispers of the Hamidi girls, "Afsaneh *Khanom* is the colonel's boarder."

In the shower, she turned the knob all the way to the left, releasing a stream of water and thoughts. Perhaps it was because of the wheelchair that the sewing machine could catch and squash everyone. *But you must not forget: it is not just one person who constructs history. It is not just one event that can produce a golden rose. If you search, you'll come upon those earlier days when Medes roamed the map on horseback. You can start with why a person gets their shirt caught under the sewing machine and then gets devoured.* It is the fault of that first horseman who suddenly, upon reaching the spacious green field, yelled out, "We'll settle down right here."

Then he forced all the alien horsemen to remain in front of all the Khan Qajars, with their hands and feet bound ...

"*Khanom. Khanom!*"

Because of the noise of the shower, the woman did not hear at first. Then she realized that the old lady was pounding on the bathroom door with her fist. Frightened, confused, as several pairs of worried eyes stared at her from behind the door, "Oh, *Khanom*, we can't breathe anymore."

She stared at them blankly, responding, "Why not?"

So she committed suicide in this very *hammam* chamber? Perhaps the weight of the sewing machine crushed her. It is no different from all those who lose their strength and, in the final moment, fire a bullet. But do they finally understand? Surely they do not regret the shot they fired but only the strength they have lost—but sometimes it is regret. Then you see that you did not fire a bullet. For example, if you are obsessed with bathing and cleanliness, or are in the vicinity of the sewing machine and the wheelchair, you suddenly see that your hands are empty. The alien Horseman escapes. Your father and all the people who don't even want to see point to this bitter orange tree and giggle.

When the woman came out of the shower, she peered through the window and saw that Siyavash was out in the street, his head resting against a wall. He was standing and smoking a cigarette, perhaps a *Zar*. She wanted to tell him not to smoke, but what business was it of hers? He was a prisoner and perhaps he had forgotten Farangis and Afrasiyab.

Now it was 1986, and five years of war burdened Rostam. *So, what are you doing in this place?* And they are saying that Key Kavus has escaped on an airplane. Who has escaped?

He dropped his cigarette and she watched him run. The two leaning against the wall alongside him ran as well. Why did they flee? She laughed at the child who wanted to get closer but escaped. How old was the young man? Twenty, twenty–five … and she? *Why are you counting? What is it that you are counting?*

18

"Will you let me in, Afsaneh *Khanom*?"

"No, no."

She stood still between the sound at the door and the voice of the Dictator.

"First tell me again what you're saying," she said.

"It's not necessary. Open the door."

She relinquished. His eyes were bloodshot, crazy, drunken, but she was not greeted by the smell of wine. The eyes were perplexed and stormy. They wanted to pick up all the fallen leaves and hide them behind a black mountain where no color could show. Rich, red wine had not caused these eyes, but rather something un-drinkable.

"The Mr. and Mrs. have gone out," he announced.

She was frightened. She was very frightened. No one was home. He was young and he had eyes that were drunk and drowsy. He took out his cigarette and lit it, and he puffed on it with one greedy drag after another. She was in a bad mood, and if she did not control herself, she would attack.

The sound of his congested chest made her grimace.

"You smoke too much."

The young man nodded his head and sighed.

"I know."

"Your cigarette smells awful, really awful."

She yearned to tell him that smoking was bad for him but she did not utter a word, and she pointed to the vases instead.

"It's bad for them."

The young man looked straight into her eyes. "You smoke too."

She remained silent, and the young man laughed.

"You stay up late standing at the window and smoking. But not *Zar* cigarettes."

Silence. What else had he seen? Those times when she was happy with herself and the Dictator had given her permission to dance around in circles? Fortunately, the middle of the room cannot be seen from the garden. You must be next to the window for that, and she never danced by the window. She was certain of that because the bed was there. Sometimes, though, she would sit on it and smoke a cigarette.

She frowned.

"I don't smoke much."

Something had cracked and would soon break. The young man chuckled and appeared to be waiting for her to open up about her private life. She sat down with a scowl and stuck a piece of paper into the typewriter.

"Am I interrupting you?"

Under her breath she said, "No."

She got busy writing. Passengers were sitting on the horse saddles behind their attacking horsemen. Among the young women who survived was one who was writing a history of the attacks and the ensuing events. He bent down over her notebook.

"Where did you learn to read and write?"

"When I was a child, my father taught me under a bitter orange tree."

"Does he read your work?"

With her big black eyes, the woman looked up at him. She felt cold and embarrassed. Fathers do not all work the same way. She had heard nothing from him, though copies of her novel reached Shiraz days ago. That could only mean he had not read her first book. Father could devour books; he could finish them in one sitting. He was probably too busy, but he would certainly read her work on the Horseman ...

The sound of the colonel closing the door to the garden mixed with the pattern of footfalls on the stairs. The old lady reached the top and opened the door to the woman's room. Her eyes lit up when she entered. She looked at Siyavash—*where is Farangis?*

Then the colonel's wife kissed the woman.

"Perhaps you are God-sent."

19

On Tuesday evening, the two spinsters invaded her room. The doorbell rang and Pari stood behind the door.

"Afsaneh *Khanom* …"

Breathing heavily, they sat down on the sofa.

"We brought the dresses for you."

Both of them unknotted the knapsack: two musty wedding dresses.

Pari said, "Come and try it on so we can see if it fits you."

Zari pushed her back, "Mine will fit her."

She saw that they were both sitting in wheelchairs and laughing. They were putting her under the needle of their sewing machine, feeding her through. They could not—or could they? Perhaps. She was afraid, and scorned her own fear.

"These belong to you!" she said.

"No! No, we'll sew another one."

Pari came closer and put her dress under the woman's neck. "It fits!" she said with a whistle.

Zari also measured her.

"It's so cheap, so cheap!"

The woman took the dresses and threw them on the bed. She tried to laugh.

"First sit down, and then …"

Both of them sat down calmly.

"We … We didn't want our mother to die so soon."

She brought them down from the wheelchairs and put the handle of the sewing machine's flywheel in their hands. Should she just sit there? No! She could neither sit there by herself nor allow someone sitting in a wheelchair to look into her heart.

"Ask them—perhaps it'll be useful for a story."

It was the voice of the Dictator. Maybe he wished to increase his own knowledge and power.

"Where's your home?"

Zari said, "Far away, very far away and very small, only two rooms."

Pari began to cry. "Mama, poor Mama! How can we possibly come here anymore?"

The woman sat nervously on her chair, anxious to get up. How distasteful it was of the old rulers to allow them to come here. Why couldn't the illusions of the black-clad spinsters help the rulers open the city gates? Everyone frantically tried to flee. But the Horseman watering his horse at the pool said, "It couldn't happen. During those times there were no spinsters—the girls were just nine years old."

The Horseman laughed. Father shouted, "None of you knows a thing about history!"

"Calm down, Father. I'll give you my manuscript on the Hero of Zand to read before it is published."

Zari said, "We'll live in a room in the corner of the garden."

Pari laughed, "It belonged to two students who became the wives of our step-brothers, Hassan and Husayn."

They looked at her, giggling and biting their nails.

"When did your mother die?"

She told them to stop laughing so much. They stuck together and started to cry.

"We didn't want her to die."

"Can you prove that?"

It was the voice of the Dictator, not her own. They sat glued to each other, piercing her with frightened eyes. They could no longer sit in front of her in wheelchairs. Fear. Once one instills fear, it is enough for obedience and slavery.

"If your mother were to come back to life ..."

The eyes of the two girls clad in black reflected a mysterious and sickening light.

"How wonderful, wonderful."

The woman flashed a naïve smile. "Really? So that she can sew you up with the sewing machine little by little?"

Time went back to thirty–five years ago, when the hands of the girls busily worked.

"Don't stand by the window ... get me the bed pan."

Pari put the bedpan underneath their mother. But a song in the street distracted her, the bedpan fell over, and ... shit. Shit everywhere.

"Now the two of you can eat all of it up so that you'll forget the song forever."

"I'm going to die today," remarked the woman in the wheelchair.

She did not die. She did not die until thirty–five years later. Would you try to look for that person who took away thirty–five years of your life? Would you try to reclaim those thirty–five years from her? From a corpse that is a part of you, and you a part of it? No court would judge her guilty. History is useless and time is blameless. The court only takes action when a death is sudden and obvious. If it happens over thirty–five years with the needle of a sewing machine, with tiny punctured holes, stitched seams, and sewn fates, the death is normal. Nobody will see the poison in the seams, or the tidal wave of white lace.

Pari said, "I swear to God, we didn't wish for her to die."

The woman could stand it no longer. She could not bear the thought that someone would remain so helpless and desperate.

"I'll buy it. How much?"

The colonel's daughters jumped from their seats.

"I offer one thousand *tomans.*"

"One thousand five hundred *tomans.*"

She opened her purse. The money was already in her hand when Zari asked slyly, "So now who should we sew a dress for?"

Pari replied, "Why, for Nahid, of course."

Both of them looked at her and said, "She was Siyavash's fiancée, but he broke it off with her."

The woman did not ask why. She moved aside so that her shirt did not catch under the sewing machine. When you have lost your whole life and nothing remains but desperation, you could easily commit a crime. Then all of history would go on, not for the sake of power but because of desperation. *These girls in black want to pour the bitterness of lost years into your soul and turn you into a corpse.*

"We're sorry, so sorry. We're afraid that our mother's spirit will curse us."

When she reached out her hand with the money, they knocked it aside, picked up the dresses, and fled.

— 20 —

It was eleven o'clock and she was still planted behind her desk. She needed to sharpen her pencil and open her door to allow the air to flow and the whispers to float up the stairs. She closed the door firmly but could not stifle the voices. As she opened the table drawer to take out her pencil sharpener, her heart stopped. The box of earrings was empty. They had been stolen.

"Thief ... Thief!" escaped from her.

Someone downstairs was yelling. It was the colonel hitting someone, and the brief screams of the spinsters pierced her ears.

She closed the drawer. The room became suffocating. The earrings had been stolen and sold for half price. She heard the colonel's screams: "My suit, you sold my suit for half price, you dirty addict!"

She heard the young man saying, "Hit me! Hit me, Father. You have the right!"

And now nothing else remained for her. Nothing. Her legs trembled. She stood at the top of the staircase and collapsed against the wall. Then she pulled herself inside the room.

❦ ❦ ❦ ❦

Everything was destroyed—even the Horseman who perched on his horse, and even the Dictator who shook with laughter. The walls were cracking from the bursts of his laughter.

"Siyavash ... ha, ha, ha! And Key Kavus ... ha, ha, ha!"

The bitter oranges dried up in the moonlight, and those two rebellious pigeons returned. The colonel whipped both of them until they stopped, motionless, paralyzed with pain. Only one of them submitted to his blows. The other tried to escape, but could not move his bloody wings out from under the whipping.

A haze of cigarette smoke masked the Horseman's face. He threw down his box of *Zar* cigarettes and stomped on it. His face was the same as the man in the picture, standing with a sword on both his left and right side.

"It hasn't dried up! It hasn't dried up at all!"

It was the voice of the Dictator, who was no longer laughing. He paced the room and shook his head, struggling with a decision.

She knew. One jug of salt-water was hardly enough to dry up a bitter orange tree. A single jar, poured under her own feet, would hardly make her disappear.

⁂ ⁂ ⁂ ⁂

"Shut up!"

The woman immediately quieted. *I need to move to another house. A house inhabited by no one, with no opium addict in it.* She saw that the Dictator was irritated and wanted to make a joke of her situation. He sat on the bed and shook with laughter.

The colonel's wife, frightened and in tears, knocked on the door.

"I wish he had become a martyr," the old lady said.

The woman frowned. "*Khanom Jan*—I wanted a peaceful home, not a hell."

"What should we do? What should we do?"

Then the woman heard a story she did not for one moment believe.

"How does one spoiled rotten kid go to the war front and leave with the first gunshot? He is afraid. So with the money he has, he wanders around for a year. When the money runs out, he returns home. And what does he tell us? He tells us stories of war and prison."

"*Khanom,* I have work to do, and under these circumstances, I need to think about a house!"

The old lady cried.

"Perhaps—perhaps you'll be able to work anyway."

"*Khanom,* I've never dealt with an addict before. My studies aren't of help here!" She grabbed a cigarette. She locked the door and turned the lights out so no one would knock on the door with a cup of tea. She no longer had earrings that could be stolen. *Just let me get back my book, Jean-Christophe.*

She was upset with herself and everyone else, like a proud beggar drowning in her own misery. No one understood that she had begged, except for the one person who was making more plans for her and the poor Horseman. He stomped on his cigarettes, not saying a word. He left calmly and no one knew where he went. The gates of the city of Shiraz were not open; the doorkeepers smoked opium.

She sat behind the desk so she could compensate for her defeat. She would force herself to work, even if someone were screaming in her soul until judgment day.

⁂ ⁂ ⁂ ⁂

This time the city gates opened easily. The gatekeepers gathered opium plants until dawn. The masses occupied themselves with planting opium seeds. Where was the Horseman? The alien Horseman?

She found him, a bitter smile on his lips.

"This is unfair," he said.

"You're more unfair …"

"This wasn't how the story …"

"You're lying so that I …"

The Dictator smirked.

"Just stop it. You need to leave this place. You've lost enough time."

The attackers whipped everyone violently. The body of the young girl writer was burning, her skin swelling with the beating. Deep red welts covered her arms and back, and the attackers subdued her as they searched her life for stories. The attackers found her scraps of papers, and the Horseman disappeared. Her body folded beneath the whips, screams erupting from her throat.

"Tear up everything that she has written."

They tore it up. The scraps of paper caught fire and her screaming suffocated the flames. The pregnant weavers laughed. She had spent the whole day searching the twisted alleyways of Shiraz and of her mind until she found her footsteps from that lost night. The whole day she walked next to that man who once had silver eyes. No one knows that he has lost them now. How comfortably Father and the pregnant weaving sisters were sitting next to him, without noticing the caverns his eyes had once inhabited. What did it matter who lit the fire, whether it was an alien Horseman or a man with empty eye sockets?

※ ※ ※ ※

"What are you writing?"

"Memoirs."

He leafed through the pages. Then, as if he were tired of humoring a lunatic, he threw the notebook aside. She was relieved that she had not written anything in its pages—especially, the names of men who had called her. In the end the man said, "Look, if I said no, I'd be lying. I have a wife, but what a wife!"

Then she, with telephone in hand, finally listened to what he had to say. "So make note of my home number. I realize that you can't talk now, but I'm home in the evenings."

She jumped every time the telephone rang. One time she wanted to say, "It's me—right here in front of you." But she was afraid, and her voice remained trapped for some time in her throat.

— 21 —

She left the house at six o'clock in the morning so that she would not have to see the young man, who remained fast asleep. Everything was closed. She wandered the streets, crossing one intersection after another. Where were the policemen? She continued her search for a home. Then she heard the faint sound of a whistle—the whistle of the policemen pierced her ears again and again, shrill in the morning air. *She does not have a home.*

Her heart trembled as she reached Pastor Square. She thought of her own doll-like old lady. She usually came out at this time of the day to water the trees that lined the streets.

The woman would say that her house had burned down. It seemed so much better to have one's house burn down than to have no house at all. A burnt down house had existed at some point; you could almost put a price on it. Then no one could blow the whistle. What if the old lady whistled and alerted all the neighbors? They would hurry outside and yell to the world about her missing house, her missing night, and her missing bitter orange tree as well.

"Come back soon, *Koofti*—you little shit."

She went no further. She turned around and headed back ... *You close your eyes for just a moment and then, suddenly, one picture morphs into another. I warned you not to close them. I told you that if you close them, it is all over. It shall all end. Is there anything left, now that it is all over?* A bitter orange tree, a house, and a city by the name of Shiraz or Kerman—she did not recognize them. She could not recognize anyone—not the old lady of Pastor Street, not the old lady of Gorgan Street. Grief overcame her and she choked on her own tears. She saw that same woman with a green headscarf getting into a green-colored *Paykan*. The woman smeared her lips with lipstick and cried. No one should know that she had lost her doll-like old lady, that she no longer had anyone. She knew that even a truck filled with salt-water could not dry up the tiniest bitter orange seed.

22

The walls of the publishing house began to close in. Ominously, they inched closer each time she looked up from her work, threatening to squeeze the life out of her with the same intensity as the punches and kicks showered upon the youth who had stolen her earrings.

"They called from the printer's—your book's almost finished."

The secretary's words were a chink in the wall, a chance to escape. The woman stood up.

"I'm going to the printer's. I need to see the work."

First she had to endure the rumble of the company's car, and then the strange pounding of the printer's mechanical equipment. She could block out sounds. She could block out all sounds: the sound of the Horseman, the sound of the earrings, all the sounds that were or were not of this world. She blocked out the sounds of being and not being.

The woman spent the entire day at the printer's studio. The attackers galloped toward her, urging their horses to trample her with their hooves. She did not scream. No one else could tell that the razor-thin silver sword blades butchered her—slowly slicing her from head to toe. As soon as the attackers grew weary, they would leave. Then she would rise and wash her face with a stream of water. The woman would leave calmly, blouse straightened, manuscript tucked under her arm. Nevertheless, the young girl writer trembled violently, and the papers that told her story swirled, scattered in the air.

❦ ❦ ❦ ❦

She bent over the printer's proofs. Outwardly she was reading, but she could not concentrate. The attackers surrounded her and cried out, "Leave her alone, she's working! Ms. Sar-Boland is working."

The print shop workers nodded their heads. They did not dare to come closer with a glass of tea or to say that it was lunchtime.

As soon as she left the printer's, she sought out the real estate agency. She had to salvage whatever remnant of herself was left. Now that the attackers had exiled the young girl writer to the desert, she needed to gather the papers scattered by the wind. History would read that once in such-and-such a desert, a young girl writer had wandered.

"Yes, *Khanom*, we have one—it would be 500,000 *tomans*."

"Let me see, the cost is 600,000 *tomans* for that one."

"Yes, *Khanom*, it's a very nice place. A gentleman lives there all alone."

"Why do you want to live alone, *Khanom*?"

"Because of the papers!" she cried.

The real estate agent stared at her and she left. Now she had to live her life, if only because of the papers—even if it were only one room, one tight, dark room.

It was nine o'clock—late—by the time she got home. Shoes lined the inside of the door and she heard more voices than usual. Lieutenant Mohsen Hamidi had arrived. The old lady with puffy eyes opened the door, but the woman went up the stairs without saying a word so that she could put the young girl writer to work.

"Lock the door!"

She did as the Dictator commanded. But she felt drowsy and told the young girl writer, "Write yourself—sit on the chair and write!"

But the young girl writer showed the woman her wounded hands and wept, "I can't! The sword has pierced my hands and the horse's footsteps have trampled my fingers. Help me!"

The woman sat down but her concentration was soon lost to the noise and commotion below—what was going on? Those noises, those screams. What was all the talk about? Something crashed against a door, where it fell with a sickening thud in the hallway.

A knock at the door startled the young girl writer. She rose, but the Dictator stood before her and blocked her way.

"Don't go."

She took a few timid steps toward the door.

"Don't open it."

"Let me see who it is. Perhaps it isn't who you think—perhaps it is someone who is lost and searching for the road."

"No! It's the Qajar horsemen who are pounding on the city gates."

"You're lying. It's probably the colonel's wife or ..."

The Dictator turned red with indignation. The young girl writer crouched in a corner and shook with fright as the woman placed herself behind the door.

Now she could hear the colonel's wife begging, "Open the door, Afsaneh *Khanom*. Please open up the door."

The puffy-eyed old lady was carrying a tray of dinner. The woman collapsed in her chair. It was evident that the old lady had been crying and that she had hit herself or someone had pulled her hair.

"You came home late, Afsaneh *Khanom*."

Now began the chess game of words. *You say one sentence and provoke your opponent to defend herself* ... The woman had done the opposite of what they had wanted, so she would have to play hard in order to win.

"I went searching for a new house."

The old lady started to cry and hid her face in her hands.

"*Madar Jan*—My dearest ..."

"It's impossible for me to work under these conditions."

She felt the exquisite joy of vengeance. The young girl writer had trusted the old lady. Now she sat down purposefully behind her desk, straightened a few piles of paper and began to write. Her heart swelled with the sweetness of revenge.

"Siyavash ..."

What did the old lady want to say? Siyavash! He had died somewhere in the boundaries of Iran and Turan-Zamin. *Give him another name ...*

"He was very worried. He was afraid that you'd find out."

"Find out what, *Khanom!* I haven't found out anything and I don't want to know more, because it isn't my problem. It's your problem. If only you'd let me get my work done until I find a new house."

The old lady cried inconsolably, and the woman felt the sweetness fill her body more than ever. She had been wandering for hours in the waning light. Now, she just nodded her head.

She was about to say something about the earrings, but the young girl writer stopped her. "If you tell them, there will be such screaming that you'll never be able to write."

Perhaps she was right. The old lady wiped her tears.

"You have studied psychology—you could help."

People like this, she thought? People who have innocent brown eyes but the hands of thieves? Were the missing earrings really his doing? Perhaps the two spinsters were responsible. It did not matter either way—they had left. She, too, was leaving and would open no more windows. She would open no more windows on moonlit nights.

"Kick her out. Time's passing you by," the Dictator said.

But the old lady would not budge. The woman took out her *Zar* cigarettes and smoked. She no longer coughed at the first drag. The young girl writer and these vases of *Hosn-e Yusof* flowers would soon need the curling tobacco fumes to work.

"Sometimes I think that you were sent by God to help us."

Silence—don't say a word—this is a chess game. Instead of moving elephants around the board, the old lady played with a two-headed dragon.

"Two university girls once rented this very room, and my other two sons soon married them."

"But my dear lady, I'm not a university student."

"I know that, Afsaneh *Khanom*, but you can at least help. He's young. Something happened to him during the war."

Again, the sound of crying and the roar of a whirlwind filled her. The old lady's shoulders shook like the shoulders of Mother, who had smoked a hookah. She would sit in the corner of the room and cry as the four pregnant weaving sisters came and went.

"It's your fault, it's your fault. It is you, Mother, who is responsible ..."

The woman was lost in thought. Father opened his history books and read to them.

"Persepolis, even Persepolis was set on fire by a woman."

The young girl writer said, "But that woman who set Persepolis on fire didn't smoke a hookah."

"I know. But Father doesn't know. And he says that whether a woman smokes a hookah or not, she'll set her beloved surroundings on fire."

"Perhaps. But some will only set themselves on fire ..."

The woman felt hot. Parts of her body began burning and Mrs. Hamidi was crying. She too burned, a mother aflame with anguish.

"How can I help, Mrs. Hamidi?"

In disbelief at her sudden change of heart, the old lady answered, "You can help in many ways. Before you arrived, nothing mattered to Siyavash. But now in the evenings he comes home early, anxious that there be no fight that will cause you to flee this home. All day his eyes are pointed up toward your room."

The woman wished to inform the old lady that perhaps it was because up here in her room it would be easier for him to get high. That her mother had smoked a hookah and cried. Instead, the young woman did not say a word. She moved her hands indifferently, not knowing what else to do.

"I'll see what I can do for him. But right now, I must get back to work."

"You can speak to him—give him advice, give him shelter."

The Dictator scolded, "Then he'll come up here, lie down, and smoke until morning."

❧ ❧ ❧ ❧

Mother removed the snaking hookah pipe from the corner of her mouth. She wanted to say something, but thought better of it. The woman said, "It's because of you, Mother, and that lost night."

And the Dictator said, "History is a lie, and so is life itself. The two are inseparable."

23

"Pretend that you don't know."

So, she would pretend that she hadn't seen his opium-crazed eyes, too warm and blank for wine. To her, his name ceased to be Siyavash. He came upstairs that night. She was frightened, but not of him—because she was certain now that he did not know anything about the earrings. Now she was frightened of what was taking place downstairs and on the roof, and most of all, she was afraid of Lieutenant Mohsen Hamidi. He was a fighter and could strike fear into anyone's heart.

There was no glimmer of the earrings in the young man's eyes. They were clear of any image except that of the chain links that bound him. His hands clasped together tightly and he trembled. It was as if he wanted to tell her something but choked on his words. The tribe abandoned the Horseman, and he remained by the side of a horse that reared up on its hind legs, bucking and neighing. The Horseman's hands were filled with rusty old swords, metal armor, and helmets. He faced the horizon. Sighing with grief, he looked out on a desert littered with burnt tanks. Finally, he took out his cigarettes, his *Zar* cigarettes, and lifted one to his bloodied lips.

The young man's hands shook uncontrollably. He puffed smoke rings into the air. He did not say a word—so what should she say? Should she just sit and watch? She needed to do something. Where was Dr. Mehrsayi? He would be able to help, to talk to the young man. All those nights in the hospital, he used to sit next to injured men riddled with fragments of mortar shells that still wanted to explode in their bodies. He would sit and talk. Now, at this hour in the evening, she could not be like he had been so long ago.

※ ※ ※ ※

"Would you like to read a book?" she asked herself.

She needed to work; she could not take the time to read anything. The woman flung words into the air, and they landed with a crash on the paper in the typewriter. Each word was like a light bulb exploding with the fear of Father's yells, the cynical smiles of the pregnant weaving sisters, and Mother drying up as she smoked the hookah.

She had promised Mother, hadn't she? This image, the one that came to her so often, must cease to repeat itself. She tried desperately to escape so that she would not see herself crouched in the corner of the house, terrified of the belt raised above her head. She had been terrified of everything. And then he had come, he who could destroy all the old images in the print shop, and she had to escape again. In the same way that she had escaped from Shiraz and Pastor Street. She had to find a house where there was not someone always knocking on her door and coming in to sit with her—neither a young man nor an old lady. They would never be able to erase the memory of that lost night. Never.

"You must leave."

It was the Dictator; he frowned at the young man. The young girl writer with the mysterious smile on her lips did not budge from her chair. She was not used to this, but she would learn. She adjusted herself in her seat. A few times, she looked over at the young man and the Dictator. She brought the typewriter forward. Her typing was all-wrong and she had no idea what to do.

"Look—you put the paper in this way, and these are the letters. You place these five fingers here and your other five fingers here on this line. Now start. This way."

She hit one key and then another until she learned. How quickly she learned.

"She could write a book in just one night."

You imagine that writing is as simple as that. It is not just about a typewriter and yourself. This place is full of pigeons. Look at the bitter orange tree that has come out of the moon, just look at it.

The Dictator wanted to show the moon to the young girl writer, but it was not there. The young girl writer sat down to work and the sounds of a thousand wounded birds filled the room.

He bent over and read the paper that the young girl writer was typing on.

"You made a mistake. Look."

He tore the paper out of the typewriter. Startled, the young girl writer observed him. He read aloud, "The faraway sound of war tanks' sirens ... air attacks."

"What time period are you writing about?" the Dictator asked.

The young girl writer snatched the paper from him and put it back into the typewriter.

"What difference does it make? Horsemen were always alone, alien horsemen."

Then, without looking at anyone, she delved into her work. The Dictator was fed up. She took a cup of water and sipped it, lit a *Zar* and coughed. She was disappointed; all her plans for work had come to nothing.

At eleven thirty, the young girl writer rose. The Dictator examined her work and stacked the pages. The young girl writer suddenly noticed the young man and pointed at him in surprise.

"It's Siyavash. He has been right here the whole time, don't you remember?" The young girl writer continued, "Like *Hosn-e Yusof* flowers!"

The woman went to the vases and stroked the bright red petals and laughed, "In those days, when the invaders came, the flower vases stood empty."

The young girl writer put her hands up to her face and cried, "All the flowers were crushed and everything was set on fire."

"Like all the red flowers in Khorramshahr and Abadan."

"That's true."

"But you didn't see it, did you?"

"Yes, I saw it. Many times I went and watched it."

She was probably so sleepy that she was confusing the times.

"Sleep—you're tired."

The young girl writer pointed to the young man. "No, he's still here ..."

Then Siyavash got up, reacting to their words; after all, now it was midnight.

"Thanks so much, Afsaneh *Khanom*."

He left. Now it was time for the Dictator to read the pages, to nod his head and smile contentedly. "You and the young girl writer can work together. Work will go faster, but not if you continue to live here."

She accepted. Until she found a house, she would have to stay here with the young girl writer. But until then, the Dictator instructed, "He must come upstairs. We're no longer concerned about downstairs. No one is being beaten. Things are peaceful down there after all."

"As long as this isn't an excuse for staying, I suppose it's all right."

The Dictator seemed to know something, something from the past. He chuckled heartily and sat in the very place the young man sat moments before. The young girl writer held her hands over her ears. She went to bed and pulled the blanket over her head so that she could not hear.

Soon the Dictator ceased his laughter and the young girl writer fell asleep. The woman tossed the sheets aside. She was thirsty and the water jug was empty. She got up calmly and took it downstairs. It was one thirty. As she descended the steps, she saw that the door to the room on the left was open.

His cigarette lingered in the ashtray, still burning. It was as if the glow of its tip followed her steps in the dark. She laughed. When she returned to her room, she no longer felt tired and could not fall asleep.

❧ ❧ ❧ ❧

In the morning, she woke to the crack of the colonel's whip. He stood on the rooftop and whipped the pigeons. First he dropped the seeds on the ground, and then he attacked them. They were nearly unconscious. The colonel was oblivious to everything around him; he was red with fury.

"You're being difficult and stubborn with me."

The pigeons flew up and the colonel glared at the two rebellious birds that swooped over the garden wall and pecked at each other. The colonel shouted, "My sweet children, come closer and see the daylight!"

The pigeons indifferently rubbed their wings together in front of him. The colonel threw the empty bag into the garden from the roof. He hid the whip behind his back and calmly climbed down the ladder.

❧ ❧ ❧ ❧

The woman threw aside the sheets and opened the window. The colonel and his evil laughter filled her room. A wicked light shone in his eyes. Walking slowly, he approached the two rebellious pigeons. The woman leaned out of the window and cupped her hands around her mouth to yell "Shoo!" when she heard the young man shout it before she was able to, "Shoo!"

By the time the colonel's whip came down, the pigeons had escaped. Furious with his unsuccessful attempt, the colonel whipped the walls and roared. The terrified old lady hurried into the yard. The woman heard the sound of the spinsters snickering—or perhaps it was Lieutenant Mohsen Hamidi, a short but broad-shouldered man with a round, brooding face and bulging eyes. The spinsters took the colonel's hand. Like an obedient child with downcast eyes, he left.

24

She demanded more from herself than ever before, but the Dictator would not loosen his grip. He would grimace and slant his eyes at her, making faces more clown-like than intimidating. In the end, all the world's dictators turn into clowns.

She did not express this sentiment aloud. Despite her fear of his actions, she was more afraid of losing him than she was of him hurting her. She had leaned so heavily on him before, and if she lost him she knew she would tumble. He was the root system to her bitter orange tree.

❧ ❧ ❧ ❧

The secretary knocked on the door with a set of typed proofs. Reading over them, the woman noticed that the girl had again ignored many of her edits. The very first sentence was missing a word, and there were grammatical errors throughout. This was the second time in a week that the secretary had to take her work back and type it again. The woman yelled at her, "Where's your concentration, *Khanom?!*"

She threw the typed pages on the floor. Mr. Mohajerani came by.

"Where's your concentration, girl?" she demanded.

The secretary's face lost its color as she bent over to pick up the papers. Mr. Mohajerani said, "If you make a mistake this time ..."

The woman became aware of someone standing near her, holding a cigarette between his fingers. She felt foolish beneath his gaze and did not know how to explain her outburst. She fished a cigarette from her purse and lit it with a deep inhale. A satisfied smile played across his lips.

She did not answer Mr. Mohajerani's smile yet; it did not bother her that he was waiting for her to smile in return. It had always been like that and always would be. *What does turning a person into an idea get you? You end up with someone so flawless and pristine that it is impossible to find fault with them. Beware the faultless acquaintance—she will lead you to the ends of the earth. You can be a follower or a leader—you choose. If the Dictator were to sense that you surrendered, then he would crush you forever. The sewing machine that fashions followers, would pull you in, its needles shredding you into so many tiny pieces that you would have to try to sew yourself back together. But then the scraps would create something new, something not truly you.*

A musty wedding dress and fading spinsters—perhaps she was brought out from under the bitter orange tree to rule. If she led, she could also be destroyed. At work she was clearly a leader, but what was she in the colonel's house? A leader or a follower? She was a leader. As a leader, she had to build up the young boy—she needed to influence him. This is what the old lady had said: "You can. You have studied psychology."

Could she though? How? Should she call Dr. Mehrsayi? What would she say? What business was it of hers? She was depending on the young man's existence to write her story. Every night, before she and the young girl writer would be able to work, he had to come upstairs and be sucked into the abyss of smoke as dark as opium and memories as black as her shriveled bitter orange trees. But what if the colonel also came, and the spinsters, and the old lady? She would be obligated to keep quiet, even if the colonel came upstairs and whipped everything in sight. Even if he whipped the young girl writer until her bright blood frosted the blue walls, she would have to keep quiet and write.

She wanted to be a leader here and everywhere. But until she found another home, she would have to wait and allow the young man upstairs. She would not say one word to him. She had lost interest in saving him. Although she was still young, the girl writer did not put her heart into anything. She just wrote for insurance, so that nothing would be omitted from history.

ﻲ ﻲ ﻲ ﻲ

"You're exhausted. You should rest."

She stared into Mr. Mohajerani's eyes. His voice had suddenly intruded upon her thoughts.

"Why?"

She did not understand why she had said "why." Sometimes you move a chess piece without giving it a lot of thought; but the move had the effect of disarming Mr. Mohajerani, and he knew he had lost. This latest move was really just the continuation of a game started five years earlier. When you lead someone to a dead end, you are the winner.

Mr. Mohajerani was taken aback.

"I'm not criticizing you, but you work night and day. A vacation couldn't be a bad idea!"

His triumphant smile could beat any opponent.

"I surrender. I'm leaving."

He stayed and put away the chessboard. He knew how to set the pieces up again. Playing with Mr. Mohajerani was pointless. He may have been temporarily defeated but it was only a matter of time before he would incite another competition.

⁂ ⁂ ⁂ ⁂

Every night the young man came upstairs and sat until eleven or sometimes even twelve o'clock. The woman and the young girl writer would be absorbed in work. The young man would not say a word. He would read a book as a rare silence drifted up from downstairs. When he left, he was calm and relaxed. Sometimes the colonel's wife brought something upstairs and kissed her forehead as she wrote. By the time she found a new home, the young man would have grown used to coming upstairs. Perhaps he would still come upstairs and sit in the room alone with his thoughts. Then he would smoke his opium, and the traces of blood would splatter on the walls once again.

She picked up the phone, looking for an excuse to call the young man. Mr. Mohajerani said that he was advertising for an editor. On Saturday, the printer would begin the run. The game's losers always had an excuse, though. She hung up the phone.

It was Thursday and almost two o'clock. The publishing house would be closing soon. She always stuck around late, sitting at her desk in the quiet after everyone else had left. Today there was no literary discussion and no party. She could go home and get to work with the young girl writer. If she maintained her current pace, the manuscript would be finished soon.

She wanted it to be two o'clock on the dot so that Mr. Mohajerani and the secretary would leave, and she could get her purse and hurry out of there. If she left earlier than usual and Mr. Mohajerani saw her, he would probably laugh to himself and assume that he was right about her exhaustion.

One chess piece would move to his advantage, and she did not want that.

Mr. Mohajerani would not leave. At two o'clock the secretary opened the door.

"Do you need anything, Ms. Sar-Boland?"

"No."

The girl left. She always went home early. She had a home and a family—a father, mother, and sisters who were not weavers or pregnant. It was for this reason that she would leave. How long did Mr. Mohajerani intend to stay?

She heard him on the telephone and began to lose her patience—what if he stayed until evening? She grew tired as he continued to talk.

-127-

Finally, at four o'clock, she arrived home. She took a cab so that she could arrive as quickly as possible. Home: two rooms opening into each other. The smell of *Zar* cigarettes accented the scent of blossoms in their vases.

The colonel was sitting in the hallway with a chess set in front of him. He played by himself, and the world was set out before him. Times gone by stretched from his fingertips to the ends of the earth. Sometimes he would shake his head in anger. With his left hand he would tug at his left ear. When it was the white pieces' turn to move, he would play with the hair on the right side of his head with his right hand. The old lady brought a tray of tea. The woman sat on the stairs, her feet pulled up beneath her, and her eyes fell on the walls of the hallway, which had once again grown dirty. The old lady followed her glances.

"Mohsen's shocked at the state of the house."

The woman stared at her, and the old lady explained, "It's so clean and orderly—obviously the work of Afsaneh."

The woman did not say that she thought it was getting dirty again. If she stayed one more moment, she would have no time to work and would lose the chess game to the old lady. The woman had to checkmate her and always be prepared to win—but could she play the game with everyone?

It was eight o'clock when the young man came upstairs with a tray of tea. He was agitated and upset. He would not stay. Anxiety, she knew, was contagious, and she could feel it worrying not only her but also the young girl writer. She needed to concentrate on her work. The young man got up; he would stay only ten more minutes. She saw that his hands trembled and his *Zar* cigarette shook between his fingers. Then she heard the sounds of the colonel's screams: "My watch! My watch is gone!"

He stole again today, or maybe it was yesterday that he did it. Time was leaving its marks on her face and that of the young girl writer, who was suddenly tired and old. The woman realized that she would soon be disheveled, wrinkled, and turning to dust. The woman pleaded with the young girl, frustrated and dependent. "You have to stay with me. You have to stay alive."

The young girl writer was fading. A weak smile lingered on her lips and she said, "Don't be scared. Just tell me what time it is."

ᘯ ᘯ ᘯ ᘯ

She did not have her wristwatch. When she had come out of the shower, it was in her hands. She had put her watch down in the bathroom and forgotten it. Oh, what a whirlwind, what a strange whirlwind that could move time.

The young girl writer sighed. In the whirlwind she saw all the watches in the world being hoisted high.

"Let the whirlwind take them. If there is no time, then I can stay here."

"So go. Let the strange whirlwind take them."

The whirlwind carried away all the watches. Only one watch remained on the table, and the young girl writer pointed to it.

"If I get distracted again, you must make all the watches stop working."

She was obedient to the young girl writer. It was not possible to play chess with her. The young girl writer would pull herself together—she would become herself again and live her life.

�� �� �� ��

She stood at the top of the stairs and listened. They were holding him by the chin and hitting him. The two spinsters laughed and the old lady begged.

"You've killed him. Mohsen, you've killed him!"

The voice of the colonel: "I told you that if you let the general come home, I'd take care of him."

Then the voice of Lieutenant Mohsen Hamidi, who was breathing deeply: "Where are the chains?"

�� �� �� ��

The young girl writer screamed. She was in the room upstairs, surrounded by many prisoners with bound hands and feet. They took the Horseman, his hands cut by the edges of the sword, toward the Qajar palace. Khan Qajar was laughing and yelling, "Stay here until you die!"

The sounds of chains and the rasp of the Horseman pressing his swollen, cracked lips together; he was thirsty, parched. The young girl writer's pen fell from her hands, but her ink could not wet his lips.

Silence fell. It was late at night and everyone but the woman was sleeping. Like each night before, she came downstairs to fill a jug of water and see the cigarette, an ephemeral light in his dark room. Tonight the small disembodied glow did not illuminate her walk down the stairs. No one was in the room. She went into the kitchen, afraid of the threatening darkness. There was the sound of the wind and the clashing of swords. If she turned on the lights, the sounds would fade away. In the dark, sounds take on a life of their own. She turned the lights on. She took the jug out from under the faucet and froze at the sound of tortured human moans.

"My God, please stop!"

She stood at the entrance to the kitchen and listened; it was the sound of the young man, but from where?

"Get closer—the sound's coming from there."

It was the young girl writer, who was also not able to sleep. She stood on the stairs, next to the storage room.

She was right. The sound was coming from within the door beside her. The woman inched closer. Slowly, she pushed on the door, but it did not open. She moved her hand. There was an enormous lock on the door. The moans continued quietly. It was no business of hers to open the door.

"It's bedtime now—go, go, tomorrow you have to work. You'll be tired."

She turned around and ascended the stairs, but the young girl writer was facing her and crying, "Please don't close them! Don't close your eyes. Don't blink, because for that one moment they're shut, the picture will become another picture ..."

"What does it have to do with him? Let him go."

The young girl writer pounded on the Dictator's chest, and she said to the woman who was coming up the stairs, "But he'll die. The convulsions will kill him. Another picture with eyes that look at nothing. The portrait of death."

The woman descended the stairs again. She did not want to close her eyes. Whose quavering voice was this? For a moment, she became scared and imagined again that the young girl writer was growing old. This time, her image was transposed with that of the colonel's wife. She held one finger to her lips, and with the other hand she extended the key to the woman. Her hand trembled so badly that she was not able to open the door, so the young girl writer helped her open it. The woman could no longer make out the old lady, who either fled out of fear or remained standing, hidden.

It was dark, very dark. The young girl writer brought out the woman's cigarette lighter and flicked it on.

"Please, Mohsen, my dear brother, this is enough for me."

The woman moved the flame of the lighter in the direction of the moans and then recoiled. She had never seen such a thing, so bloody and malformed. She had never looked into the mirror to find her eyes blackened because she had feared becoming a stranger to herself. She never wanted affirmation of what her father or her husband had done to her. What she saw now before her was indeed a stranger, a bloody and bruised face and swollen, cracked lips and eyes that winced even at the weak flame of the lighter. It was as if he recognized the woman who stood before him. Tears started to pour from his eyes.

Oh kindness, oh lost perfume.

The young girl writer held his shoulders.

ꗷ ꗷ ꗷ ꗷ

The Horseman bent his head. He smelled the young girl writer's hands, hands that did not smell of whips but instead the blossoming scent of paper. She removed her headscarf. Like a young child, the Horseman let his head drop into her hands. The girl washed his face as his horse stood far away on the horizon. It was neighing, worried. The early morning dawn was breaking. She gave him some water and all the pigeons flapped their wings. The Horseman laughed and so did the young girl writer. The young man stirred. His swollen, cracked lips opened with difficulty.

"Afsaneh ... Afsaneh *Khanom!*"

"Please, don't try to move."

The young man started to cry again. He turned his arms toward her, gesturing, "Look here."

She brought the cigarette lighter closer to the young man's hands: black veins pitted with needle marks, snaking traces of morphine.

When she left the storage room, she handed the keys over to the colonel's wife, who was lingering on the stairs in the dark. The old lady kissed her. The woman took the pitcher of water to the kitchen. It was bloody water now. Exhausted, she set it down and put her face under the stream of water; she would stay in that position until the fire in her head cooled. It did not cool, however, and eventually she went upstairs. A faraway rooster crowed. It crowed three times. It was not clear who was denying whom or where the denial was taking place.

The young girl writer said, "Nowhere is there anyone denying anything."

— 25 —

In the morning, she peered out her window and saw Lieutenant Mohsen Hamidi exercising in the yard. His massive body shone golden in the new sun, and he opened and closed his fists in a gesture of punishment. The colonel climbed down the ladder. He stood with the empty bag in his hand and gazed lovingly at his son.

She was terrified of the lieutenant's roving fists, and she quickly left the house. What if they brought out the wounded body and beat him again? Where would this game end? What would become of her work? She saw that the Dictator had become short. His shoulders were broad, like the lieutenant's shoulder's. He nodded his head at her and left.

She had to find a home and leave. There was no way she could work late at night with him in the storage room. She counted on his presence –on his abyss, his whirlwind, and the smoke of his *Zar* cigarettes. What if he died? She needed to tell Dr. Mehrsayi, but how could talking to him give the young man strength? Whether he was strong or not, he would die, and if he did not die in the storage room, he was sure to die in some alleyway. This was just the way things were. What could she do with his needle-marked hands and black blood?

❧ ❧ ❧ ❧

She sat at her desk at the publisher's, staring at the page in front of her. It was impossible to work. These meaningless squiggles of lines and dots: what did their sinuous shapes mean? They were really nothing more than fine rings linking one sheet of paper to the next in a long serpentine trail. They hoped to jump out and sink their fangs into her.

There was a knock at the door, and the secretary carefully poked in her head.

"Nasrin *Khanom* is outside. What should I say to her?"

Without a word, Nasrin came in and sat down—swollen eyes and puffy face. She bit her lips nervously. Afsanah suspected a sly happiness in Nasrin … *With your perpetual confusion, Nasrin, we never speak of mine,* she thought to herself. *If I revealed my problems, you would certainly laugh and say, "Why do you care what goes on downstairs? Don't you want to work? Why should you have to go down to the storage room in the middle of the night and clean the wounds of a young man? Just out of pity? I don't believe it. No one can believe it. There should be no pity for such a person."*

Then all of my pawns would be captured, and I would be forced to raise my hands in surrender; you, Nasrin, would say between incredulous laughs, "It's your own fault."

Was Nasrin the one who would say it, or she herself? Neither or both of them. Nasrin was crying once again. Watch. Now she will mention Khosrow, that same man who let her go once so that she could make something of herself, but she had made nothing; now she was no one. All she could do was cry.

"I went to his company. They said that he had just left. I went there to tell him ..."

She was stuck in the mud. When a bitter orange tree is fresh with all its globes glittering on the branches, you are left behind if you let go. Instead of thinking of a bitter orange tree, you are forced to think of an old lady who sits by a window and keeps track of your every move, controlling your life with her calculator.

"He wanted a traditional wife, do you know? He complained to me, 'How stupid of me to have married an enlightened woman!'"

Nasrin used to be enlightened, but she had gone outside, and then that old lady who kept tabs with her calculator made a traditional woman out of her.

"I'm afraid—I'm afraid that I'll never be able to find him again."

The woman snickered to herself. She told herself to keep quiet but spoke anyway.

"Why do you speak this way?"

"How could I have known he was like this? And anyway, I ... I love him."

'Love him.' What a lie. She was only frightened of the old lady. Now Nasrin was deceiving herself and the woman. She knew that all horsemen built these same lies, *and* that she hated all horsemen. She was frustrated with herself, with the bitter orange tree that had not dried up, and with all the storage rooms that contained someone who was dying and panting loudly. She pounded on the table.

"Lie ... all a lie ... I'll also make up some lies—lies!"

Nasrin stared at her. Only in those days—the days of the revolution—had she yelled like this and pounded on the walls. Nasrin pleaded, *"Be Khoda*—I swear to God, I'm telling the truth ... Before, the medicine made me indifferent to everything. Now, believe me, I really miss my medicine."

The woman tried to calm down. She saw the secretary's feet beneath the closed door. She listened. Only her hand clamped firmly over her mouth kept the woman from laughing aloud. An amateur thief does not steal earrings; he goes for the worthless sack.

"This is masochism!"

The woman laughed good-naturedly and Nasrin composed herself. The woman's concern was not Nasrin, but rather masochism itself. She saw that the word rode the horse and the young girl writer was running after it; the word commanded the horse to go faster so the horse began to gallop. Damn—she was tired and she was mixing everything up. In any case, Nasrin had asked for suffering by purposefully complicating her life. And what about herself? Why should she care about the storage room? Was she too asking for suffering? She should not be. She should no longer let anyone into her room, and then she should flee.

In an authoritative, unrecognizable voice, she said, "You're weak. Everything is just empty words."

Who was she talking to? To Nasrin or to the young girl writer, who was still chasing that word and that horse? Everyone frustrated her—Nasrin, the secretary, and the young girl writer. Mostly the young girl writer, whose concentration was slowly being leached by the colonel's house.

❧ ❧ ❧ ❧

The young girl writer asked her, "But will these too become stories?"

"No, we're the stories—they're reality," the woman said.

The young girl writer lifted up her head and cried as if to say it could not be. She yelled, "What are you saying? Isn't it a story that in the middle of the night, you stand on the stairs and you listen to what's going on below—who is being hit, who is in the storage room? They brought me into their house, and now you say that I'm the story. They're just having have fun with me, is that it?"

❧ ❧ ❧ ❧

Nasrin said, "Like you, I thought I could …"

Nasrin set up the chess pieces. *This time*, the woman thought, *I am not going to play.*

She broke in, "My situation was different."

❧ ❧ ❧ ❧

In the evening, the woman made more visits to the real estate offices. She was irritated with herself and the entire world, and the young girl writer would not let go of her.

"Don't you want to continue working? You're falling behind."

She did not leave the office until all the streets were empty. The policemen began whistling again, pointing her out to each other and laughing.

"Surely she isn't searching for a house!"

The city churned with noise; even the sky echoed with the trill of the policemen's whistles.

"Of course she isn't looking."

She returned to her house at nine o'clock. In the room on the left, the old colonel cut up pieces of bread for the pigeons and chuckled to himself. The old lady sat on the steps, anxiously glancing at the storage room. This time the woman did not ring the bell. She let herself in with the key.

I'll go up the stairs without making any noise. I won't even turn on the light.

She stopped at the kitchen because she was thirsty. The old lady, with worried eyes and tousled white hair, followed her.

"What do you need?"

She spoke loudly so that the colonel would hear. Then she took the woman's hand and signaled that she should go upstairs and the old lady would follow.

The woman did not move.

"I just came to get some water."

"Go, I'll bring some for you."

Surrender.

The old lady sat down on the sofa and cried. It was as if she were just waiting for the door of the upstairs room to be opened so that she could pour out her tears. "He bolts the door against me and won't let me in. He says he'll get better right there or he'll die."

The old lady cried so much and moved her chess pieces so aggressively that the woman found herself asking, "Has he eaten anything?"

"No! Mohsen will not permit it. He says we should just let him wither away."

❧ ❧ ❧ ❧

A pain twisted her whole stomach. The young girl writer fled the room. Time drifted back to the years of drought. Attackers surrounded Shiraz and closed the city gates. The young girl writer ran to the dry garden alleyways of Shiraz. With thin, starving eyes, she sat on top of a dump. The sounds of moans from the city funneled up the alleys and made the blue skies cloudy. She smelled something, and moved forward slowly.

"Bread ..."

The smell of bread, the smell of meat ... They were attacking the shops. Coffin shops. Men and women ran through the shadows of the streets, hiding bundles in their clothes. She went down a narrow alleyway and found a door; inside there were storage rooms full of bread and meat. An older man with a beard and a younger, clean-shaven man were having a good laugh.

The first one said, "There are no raw materials. The city's surrounded. We're forced to ..."

The second followed, "We can strike from right inside the city, and it will fall down quickly."

The young girl writer screamed, pleading with the men. "What about the people? The people are dying of hunger!"

The first one said, "Pray for them, *Khanom*. The lives of the people aren't in our hands."

The second one laughed, "They were the ones who wanted this in the first place, so let them suffer."

The young girl writer cried. *Zar* cigarettes filled the boxes. She stretched out her hands and took a box.

The first one said, "It's cheap—it isn't bread, so it won't be expensive."

And the second one said, "Let them sit and suffer now."

Dr. Mehrsayi screamed, "But why so expensive? One coffin shouldn't be this expensive!"

The voice of the salesman: "It can only be used once. These people are strangers, you know. You have to bury them in a coffin. Their bodies won't even be washed ..."

緑 緑 緑 緑

"I just had a key made."

The old lady thrust the key to the storage room at the woman,

"Please be gentle with him. Just like you were last night. Give him something to eat. Tonight I'll set up the colonel's and Mohsen's beds in those two rooms at the corner of the yard. Be gentle with him."

She looked at the old lady. Silence. She should not say anything; she did not know what to say.

"You have no idea what a boy he used to be. The colonel, who is so mean to him now—how he used to love him, before all of this."

The woman trembled. All the coffins were expensive and not reusable. Someone downstairs in the storage room was struggling and dying. She had heard once before that the only reason for a person to quit suddenly was fear of death. No one can rid himself of a habit that easily—even the habit of smoking cigarettes. Perhaps he has already died. Dried up, just like that, in the chains.

The old lady left and the woman remained alone in front of the storage room. Her brow tightened with confusion. She had to tell Lieutenant Mohsen Hamidi to open the door, or else his brother would die. The colonel must know, too. She had to introduce the young girl writer to him and make the girl tell him all that she had seen in the years of drought. *Coffins are expensive, and they can only be used once.*

❧ ❧ ❧ ❧

Pained moans emerged from the storage room. They were hitting him again, or perhaps he was shaking with death convulsions. Why wasn't anyone helping? Why had the old lady gone? Why did the woman let her go? She shivered.

When the two spinsters arrived, her heart became lighter. The smell of humans. They were human, weren't they? They walked on two legs and laughed.

Pari showed the book that she carried under her arm: *"The Summoning of the Spirit.* We're going to talk with the author."

Zari bit her nails, and said, "Someone gave this to us so we could summon our mother's spirit."

Don't just sit there. Do something. You can bring them back to reality.

"Why don't you sit down, girls."

It could not be done with chess pieces. They did not know the game at all. *You must make them prisoners—you have to sit in a wheelchair and grow more powerful. If you have a wheelchair, who knows what you are capable of.*

She laughed, "Perhaps now I can work again."

The two spinsters sat close together, as if they had come to listen to her tell a story. They stared at her eagerly. "Do you want us to bring you a glass?"

She had forgotten what they had told her and asked, "For what?"

"To put our mother's spirit in."

The second one said, "So she can't come out anymore."

The woman was tired. She saw that even the wheelchair was moving farther away, diminishing her power. It was a warning. She should not have stayed any longer.

"So when did your mother die?"

Pari said, "Six months ago."

Zari cried, "No! Nine months and six days."

The two of them cried together, "It's as if it were just yesterday—just yesterday."

She took a breath. The wheelchair came closer.

"So why isn't Siyavash upset like you two?"

"Zari said, "He's *this* woman's child."

Pari giggled, "Boys! They're all boys!"

"Where is Siyavash? Did he go on a trip?"

Both of the spinsters laughed. Zari said, "No! His mother's lying. He's in the storage room."

Pari whispered, "Shh!"

The woman rose. She lit her cigarette. This was a stupid, ugly game.

"I already knew that."

The two girls shifted in their seats and shot each other a glance that implied, *She knows everything.*

"I also know that he isn't well and that he might die."

She lingered on the last word. The girls fidgeted and watched her quietly. How much power could a woman sitting in a wheelchair have, anyway? She would test it. *Put down a chess piece and test their concentration.*

"He's your brother, isn't he?"

Zari said, "It's his mother's fault—his mother spoiled him."

Pari hit Zari's side with her elbow and said, "Everyone has spoiled him. How could you have forgotten?"

The woman angrily put out her cigarette with trembling hands.

"To torture him like this is terrible. He might have a heart attack. He might die!"

The two spinsters exchanged a meaningful look. They giggled wickedly and asked in unison, "Would you like us to sew you a wedding dress?"

Defeated. First a warning, and then a defeat. They are powerful chess players.

"Out! Get out of here!"

They had conquered her. The walls of the room closed in on her as someone lay dying downstairs.

Let go. It has nothing to do with you. Do you understand?

Those plain, innocent eyes and the way he cried affirmed that she could not let go. No, she could not. She would not be able to let go. She paced the room and lit a cigarette. The young girl writer stood in a corner and gaped. Even when the old lady entered with two trays of food, she did not move. Perhaps one was for the young girl writer.

The old lady silently pointed downstairs with pleading eyes. "This is for him."

"Perhaps your son will have a heart attack from the torture."

The old lady barely answered through her tears. "His brother—his brother won't allow it."

"But torturing is dangerous. Food isn't important right now."

"Please, talk to him."

Where would she start? What did she have to say? That Lieutenant Mohsen Hamidi wanted to sew her a wedding dress. The Dictator would grow taller. His head would reach the sky and downstairs someone would die, buried in a coffin that could only be used once.

❦ ❦ ❦ ❦

The clock had struck midnight by the time the old lady summoned her. Everyone else was asleep when she tiptoed downstairs and entered the storage room.

"Is it you?" came a voice from the darkness.

She knelt down and forced him to eat, morsel by morsel. The young girl writer brought a blanket from upstairs. With every minute that passed, the young man's arms and legs became increasingly agitated. The woman spread the blanket over him. She needed to contact Dr. Mehrsayi and tell him. In the meantime, she washed the young man's face with warm water. His arms and legs rebelled against the chains. She held them tightly to keep them from jumping, but she was not strong enough. Distressed, she looked down at his body and signaled to the young girl writer to hold down his feet as best she could. Within moments, they were convulsing again—legs, arms, chains. He heard the groans of the young girl writer: "How can you ... up here?"

It was as if he felt sorry for the young girl writer—or perhaps he was feeling sorry for himself.

"This happened to me during the war."

The woman remained still. He was lying. There was only blood and the sound of mortar shells at the front. These kinds of people were always like this. She heard that they could talk and make up such nonsense that you would turn around and laugh behind their backs. Those asking for kindness have many demands and will not give up, even on those who are prisoners to their habits: the humanity of asking for help.

"It started when I was a prisoner, in a hospital in Iraq."

The killing shot. It ended. Was it just a sly story or the truth? The young girl writer said, "Let's listen. It would be better that way."

"But he's lying."

"How do you know?"

"I know. He escaped."

The young girl writer asked, "But didn't you escape?"

She heard a strange sound coming from the young man. By the flame of the cigarette lighter, she could see that he was laughing.

"No! No!"

She could not say anything else, and her cheeks were wet with tears.

In the morning, nothing mattered to her anymore. *Let them think they won. One warning and then, boom—defeat. That's all it was. If he lied, then you have heard a tall tale, and if it is true, you have discovered a story—nothing else. Then you can continue with your writing.*

When all the members of the colonel's house had gathered for the meal, she descended the staircase. She stepped forward like the dictator. She needed to attack; in order to defend herself, she would attack. Wherever you might be, if you forget yourself, you will be conquered.

Her presence in the doorway caused everyone to stop eating and sit still. Silent, cold faces turned toward her.

"Mr. Colonel, there's something I need to speak to you about."

The chubby colonel was taken aback by her directness. Indeed, all forceful people who find themselves face to face with power are panic-stricken and intimidated.

"Yes ... Afsaneh *Khanom* ..."

"With what's going on with the lieutenant, I'm not able to work. I pay rent here to ..."

The old lady quickly overwhelmed her with compliments: "You don't have to pay it. You're worth more than the money."

The two spinsters giggled; with a dark look from the lieutenant, they choked back their laughter. The woman did not want to lose, but she was not sure that she could play. The game was bound to prove too difficult.

"What you're doing is dangerous. You might kill him," she said.

"And so we'll finally be relieved."

The lieutenant caught himself and hastened to justify his statement, "My dear lady, for seven years it's been the same old story. Seven years."

Her spell was broken—they were no longer frightened by her. The colonel smirked, and one of the pregnant weaving girls shouted, "You must treat him like a dog, Daddy."

The second cried, "You raised him spoiled rotten, to wander the streets aimlessly."

Mother, her body scarred, threw herself down at Father's feet.

"But he'll die. You have been beating him for a week, Colonel. You and—this man."

Father brought down the whip and yelled, "Throw him into Nader's storage room! Don't let him get soft, like a woman."

Mother paced back and forth several times. Finally, she put her head on his chest and broke down. Father said, "Let him die—what could be better?"

Relaxed and unconcerned, the lieutenant put a bite of food in his mouth. "Nothing will happen to him."

Mother burst out, "I'll file a complaint!"

The woman said, "Lieutenant, sir, because of my own personal circumstances, I'm forced to do something."

Father and the pregnant weaving girls dragged Mother into the house. The man said, "We are all going to be shamed in front of the neighbors."

From the colonel's house she called Dr. Mehrsayi, who laughed aloud. "Let's see—that makes it thirty-one, doesn't it?"

"No! You don't understand. He isn't among the dead."

What strange nights there were at the hospital during the first years of the war! Particularly the night they wrapped thirty fighters in canvas shrouds and sent them to the morgue's fridge. The doctor laughed. "He's telling a story, isn't he?"

"I know, but anyway—"

"There's always a 'but anyway.'"

"How can it be otherwise? For anyone who yearns for something, there will always be a 'but anyway.'"

— 26 —

"He shouldn't come out of the storage room."

Lieutenant Mohsen Hamidi clenched his teeth and, although it was difficult, she obeyed. Even Dr. Mehrsayi agreed. As soon as Mr. Mohajerani found out, he was happy.

"A good deed."

Yes, they proclaimed that she had done a good deed. The eyes of the secretary, Mr. Mohajerani, and everyone else glittered with pleasure—except for the lieutenant, who would not come down from his wobbly wheelchair. He would not allow the young man to admit himself to the hospital. The young man was suffering from a strange thirst. His whole body was drenched in sweat and the brilliance of his eyes was slowly fading. They had freed his hands from the chains, but his legs were still bound.

The woman rolled up his sleeve and injected a syringe into his bulging blue vein. The colonel surveyed them. He stood with one hand on his hip and a cynical smile on his lips.

"So God has given you everything you desire."

The woman turned around and looked at the colonel, but he was not fazed.

"Remember that this is the end of the game."

The young man began to doze. His head started to droop slowly, but a moment later he jumped up from his sleep in fear.

"Please, don't sit in front of the light."

Reluctantly, the old colonel changed his place. The lieutenant showed his disgust at such acquiescence. He fixed his wide, stone-filled belt and went to leave; he swiveled and returned as if he regretted it.

He tapped the old man's shoulder. "Mr. Colonel, don't be so eager to please."

He pushed the colonel aside and strode back into the storage room. Lifting his foot, he brought it down as hard as he could on the young man's leg.

"He doesn't feel a thing. He's high. High. And before everyone's eyes. What do the blind want from God?"

He stomped on the young man again. The woman rose and grabbed him by the shoulders. "Get out—get out, sir!"

She yelled so loudly that the lieutenant stepped back in surprise. The young man looked at her. His eyes were wet with tears. By this time, she was too deeply involved to turn back.

"God answered his prayers. Twenty days is good enough for me. In the future it will happen differently."

Trembling, she left the storage room. The lieutenant sat on the floor, speaking loudly. The spinsters laughed and the colonel shook his head. She stood in the doorway and the lieutenant yelled at her, "You're supposed to help, not make matters worse."

The spinsters grew silent and the lieutenant waited to see the effect of his words. The old lady quietly clapped her hand to her forehead. As the woman began to speak, the lieutenant stood up and faced her.

"Colonel, you're responsible for this house, and if we don't work together …"

The lieutenant was ready for her. "So no one has done anything, is that so?"

"Your sarcasm can only make matters worse."

The old man shook his head and sneered, "You've come too late. What do you know of our home, *Khanom*?"

"I don't want to know anything about your household. I'm just looking for a place where I can write. Until I have found such a place, this house needs to be quiet."

Mohsen got up and sat by the window; he positioned himself on the windowsill so that none of the blue sky was visible.

"Dear lady, you know he has also tired us. Did you know that the entire household used to be at this stupid boy's command?"

The colonel yelled, with a heart of renewed anger, "What did you think, *Khanom*? All the members of the household obeyed his orders—he was exactly like a general. He even chose the food. Everyone listened to his commands, and in the military salute position. I wanted to make an air force general out of him. How much I marched! How much I held my gun up in military salute, and for what? You tell me … Here are my letters of commendation."

The colonel stood up with trembling hands and tried to open a desk drawer. His head wobbled violently on his thin neck as he struggled with the lock, and he turned red. Alarmed, the old lady jumped up to help him. He drew out the bundle of letters and threw them at the woman's feet, sitting down next to her. It was as if he were by the grave of a young child. He showed each of them to her, one by one, and cried, "Here are my accolades.

Look. You're literate—look—yes, I was promoted from soldier to lieutenant. One hundred thousand soldiers were put under my command. In the morning, I'd have all of them line up and make them run. They listened to my orders—all of them—and as soon as I became a lieutenant, I was in line to become a colonel. A colonel!" The colonel continued, "But they didn't want to allow it, the enemies of the country!"

The colonel wept loudly, and the house surrounded him with silence. She did not know how to escape. The face of Lieutenant Mohsen Hamidi, sitting at the window, trapped her. His shoulders blocked the sun. The old lady went out and returned with a glass of water. The colonel took a sip. He calmed down, and for a moment he stood quietly with the glass of water in his hands; his eyes lost in thoughts of some faraway place.

"One day, His Majesty said ... to me ..., 'Bravo, Bravo, Lieutenant!'"

The old man spoke the words deliberately. His eyelashes stuck to his long black eyebrows. He put the glass on the ground. Distressed, he turned to speak to the woman.

"When the war broke out, I said to him, now is the time to serve your country, you must enlist right away—but this piece of shit didn't register in the army. He didn't even do his two years' military service. When the war broke out, he said he would go, but he didn't fight. The only thing he shot was morphine, and so his 'war wounds' are swollen, torn veins."

❧ ❧ ❧ ❧

Again night. Again darkness. Pacing, she smoked a cigarette. She was nowhere, and yet she was everywhere. She stood by the colonel, who wept next to the storage room. Next to those two big frightened brown eyes. Next to her mother, who was smoking a hookah in silence, tears streaming down her cheeks from the corners of her eyes. The woman had not seen anyone come back from war with swollen, torn veins. During all the nights of 1982 when she worked in the hospital, the fighters came back with deep, fatal wounds, but she had never had never seen such mortar-shell lacerations before.

Dr. Mehrsayi had said, "These kinds of people have so many illusions and concoct so many stories. They can think up lies no one else could ever imagine. Perhaps they never even went to the war ... One must not be too naive."

So why wouldn't he say anything? Why wouldn't he talk about it? The young girl writer remained motionless. She looked at the dusty, abandoned typewriter with longing.

"I told you it isn't just this typewriter that exists for you. There are other things, too."

Indeed, those very other things had been standing in her way. When would Father take his head out from the history books and notice her? What if he were never to see her? What if he couldn't?

She was frightened. The Dictator emerged from a thick fog. Wringing his hands, he looked directly at her. "You're losing time just because of this young man."

She stopped herself from saying anything. She saw the Horseman approaching from the left, with bloody hands and a smiling face.

"Don't listen. He doesn't know."

"If you know, say so."

"Ask him yourself."

The woman had to ask, certainly—but at this time of night, all alone? It was possible that all the seamstresses in the world were sewing her a wedding dress. She did not want to ask.

"I don't want to ask. Do you know the answer?"

The Horseman laughed, "I know."

"But why are you laughing?"

"Because you're afraid of that old lady who sits by the window."

"She has to be afraid. She has to." It was the voice of the Dictator, whom the Horseman ignored; he did not even turn around to face him.

"She has to be afraid of someone, so that she can be obedient."

The Horseman exploded, "Obedient to what? She has been afraid all her life."

— 27 —

Countless nights, nights that slowly became clear and stayed light. The young man was gradually becoming more relaxed. He hung his head and listened obediently. Every day he waited for sunset, for her to come and push the syringe into his veins. When she wanted to go upstairs, he would frown; his lips would tremble and he would ask her something to make her stay with him. What if he grew accustomed to her presence? Dr. Mehrsayi had said, "Something needs to be substituted. Not just anything: something effective."

She could not call at another time. The man was no longer there to laugh at the other end of the phone and say, "So it's you. But I gave you my home number, because I can't talk here."

When no one spoke of her long orange nightgown anymore, and there was no one to shout at her or to lash her body with a belt, she would look for Father's history books in the back room. She took the books from Mother and read them. The Dictator grew taller. He purchased a pen and paper and placed them in front of her, saying, "A human's prisoner to habits, and you're human ..."

Well, what if he got used to her? Her nightly presence? She had to break the habit. He had to know she would not always be there. She had to arrive home late to break the habit.

She searched the streets. Forgotten bookstores and flower shops ... What lingered in her memory? One alien Horseman, who did not even know why he was laughing, and a story that did not exist. As soon as she returned, the young man would start trembling, his eyes brimming with tears. She would not say anything because nothing existed between them—or was there something?

"Speak. Say something. One word. Say I made a mistake. I sinned—this is something he'd agree with ..."

It was Mother. She would come to that same back room filled with Father's history books and she would beg. Why didn't she say anything? Why couldn't she talk? Was there something there, or was something absent? Where had she gone that night dressed in orange, in a world filled with groping hands ... The tired and drunken hands of gambling men? Now they were far away from her, or perhaps she imagined that they were. Where had she been the entire night? How did she get home?

She was tired and her feet did not have the strength to continue, but she went on. Something bitter caught in her throat. It was as if she was still dressed in orange, and the attackers, the secretary, and the policemen were whistling and running after her.

"You're late, Afsaneh *Khanom*!"

All the old ladies had calculators and, for some reason or another, they each put theirs to work. Mrs. Hamidi also had one.

The woman did not say a word to the old lady. She entered the storage room and saw that he was laughing like a child.

"How are you?"

"Fine."

The old lady left them alone, and the woman could not decide whether she should go upstairs.

"If I tell you, will you believe me?"

❧ ❧ ❧ ❧

Mother stood at the entrance of the back room. The woman was afraid to leave. How she wanted to hear the sound of humans! Mother was scared that she would be stuck there forever, cowering from Father and the pregnant weaving sisters. She would say nothing. If she told anyone about that lost night, she herself would not know whether it was true.

The young girl writer said, "Come on, listen ... Perhaps it's true."

The Horseman turned and held the horse's mouth. "Stay and listen."

Mother said, "You have told me one hundred times that you stepped into a cab and went in the direction of the garden alley. What you need to explain is why you were wandering around at night wearing nothing but a thin orange nightgown."

She said, "Tomorrow night—let me remember. I'm exhausted now."

❧ ❧ ❧ ❧

In the kitchen, the woman took apart the syringe. She filled it up with clean water and came out.

Siyavash was laughing. "It's all over now, isn't it?"

"No. Three more nights left."

She injected it. The young man knew that the syringe contained nothing but water. Clean water and only that.

"Tomorrow night I'll tell you."

Like Shahrazad, each night led in anticipation of the next. The young man frowned. The woman threw the syringe into the trashcan and went back upstairs. She was tired of everything that did not exist. She lit her cigarette and paced. How could something that did not exist physically supply so much mental torture? There was no story and no bitter orange tree. And, like this story, it was as if that one night never happened.

The old lady came upstairs two or three times. She made up excuses to tempt her to come downstairs. The old lady—the chess playing old lady—made a grave error and said, "You aren't doing anything up there. Why don't you come downstairs?"

The Dictator held his stomach as he shook with laughter. "What nonsense."

He pointed to the papers and books. From the sound of the breathing of the young girl writer, the woman guessed that the pages were being torn out and burned.

"I have work to do, *Khanom*." She said this calmly, knowing that perhaps the old lady would persist.

"I'm saying it for your own sake. All this work ... You're young ... It's such a shame!"

Mother said, "I told them that if I knew where she was, I'd excuse it. It's a shame ... You're still so young ... You can't, my dear."

She said, "I can." She saw that her hair was still wet. Salty tears that had filled the small garden alleys of Shiraz soaked her thin dress and entire face. The tears rose and dried up all the *narenj* blossoms. A flood swept everything away.

She frowned, and the old lady pulled herself together. "I don't mean any harm. You know, my daughters-in-law are five or six years older than my sons. They rented these same two rooms."

The Dictator continued to shake.

"You didn't listen. Now you can be sorted out by any calculator."

"No. I brought peace to the house. There are no more fights. Even the colonel and lieutenant ..."

"What nonsense. You should know better."

She said, "Mrs. Hamidi, please go downstairs. I have work to do."

The lieutenant and the colonel remained in the woman's room. What were his hands—industrious or weak? The Horseman galloped closer: "Industrious hands."

But the Dictator jeered, "No, they're weak hands."

Anxious, she came home in a cab. Tonight Shahrazad's story would come to its close.

No one was home but the old lady, who was waiting patiently in the yard. As soon as she saw the woman, she fell upon her with hugs and kisses. A girl watched them through the window and then quickly stepped back, her eyes puffy.

"Afsaneh *Khanom*, I really miss you in the evenings."

The woman shook her head and went upstairs without a word. She changed her dress and slipped into the kitchen, where she splashed water on her hands and face. Then she stood before the mirror. She had aged. How lovely those eyes had been that she once covered with makeup. The Dictator sniggered. She tried to slap his ear, but he was tall and her hands could not reach him.

"Why this preoccupation with your appearance? Do you plan to attend a wedding?"

His sarcastic chortle rang out as she stood before the mirror. She began to brush her white hair, but when threw down her brush a bitter taste filled her mouth. Ten years had passed, and Shahrazad did not want to end her story. The young girl writer said, "I'm leaving."

❦ ❦ ❦ ❦

She held paper and a pencil. Tired, the woman shook her head and left the girl writer by the storage room. Late at night when the girl came upstairs, her eyes were swollen and all the pages were wet. She could not believe what she had heard. In the first months of the war, he had joined a partisan group and had stolen arms from the enemy. He was captured for this offense and later hospitalized after days of brutal torture. In the evenings an Iranian nurse would give him morphine, and then she helped him escape to his own country. Perhaps the woman's name was Farangis.

No, she told the young girl writer, what if you made this story up yourself? What if you made it up so I would stay?

"But listen, see how he was captured."

"Why even talk about it? I don't believe you."

"Now listen, just for a moment. Did you know that mortar shells hit one of his friends? His heart bulged out of his chest as he lay dead on the ground. A *tar* was playing and its reverberations surrounded them. He sat near his friend's heart and listened to the solemn tones of the *tar*. And then he was captured."

"Why didn't he identify himself? Why didn't he tell anyone?"

"He said that no one would have believed him."

The Dictator said, "I believe it. And now I have a story to tell you."

The woman was frightened. She sat on the bed and pulled the blanket around her neck; It was cold. The Dictator lit a cigarette. He sat on the chair in front of the young girl writer.

"Oh, young girl writer. Has anyone ever beaten you at gambling? One evening at eleven-thirty, on a dark and strange night, a man was sitting with his friends in a room. They gambled, and when a woman came to give them some fruit, she saw that they were all laughing and all were drunk. The woman was perplexed by their brutal mirth until, finally, the man said he had lost even her.

She did not believe it until the old friends demanded their spoils. He yawned and waved his tired hands toward the woman.

"Here. Collect your booty."

So, the woman fled to the rooftop. It was the month of *Azar* in the year 1977. It started to rain and she finally climbed down from the house's wall ... The garden alley, then the streets and a cab ... Where are you going, *Khanom?* She escaped by a small garden alley and wandered around in a state of confusion until morning. Why didn't she go to Father's house? Because of shame—shame for the choice she had made. She was silent. She endured the silence alone, to hide the shame of her husband's gambling.

The woman sighed deeply and corrected the Dictator, "It wasn't raining."

Suspiciously, the young girl writer looked at the Dictator.

"Dressed in orange, you say! And a nightgown at that!"

The Dictator laughed; he would not let up. "The dress isn't important. Listen to the rest of it. Behold the filth. In the morning, the husband went to the history-loving Father's home and roared that the man's daughter and his wife had been lost. No one asked why, but everyone asked where she had gone. Where? Then it started. Had I not been there, who knows how many thousands of nights she would have lost? How many thousands of nights ..."

The woman began to weep. The young girl writer rose and sat next to her. She stroked her hair and said, "I know another story, the story of a woman whose husband couldn't see her. One night, the woman pretended she was asleep. She saw the man taking his eyes out of their sockets and putting them under his pillow. He removed the silver spheres of glass just like the elderly take out their teeth. The man always used to make the woman fall asleep with a pill dissolved in liquid. That one night, through cunning, the woman didn't drink it and beheld the gruesome spectacle taking place in her own bed. Frightened, she slipped out of the room and escaped. The man searched for his eyes so he could put them back into the two empty sockets and follow her. But from the beginning, the man had been blind—he couldn't see anything. Many years ago, Khan Qajar destroyed his eyesight, but he still had his silver orbs."

— 29 —

"Write, whether you're telling the truth or a lie. Write the story. In one week, I'll publish it," Mr. Mohajerani told her.

Dr. Mehrsayi laughed at the other end of the telephone line.

"What an imagination! You have to be very careful. These types of people are dangerous."

The most truthful event must have a witness. The history-reading Father had told her that. All those truths that people believe are no more than lies without foundations. He who does not have a witness must flee. Like the one who had escaped, and now had come here to a faraway city to gather witnesses ... Ms. Sar-Boland had nothing to say ... Ms. Sar-Boland had no opinion. Orderly and responsible and ...

The courts were always open. They condemned someone until they decided to exonerate them. One morning the man went to the home of a father who read about history and yelled, "Why didn't you say anything? Why? ... What should I have said? ..." Was the Dictator telling the truth or lying? Someone stood accused until exonerated ... Perhaps the woman who was gambled off, and the young woman writer ... There is a historical justification for everything. The event had no witness. How could she prove that the man in her bed had removed his eyes and placed them softly beneath his pillow? He said he could not see at all. A witness was necessary, even for those green eyes that piled up in the hospital.

❦ ❦ ❦ ❦

The woman noticed Mr. Mohajerani and the young editor—*when did they slip in?*

"This gentleman is our new co-worker ..."

She handed him some papers, the first draft of *The Alien Horseman*, and said, "Please, you must leave me now."

The young man was about to sit down, but he took the papers; he went quickly toward the door, and Mr. Mohajerani hurried after him.

She was afraid that she would suddenly open her mouth and tell the young man and Mr. Mohajerani exactly what was on her mind. Even laughter can be a mask. Until one day when a wise man invades your mind and sees you escape across the rooftops.

He asked, "Where were you all night?"

Where had she been? The young man said, "Come, let us talk." Had he said that? At one o'clock? No, she had not seen any man, she was sure. Perhaps now there was a woman standing on a corner at Pastor Square. She wore a green headscarf, smeared on lipstick, and cried until a green *Paykan* arrived … A green *Paykan* … a green headscarf and …

※ ※ ※ ※

She trembled. Her body was ice cold, and at the sight of the pile of paper she told herself, "Hide behind the barracks so that you are not shot and your brains are not torn apart."

She wanted to talk about her life to the young man, the same young man whose feet had been released from the chains. He would come upstairs and sit quietly. If he were to ask any questions, she would no longer be able to lead. She would fold, compact herself down to his reach. He would expect her to explain herself. A leader is never interrogated about why and where.

"And why do you want to be a leader?"

It was the voice of the familiar Horseman. *How did you come in unnoticed? Where were you?*

The Horseman grinned and his face became youthful. It was as if he had grown taller.

"You haven't said why you want to be a leader."

"So that I don't have to explain myself, that's all."

"For how long?"

She did not know how long she wanted to keep her explanations her own. For the first time, the Horseman pointed toward her with his mangled hand.

"You're afraid—that's all."

"Perhaps you're right."

"Perhaps not. Even if it's a lie, tell a story. Tell a hundred kinds of stories, and, eventually, the truth will be revealed."

The Horseman took the horse's bridle and galloped off in the direction of Gorgan Street.

How he knows me—how he understand me.

After a moment's hesitation, the Dictator coughed and shifted nervously in his place.

"Everyone knows."

"No! You, no!"

"With just one word, you become a prisoner—or was it a bitter orange tree? There's no difference between the two. You'll lose again."

"No!"

Distraught, she could stay inside no longer. Even a bouquet of carnations could not help. It was dark by the time she returned home. The old lady sat waiting for her. When she saw the woman, she frowned; as if she had not expected her to arrive home so late.

"Siyavash wanted to call the publishers."

The old lady stared into her eyes until the woman retreated and picked up her chess pieces. She wanted to bring the two of them closer together under any pretext ... Siyavash and Afsaneh ... Afsaneh and Siyavash ... She knew that Farangis was not there, and that there was no more hope for curing the young man. But he was taller now. His shoulders and hands had grown manly, and his thick neck barely had room to move in its shirt collar.

⁂ ⁂ ⁂ ⁂

When she got upstairs, she threw her purse on the bed and sat down. She suddenly became aware of the distinctive rhythm of a *tar* penetrating the air. Someone downstairs was telling an ancient story. He cried and laughed as he searched for something that he had lost.

His pursuit frightened her. A bitter orange tree in the entrance of a half-opened door swam before her through a salt-water sea. The light reflected off its branches and illuminated a pair of searching, silver eyes. She lit a cigarette and saw the young girl writer, who gazed at her with strange intensity. The Horseman laughed with all his might, and the Dictator put his hands over his ears so that he could not hear.

For two hours, the melodic tones of the *tar* drifted upstairs amid the low hum of conversation from below. Suddenly the door opened and the perfume of *narenj* blossoms joined the *tar*'s notes.

"Are you free?"

This startled her; she had not heard the knock on the door or even the door open.

"No!"

Nevertheless, the young man sat down and stared at her. The woman had no choice but to sit across from him. He peered at her as if he were trying to convey a warning, but she did not want to be caught off guard. She had lost once and did not want to lose anymore. Now she would have to fiddle with the piles of paper until the young man left—but he did not budge.

"You won't be delayed for long, Afsaneh *Khanom*! Please stay."

His words angered her. She turned and shot him a glare. Her eyes burned through him with fury.

"Your work is finished, isn't it?"

"What work?"

"Your work on the laboratory rat."

She sat very still. He was now a man, and she was a single woman.

"On the war front the women also do charity work."

His voice dripped with sarcasm. He would shoot continuously until he hit his mark. Her fist pounded the table.

Dr. Mehrsayi said, "You behave as if you believed his story. Beware of when he changes it out for another one. Be careful."

It was now the month of *Azar*, the last month of fall, and every night there was the euphonic rhythm of the *tar*. The kindness of the colonel's wife, the mock-respectful attitude of the lieutenant, the giggling of the spinsters—the sounds of their voices and the noises that floated up the stairs again and again became too much. She had to pay her rent and get herself away from this. Very far away.

The old lady could not take the news. She started to cry. She kissed the woman and said, "No, please don't leave. After all, you are a woman, aren't you?"

No! She wasn't and didn't want to be.

"I'm afraid. I'm afraid that he'll go back to his habit again."

What could she do? Could she possibly trust that the young man would not sell his *tar* or break it? Now the colonel's family besieged her space as she tried to work. The lieutenant and colonel sat down and droned on for hours, the Dictator yelled, the Horseman laughed, and the same young girl writer who would yell in the city streets, alone but brave, rubbed healing ointment on the wounds of the young man.

The woman surrendered—he was a human in need, after all. Anyone who looks for it can find an 'after all'. She accepted the fact that she could not move too far away from the young man; the Dictator was making plans for her in order to prevent it. She faced the colonel's family and said about her heart, "These are the feelings of the delusional."

The young man said, "No, they aren't."

"You'll replace me with someone else."

"One person can always be replaced with another."

"I know ... Nahid."

"Please, stop it. I'm going to go."

"Where?" she asked.

"To Urmia. I have a friend there who makes *seh-tar* instruments and can also teach me how. But I need to know if you'll still be here in six months."

"I will." In jest, she raised her hands high as if swearing, "I will. But you won't."

A faint smile fluttered across the young man's lips. He gazed at her long thin hands.

The *tar*'s reverberations filled the air until late into the night. A desert full of carnations, narcissus, and a woman who was running and playing in the middle of all the flowers. It was time for her to work. Her hands began to write and the young girl writer laughed. She said, "It has been a long time since we've worked. Please, sit."

She sat down behind the desk.

❧ ❧ ❧ ❧

The Horseman reached the gates of the city—and what a city it was! A city full of carnations, red carnations. A city named Shiraz, Zarghan, Juyom ... No. It was another city. *Let go of history.* The sweet melody of the *tar* could transform history. *Let go.* What were these camels carrying? What was this caravan transporting? The Horseman stood outside the city gates as the caravan tried to enter. The Horseman inquired, "What are you carrying?"

Suddenly all the camels sat down. The Horseman saw that they were carrying boxes of *tar* and *seh-tar.*

"You may stay."

In the city, all of the swords were melted down. The *Hosn-e Yusof* flowers grew and grew, and the melody of the *tar* could be heard everywhere. Everyone came out of their homes, and the streets were filled with dancing and song. The young girl writer's cheeks grew rosy pink. She ran through the alleys and streets. She could not believe her eyes; the horses were prancing, and there was an unwaveringly sweet smile lingering on the alien Horseman's lips. The gatekeepers on the walls and towers let down their guard. At the Horseman's signal, the caravans entered the city brimming with Sufi mystical dancing.

As the spirit of the *tar* swelled in her ears, all the walls surrounding the city came tumbling down.

Nasrin cracked up on the telephone.

"What a story! The colonel's wife has taken the whole thing rather seriously."

She remained still. She just smiled a weak smile that Nasrin could not see. Nasrin was now an old lady sitting at the window; her calculator worked and she was punching in numbers. She laughed again as the woman moved the phone away from her ear to soften the blow of the deafening cackle.

"She wanted to tell me that I'm just a woman after all."

"So now how are you doing?"

"Me, I'm fine. Very well. First we spoke on the phone and then I saw him. We have both surrendered."

"Surrendered to what?"

"Surrendered to love."

The woman held the receiver farther away as Nasrin laughed and said, "You see, I'm looking for a house, do you know of any? ... Was that boy really an addict?"

Nasrin would not give up. Now that she was sitting at a window, she could no longer move. A woman must choose to pass though a small street or sit by a window. In the end, after reflecting on everything that has happened, all that exists are hills of eyes that have been picked out and men stumbling through back rooms with canes in hand.

"Do you know what all the confusion is about?"

"No."

"That is because power is in the hands of men."

❧ ❧ ❧ ❧

Now she was sitting on the windowsill. Why did the colonel's wife say this? Didn't she know this was just a game? What if the Father, lost in history, knew? Why was this Horseman sweating? He sat on a horse, drenched in sweat, and refused to look at her. An intriguing smell filled her nose, acrid and darkly sweet. She recognized it—the smell of hashish and of the Horseman, who was escaping. But Father had said that the Horseman was also a philosopher, a poet, and a *tar* player ... Now it was probably the laughter of the pregnant weaving sisters that was making the sky crack and the bitter oranges fall from their branches. What were they saying?

"Nothing else remains for us, with these things that they are doing."

Then they came together with their husbands and attacked. Father looked up from his reading, and said, "By the way that she had married, it was clear ... clear."

"Let go. Let go."

"That's correct. You're correct."

"I told you from the beginning, but you wouldn't listen."

"I didn't do anything wrong."

"Then why are they talking? I can't make up a story anymore for just one person. Not everyone is a gambler ..."

⁂ ⁂ ⁂ ⁂

The secretary stood at the door and timidly announced to the woman that someone on the telephone wanted to speak with her. Then she backed out of the office, leaving Ms. Sar-Boland alone. The woman wanted to buy a book, but she wanted him to choose it. Again, the Dictator pounded on the table with his fist. She did not look at him, nor did she listen when the secretary laughed.

The woman left the publisher's at four o'clock and saw the Horseman. He walked with the horse's bridle in his hand. She was afraid to look at him, and afraid of the wind carrying the news off to Shiraz. She wondered where that man who had gambled her away was? And Father and the pregnant weaving sisters: how unreliable they were now that she was strolling by the side of the young man and visiting the bookstores. How many years had it been since she had walked alongside a man? No policeman stared at her and whistled. The sky was blue and warm. She did not want to go home yet, with all these stores selling blue pleated skirts and green turtlenecks, and this tray with small golden rimmed tea cups, and this frame that could be hung on a wall in the house.

"Wait."

She went into a store and looked at the *melamin* flowery plates and a white pot with small *Kowkab* flowers in blue, pink, and green.

"Look, Nasser, what beautiful *Kowkab* flowers," she said.

Nasser looked, but he did not see. He never saw. The attacker galloped to the home of the young girl writer, then hit and broke everything with his sword. Even the flowers in their pots tumbled out into the bitter air. They screamed, but they escaped, and the young girl writer ran frantically after them. She held her hands high in the air, and ran through the alleys of Shiraz. The flowers jumped up and moved farther away.

※ ※ ※ ※

All the women and old ladies of Gorgan Street sat in their window frames and stared at her. Under their watchful gaze, she pulled herself together. She moved further away from the young man and saw the bitter smile on his lips. The girl who stood behind the window pulled a strand of hair into her mouth and chewed on it. When she saw them, she fled, and the young man's bitter smile turned wry.

She almost tripped at the dead end. The doors and windows opened and closed at the Dictator's hands. His words blared in her ears.

"Aha! Ms. Sar-Boland."

She did not know who it was. Who was it? *Whenever you reach a dead end, you do not know who it is. Who are you?* And as for this door, this blue door ... She still had not painted it ... *And how far away the door is ... When will we arrive?*

She threw herself into the hallway. Leaving the young man behind, she dashed upstairs and threw up. What had she done? The Dictator made a scornful face.

Suddenly, someone knocked on the door. It was Lieutenant Hamidi with the two spinsters trailing behind. She spotted Siyavash hidden behind the group.

The lieutenant said, "If in this country there existed two just like you, the world would become a garden of flowers."

The two spinsters giggled and the young man said, "Mohsen's wife works. They spend time in her house to help her. She has given birth to four children."

※ ※ ※ ※

The Dictator laughed. He pointed his finger toward the fog, and she saw the pregnant weaving sisters. Both of them would give birth to twins and triplets. Under the legs of the young girl writer, they placed a pot. Look—she washed and picked up the mess amid the screams of the babies. The big pot fell from between her hands and splashed everything in her face. They showed her the babies wrapped in a cloth blanket. They chuckled and she attempted to clean her stained white dress. She spun around and around, and the weaving sisters continued to laugh.

The first one said, "We're leaving."

-159-

And the second one, "Siya's also leaving."

Both of them faced the woman and said, "You're also leaving, aren't you? We're sure that no one will stay here."

The house was empty and the colonel circled the yard. He shook his head, watching the pigeons fly through the air. All the noise was coming from the colonel's wife, who worked busily sweeping, washing the yard, and shining her plates.

From her window, the woman could see the young man in the yard. There was a pail of paint in front of him, and splashes of blue paint covered his hands. It seemed that she was the only old thing—an ancient relic in a house full of fresh paint and shiny plates. A musty smell emanated from her being. There was dust in her soul that could only be removed by a hot shower, a steady stream of water pouring over the contours of her body for hours. Perhaps afterward she would finally feel cleansed and refreshed.

The colonel's wife spoke first: "There's a beauty parlor very close by."

She recoiled from her own words and apologized. "I don't mean anything by it, Afsaneh *Khanom*."

The old lady did not mean anything. No one meant anything. They just want you to follow them around, to do as they say. Why take it personally? Get up, take your bag, and leave.

ⅇ ⅇ ⅇ ⅇ

Sadness and bitterness crept into her heart. She saw herself with bag in hand, making her way down the street, passing the window that was always open. A puffy-eyed girl sat on its ledge, chewing on a strand of hair. The window slammed shut, and the girl refused to talk to her. *Why?*

She walked past the beauty salon and could not decide whether she should go inside. The Dictator reminded her that she could.

"Like everyone else, you have the right."

The Horseman held onto his bridle and laughed. The young girl writer's cheeks turned red.

A fat lady watching through the window of the beauty parlor stepped out to greet her.

"*Salam*, Afsaneh *Khanom*!"

Right! They knew her, remembered her name, although she did not know anyone. She was a leader—she was both a leader and a follower.

"The colonel's wife said you'd be coming!"

The old lady had made all her calculations and reported the results to the woman at the beauty salon. Two twos always equal four. The old lady's reckoning was infallible.

She hesitated at the entrance, not wanting to cross the threshold. She saw the bitter orange tree in the half-opened door; she pushed it open the rest of the way and went inside. Before her, roots pushed through the cracked floor, and a man with silver eyes stood before the tree. He emerged mysteriously from between the chairs and dryers to laugh.

"*Berfamayid*—please come in."

With a finger she pointed to the bitter orange tree, "This …"

"It's a bitter orange tree."

She knew … She had already gone and picked two big bitter oranges.

"Aren't they Shirazi oranges? There are so many bitter orange trees here."

The man laughed. His laughter was silver like his eyes. It was because of those same silver eyes floating in her husband's face and the bitter orange tree that she went to the beauty salon for the first time. The man asked, "Was the beautician a woman or man?"

She looked at him in silence. The man questioned her further, "He didn't do anything to your eyes, did he?"

She sat on the chair, with the beautician hovering over her.

"Please just cut my hair."

"How about plucking your eyebrows?"

"No!"

"How about removing your facial hair?"

"No! No!"

"Why? You're still young!"

She was still young and her eyes burned.

"It isn't a bad idea to remove the excess hair from your face."

She accepted. It hurt. She cried under the beautician's sharp thread, but since no one knew the pain she was going through, she cried for reasons other than the pain in her face. The beautician's sharp thread caught her hair. She had aged. Ten years had passed—but perhaps they were still there. The roots of her hair had grown deep. You can plant a seed of a bitter orange on the ground again …

"The land is salty and nothing can be planted in it …"

It was the Dictator, who stormed about in a rage. He looked into the mirror, on edge; had he stayed a minute longer, his fist would have risked passing through the glass.

❦ ❦ ❦ ❦

A cold breeze touched her face. The sky was blue. Like a cat, the sun crept softly over the rooftops. The young girl writer laughed. The city was calm; all of its women were on their way to the *hammam*. The ladies who worked there were bustling about, and the melody of a *tar* filled the air.

The woman in charge of the *hammam* said, "Number ten."

Why had she committed suicide in *hammam* chamber number ten? The two spinsters entered before her, removed their clothes, and giggled. A naked woman began cleaning them with a *kiseh*, carefully scrubbing off all their dead skin. As she moved the rough cloth over their bodies, she swung her body above them like a pendulum. The woman lay down on the ground and the worker's cold, white legs struck her head. She desperately wanted to remain alive ...

She pounded on the door and screamed, "Someone please come and help me!"

One of the *hammam* workers came to serve her.

"Such is the destiny of the colonel's boys—the colonel and his wife bring female renters and then ..."

୬୫ ୬୫ ୬୫ ୬୫

How could she return home with this reddened face, and that old lady sitting at the window sill? Perhaps they would believe that the redness resulted from the steam of the *hammam*, but what about above the lips? *You have to enter the house stealthily to avoid their glances. Is a widow allowed to do as she pleases? You must never say that you are a widow.*

The colonel's wife laughed aloud and said, "Congratulations!"

She answered, "Shh!"

The young man came and stood at the door. Sweat dripped off the woman's body. The colonel's wife took off the woman's headscarf and whistled. Hastening back inside, the young man warmed up his *tar* to play for her.

"He has made the right decision, Afsaneh. Siya would never forgive himself if he had to just go on like this."

"Just go on like this?"

"Yes—he'll leave the day after tomorrow ... You know, he's looking for work, because of you!"

So ... he was leaving. Now she would be free of this. Free. The pleading sound of the *tar* filled the air ... "I'll return with full hands ... Please don't leave. I'll go so that I can learn something and then I'll return. Please, please don't leave ..."

The young girl writer turned to her. "We should also get to work."

She sat behind the desk.

The sun shined brightly and the rays felt delightfully warm on her skin. Under the blue sky, carefree girls wandered leisurely through the city. The air smelled fresh, and people cleaned out their houses. The blissful modulations of musical instruments and song drifted everywhere as workers washed down the filthy streets. The Dictator said, "She hopes to get married."

"No!"

"So what's all this music for?"

"Happiness."

"That can't be the reason. It wasn't like this before. Before, this kind of festivity took place only when an army was victorious or something important happened ..."

"You're so attached to history."

The Horseman left his castle riding a different horse, a magnificent white stallion, and he wore a blue shirt clean of spattered blood. Without mounting his swords, he rode in the direction of the chariot that was descending from the sky. He stood at the very spot where it would touch the earth. The young girl writer asked him, "Who's that beautiful woman up there?"

The Horseman hesitated, but the voice of the people rose up from the city in exultation, "It's Nahid who's riding the golden chariot! Nahid, the deity of flowing streams of water, kindness, and love!"

32

"Let's go outside for a stroll, Afsaneh *Khanom*!"

The sun had descended and twilight took over the sky. The next day everything would be over—even the reverberations of the *tar*. When the young man left, she would be able to get back to work. But first, she had to walk with him to the dead end. She had to walk separately from him, not side by side. The young man wore a rueful smile. He did not approach her until they reached the end of the street and turned in the direction of the wooden bridge.

"I want to introduce you to someone."

It was a doll-like old lady, with natural, unruly hair. With her long dirty fingernails, she counted cigarettes that she laid out in a grid. The young man said, "She knows everyone's life. The past and the future. She can foresee everything, like a novelist."

The young man gave her a meaningful look.

"Her name is Nargess."

ﭼﭼﭼﭼ

Perhaps the woman could just wander around aimlessly, but she would not; in the end, she would sit down and the old doll would recount her past and present. The doll would fill in that which was lost and not yet found. The bodies of the pregnant weaving sisters would expand a thousand times, and Father would never answer any of her letters. Why hadn't he answered? And where was she in her project on the Hero of Zand?

Nargess *Khanom* yelled out to the young man, "So you're feeling better! But where is Nahid?"

The young man grimaced. He knelt down next to Nargess *Khanom*.

"She died. Nahid died."

Nargess *Khanom* yelled, "No, she hasn't died … she's over there."

She pointed her finger to a street.

At the end of the street was a golden chariot, as bright as the sun and drawn by majestic white horses. A girl stood in the window frame at a dead end of this dark city. From afar, the woman could see the girl's black eyes and her thick, long lashes. The woman's hands were at the horse's bridle, leading it in the direction of the young man. A rough whirlwind carried away the dry twigs on the street and scattered the old lady's cigarettes about. It circled around them faster and tried to sweep them all up into the air. But the young man remained grounded. The woman became Nargess, and Nargess became the woman. Both of them turned into dry yellow leaves caught in the middle of the whirlwind that dragged them upwards. At the peak of the whirlwind, her hands searched for the *Zar* cigarettes.

🕊 🕊 🕊 🕊

She said, "Let's go home. I'm tired."

33

Before the young man left, he told the woman, "I'll write, and call you as soon as I have the chance. My feelings are genuine."

The old lady, whose eyes were swollen from crying, begged the woman to be sweet and answer all his letters. The woman was tired and she wished to start from scratch, as if nothing were there, as if both the Horseman and the sound of the *tar* were absent.

First, she threw herself into organizing her room; she picked the yellow leaves off the plants and shuffled the papers on her table into neat piles. She brought a bucket of water up the stairs and scrubbed the traces of blood that remained on the wall. The old lady came by her room several times—she would shake her head and leave, each time looking more puzzled than the last. Perhaps she felt that everyone should be filled with sorrow, and the woman was not.

"Now you must throw yourself into your work and not answer anything."

"Answer what?"

"A letter or a telephone call …"

She laughed and pounded on the Dictator's shoulder.

"You were worried, weren't you?"

"Yes."

"But you should know me by now, after nine years."

"That's why I was afraid."

As in earlier days, she worked late into the night. The young girl writer sat obediently at the typewriter. A strange pitch and sweet words flew together, the tap of the keys creating phrases on the paper. She did not even see the movement of the young girl writer's hands. She typed quickly, without turning around for approval or leaning back in the chair for even a moment.

"Don't you want to relax?"

"No—I'm afraid. I'm afraid that suddenly everything will unravel."

"How?"

"You know, this typewriter isn't the only thing that exists. There are other things too."

She laughed softly and put her hand on the young girl writer's shoulders, "You'll learn everything soon enough. Relax: the worst has passed."

"You have no idea—they'll attack when we least expect it. Suddenly you'll hear the sound of the horse's hooves."

Everyone in this strange city filled with *narenj* blossoms awaited the hooves of the attacking horses. The young girl writer sat down to work. She felt at home in the kitchen, in front of the typewriter, and in this house, whose window faced the yard and the street.

The young girl writer thought to herself and said, "What if some unexpected problem comes up?"

"Why are you talking such nonsense? Those are the ideas of an earlier era."

The young girl writer looked irritated and mumbled under her breath, "No, these ideas belong to all times. They're all alike."

The woman did not feel like debating. Without uttering a word, she nodded her head in agreement. The young girl writer remained lost in thought. "Look—we're about to be attacked. The scent of attack is in the air."

It was as if ghosts inhabited the city. The people spoke calmly with one another. They moved about peacefully, gazing up at the sky from time to time. A white streak appeared in the broad field of blue. Where was this sound, so strange to the ears of the city, coming from? Suddenly the city became like a tree severed from its roots; it shook, and the woman heard the fear-filled words of the colonel's wife.

"Attack, air attack!"

A faraway radio switched on, police sirens filled the air, and the electricity went out.

"Run to the shelter!"

What shelter? She wandered around and sat down in the darkness. Nasser was sleeping right next to her. The woman took out a cigarette and searched for a lighter, looking over at the body outlined in the minimal light. She was about to strike the flint when the man yelled, "Don't light it, please keep it off ... or I won't be able to sleep."

"What—because of the glow of a cigarette?"

"Yes, this very cigarette. Everything can be seen from up there. Just one lighted speck in the dark—just one speck is enough."

Throughout the six years of war, she had lit her cigarettes secretly.

"The war must end," she pleaded to the sky.

The young girl writer disagreed. "It makes no difference. They aren't interested in ending the war. They just want to attack the other side."

"Nonsense. Night and day they're praying that we end the war soon."

"But they themselves won't do anything to make that possible."

"But the stronghold of Khorramshahr was taken a long time ago. From that very day, they should have …"

"They deny it."

"That's what you think. But they'll come to their senses again."

"We can't just go on fighting forever with the increasing magnitude of casualties. The war has to end somewhere."

The white sirens blasted their all-clear signals. The electricity came back on and the radio announced that the air attacks had ended. Everyone could come out from their shelters. The woman laughed. She was thirsty, so she climbed downstairs to the kitchen. The colonel trembled like a willow tree, and his wife covered him with four thick blankets. Even this display of warmth could not penetrate the cold that spread throughout his body.

— 34 —

The secretary was no longer beaming; a fog of unhappiness blanketed her, and she drummed her fingers on the desk nervously. The woman wanted to say something to someone, but she did not know which words would connect. She felt depressed. It was better for the woman to ask the girl ... *Why are you playing with your fingers ...* No, it wasn't necessary. All she had to do was look to the air attacks. There was her answer—prefabricated topics of conversation.

"Where did they strike yesterday, Ms. Azeri?"

"The barracks of Louizan."

Then the secretary did not say anything else and once again retreated into herself, indifferent to the environment surrounding her. She did not even see Ms. Sar-Boland. *Why was the girl frowning? What does it matter to you? You are not obligated to befriend her. Go to your desk ... Why should I go? To work! I can't. I don't feel like it—they might begin pounding down again ... Is that really why you cannot work?*

🦎 🦎 🦎 🦎

The telephone rang. The secretary tentatively picked up the receiver and said, "Yes, she's in." Without another word, she pointed at the phone. The woman ran to her room and picked it up. It was Nasrin, lighthearted and jovial.

"You didn't get hit by the attack, did you?"

"No."

"*Khoda ra Shokr*—Thank God!"

Yes, *Khoda ra Shokr*! Always, after each air attack, *Khoda ra Shokr*— everything was fine. *It did not fall on my head. How nice of it to have spared me. My God, for how long will this city be without defense, without shelter?*

Morning was on its way. The exhausted masses spoke hesitantly. They glanced toward the sky ... Yes—*Khoda ra Shokr*!

"I heard that Romeo has left."

Nasrin and that distinctive laugh of hers.

"You're free. What a useless boy. I told Khosrow everything and he laughed. He said you were doing too much for him, trying to bite off more than you could chew."

Apparently, everything was going well with Nasrin, what with Khosrow *jan* no longer considered her feudal lord and oppressor ... She had gone back to him; there was just no telling what would happen next.

"I found a house and I'll sign the papers soon. How about you? Are you going to stay alone forever like this?"

Nasrin sat by a window frame. As she spoke, she worked hard on her calculator. Yes, she was going to sign the papers and then, once again, everyone would see that she was not standing on a street corner. The old lady would make room and Nasrin would sit down comfortably next to her. The clock ticked rhythmically and she would begin counting. *They will force you to do the very thing they want you to do!* No one could force the woman to do anything.

❧ ❧ ❧ ❧

She heard the Dictator's bursts of laughter. The sun was setting, washing the streets and flower stores with soft pink light. She did not buy anything. The petals of storefront plants wilted in anticipation of the bombing. People seemed too scared to return to their homes, knowing that bricks and iron beams might collapse on their heads. Everyone was bewildered, hesitant, holding their breath. Why didn't she go home? Why? She had no idea. *If you stay in the streets long enough, all the policemen will look at you, and soon they will blow their whistles. What will they say? You have a home this time. So what don't you have?*

❧ ❧ ❧ ❧

Tonight, if the lights do not go out, I will be able to work. In what part of town did they expect the next strike? It did not matter. The young girl writer had already lost her train of thought. She confused everything-time, place ... Why wasn't the Horseman there last night? Where had he gone? Perhaps tonight she would find him. *Now it is better if you go home. The streets are becoming empty. Do you want to keep treading on foot until you reach the wooden bridge? You will exhaust yourself—and how will you work after that? You will fall asleep as soon as you get home. The old lady will come in again and observe you with such censure that you will shiver. My, how high his expectations where when he hired you, Ms. Sar-Boland ...*

❧ ❧ ❧ ❧

When she arrived at the house, it was dark. Under the streetlights, she saw that the door was ocean blue. She might as well have been seeing it for the first time. On the day she had come with Nasrin, the door was not blue. Or maybe it was this same color, but she had not noticed it then. All the doors in the world are blue. You just have to notice ...

She stood in the hallway and the house felt surprisingly bare. Something was missing. Suddenly it came to her—the omnipresent music of the *tar* was gone. Such is the power of habits. She had grown accustomed to hearing the *tar* every evening when she came home, accustomed to someone warming up the strings. Now, he was not here. How cold the weather had become. Cold. She guessed they had guests due to the closed door. What if they saw her? Those looks of theirs ... They made her feel as guilty as a sinner. She quickly went up the stairs, but she could not work. She was freezing, and the young girl writer trembled. She gave her coat to the young girl writer but it was of no use; her teeth chattered, and the colonel's wife did not bring up tea. Why did she no longer bring tea? Perhaps she was crying downstairs or perhaps she was sitting with the guests, talking and crying. She had probably stopped speaking to her because she now understood that the woman had work to do. She knew ... The woman went downstairs. At the sound of her footsteps, the old lady shut the door. Whose whispering was this? A bitter orange tree does not cry.

"Why didn't you tell me he was leaving?"

It was the sound of a girl, certainly a young girl—Nahid, that same girl who was riding the chariot and waiting ... Nahid, goddess of streams of flowing water.

The woman lingered in the kitchen, but did not know why. What if Nahid were to get up and ride the chariot out the door, looking heavenly even with her puffy eyes?

"It was your own fault, you left ..."

The sound of the colonel's voice first, and then the cries of the young girl whose chariot was the color of the sun.

The woman shook her head and went upstairs. Let the whole world ride on the chariot. She did not want to see anyone or hear anything. It had nothing to do with her. The yard had fallen to pieces ... She regretted leaving and returned downstairs. Perhaps she was mistaken and it was not Nahid but someone else. She opened the window that looked overlooked the streets. Nahid, who was riding the chariot, looked at her angrily; the woman shut the window quickly, feigning indifference.

The young girl writer said, "Let's work—the electricity hasn't gone out yet."

She was right, but where should they start?

"From the time that the city was bombed."

"Perhaps we'll have to gather the dead."

"That's always the way it is …"

"And what about that chariot? Will it also be destroyed?

The young girl writer sat down.

A bomb went off in the center of the city, but the chariot, made of sunlight, slipped easily out of range. There was no bomb in the world that could make it disappear. The people of the city were once again peering at the sky. The chariot rode toward the sun, drawing its energy from the brilliant golden light.

※ ※ ※ ※

A whirlwind sprung up from the earth. A woman's hands reached toward the chariot, trying to guide it to the ground, but the horses fled and a woman's scream rose from the eye of the whirlwind. Now all the dead climbed from their graves, brushing dirt from their sodden bodies. No one had died; rather, they were renovating houses. The blasted doors and windowpanes flew back into place. The woman yelled over the sounds of reconstruction, "We've been bombed, and now what?"

The young girl writer said, "It's not in my hands. It's all because of the chariot."

"Where's the Horseman?"

"I don't know, but he hasn't gone up with the chariot. Perhaps he's somewhere in this city. Or maybe he's wandering through the country somewhere else."

※ ※ ※ ※

The electricity went out, and the now-familiar call sounded: *Run to the shelters …*

It is always like this. First they strike and then you seek shelter—backwards from how it should be ….

※ ※ ※ ※

She puffed on her last *Zar* cigarette. Dried and forgotten, it lit easily. There was no shelter for her. Perhaps an exhausted Dr. Mehrsayi was already waving his hands and yelling, "Oh, my God, all of their eyes will have to be removed …"

"Why are you still here, doctor? Go home and rest …"

"I want to know what's going to happen," Dr. Mehrsayi insisted.

"The laboratory rats. You want to test them, like all the others?" the woman asked.

The young girl writer's lips trembled. "What's he testing?"

"The threshold of pain, the threshold of patience, the threshold of everything."

ʔ҉ ʔ҉ ʔ҉ ʔ҉

Once the electricity came back on, the young girl writer again sat down to work. She pressed her lips together tightly, chasing distant thoughts. She rolled a piece of paper into the typewriter. Then, without paying attention to the one who read over her shoulder, she started to work. The woman devoured her words, not knowing what else to do. She would sit still for hours. This time it seemed like war had devastated the chariot. Fire poured from the sky and homes burned, crackling beneath the flames. The girl waited, and the alien Horseman searched for her. It was not clear whether the thunderous roars were dropping closer or farther away. *Let us go and put out the flames ...*

ʔ҉ ʔ҉ ʔ҉ ʔ҉

Nothing was there, no fire—only the fog and the chariot were waiting. It was neither night nor day. No one could feel the warmth. No one could feel the cold. The young carriage drivers moved in the direction of the Horseman, drawn to him. No one knew whether the deadly sound was flickering further away or coming closer.

"Tomorrow it'll all be over."

The young girl writer stopped working and nervously took her hand.

"You mean the war?"

Yes. They are not striking anymore. The chariot, meandering through the sky in pursuit of the Horseman, has dissuaded them.

The Horseman galloped away from the chariot, and the puffy-eyed girl shouted down to him.

"Who are you moving away from? Who are you approaching?"

ʔ҉ ʔ҉ ʔ҉ ʔ҉

She tossed and turned until morning. Fear had no shelter. Was it the sound of the police sirens, or something else that was playing tricks on her? What if they struck again tomorrow? Fortunately, the Horseman had galloped far away. She saw with her own eyes that he was moving further away from the chariot, from time, from everything. Could he ever be found again?

-174-

The nights were dark and without electricity. The young girl writer had lost her discipline. She was no longer even listening to the woman who was supposed to turn in her work in four months or ... *No, you said six months. Six months. Still a lot of time left, but it will pass quickly. You have to tell the young girl writer to take charge of her work again.*

❧ ❧ ❧ ❧

The enemies did not strike. The foreign radio station said that they were no longer attacking. This was indeed good news. Even with this new safety, the secretary had grown thin and was not uttering a word. Was she frightened of the bombs, or something else? *Let go, it's none of your concern. You're behind and you need to finish your work ... But what if the young girl writer will no longer write? ... Let go of her too—just write yourself.*

❧ ❧ ❧ ❧

Mr. Mohajerani said, "How's your book coming along?"

The woman, sitting behind the desk, was taken aback. Mr. Mohajerani saw this and laughed.

"Perhaps this bombing is preventing you from working?"

She went into the role of Ms. Sar-Boland, and said assertively, "No. I intend to meet my deadline."

Four days of continuous work. It was as if Mr. Mohajerani's words were a whirlwind that pushed her forward. All the leaves separated from the branches in her mind and she became fresh, devoid of withered leaves on her limbs.

On the fourth day, the old lady stood empty-handed at the bottom of the stairs.

If he would just send her one more letter ... if only he would write just one more line for her!

She remembered that he had promised to call—would it be today or tomorrow? A week had passed already.

At five-thirty in the morning, the sound of the phone woke her. The sky was still dark. She heard the sound of laughter, the laughter of the Dictator.

"Perhaps you were dreaming."

She lay very still. Would he call her here or at the company? If he called at the company, perhaps the secretary would ask who he was and what he wanted. What if he called here? Then the old lady would pick up the phone. Yes—it would be better that way. *You have to get word to him, tell him to call you at the house, not the publisher's. What if the secretary or Mr. Mohajerani overheard your conversation? What explanation do you need to give them, anyway? They would only hear a dispassionate conversation.*

⁂ ⁂ ⁂ ⁂

In the end, no one ever called. She jumped up from her seat with every sound. She was sweating and felt feverish, but no one said a word to her. Not even a word. Finally, it was two o'clock. Tired and sad, she picked up the phone.

I need to gain control of what is happening. I cannot continue like this, without having written anything by one o'clock. But what should I say? How can I ask the colonel's wife? ... Don't worry, dial the number. The words will flow naturally and take care of themselves.

"Is there any news, Mrs. Hamidi? My father was supposed to mail me a package from Shiraz."

No deliveries—so what should she do now, work? No, she couldn't ... Speak to the secretary so that time will pass—but pass for what? So you can go ... But where ...? Home. Perhaps there is something going on there. Perhaps the young man had said that he would call after eight days ... *The young man needs you. Now speak firmly into the phone and find out if he has sent you another letter ... So now this damned dictator is laughing again. Leave him alone. These days all he can do is laugh. All dictators become clowns.*

She told the secretary, "I have an appointment with a designer."

She left before the publisher closed. A feeling of panic overcame her; all the images in her mind were being erased. She dragged her legs uncertainly toward Gorgan Street, and the Dictator laughed as she stepped into a cab.

"Here's one hundred *tomans*—take me to the wooden bridge."

She wished that the driver would slow down for the toll and then speed up.

"Drive faster, *Agha*, I'm late," the woman ordered the cab driver.

⁂ ⁂ ⁂ ⁂

Nargess *Khanom* loomed larger than ever and her body stretched out, covering all the intersections. She played with the cigarettes that had fallen on the ground and turned to the sky looking for the golden chariot.

"Nahid ... Where's Nahid?"

At another intersection, Nargess *Khanom* stretched out her arms. With a span as big as an iron-beam, she brought a cigarette closer to her and said, "Smoke it! Soon even *Zar* cigarettes will be extinct."

The woman shook her head and ran until she reached the dead end. Panting, she leaned on the wall. Why was she running? What had caught

-176-

fire? What if someone had seen her? Now what should she tell the colonel's wife? How should she speak to her? The colonel's wife no longer came upstairs, and instead left a tray of tea or placed dinner on the steps. She must know that she should not be a stranger to upstairs or her heart ... what about it? Silence ... This blue door had once been an ugly color ... You have to reach all the doors of the world so that they can become blue, or else the whirlwind will hide behind them and steal their color.

⁂ ⁂ ⁂ ⁂

She stood at the door breathing hard.

She could not let anyone see her so distraught. She took a deep breath and forced a laugh. Then she rang the doorbell. The colonel's wife opened the door.

"How are you, Mrs. Hamidi?

The colonel's wife let her in, and she slowly entered the kitchen. She waited for Mrs. Hamadi to make a polite gesture for her to stay and eat but she did not. She simply placed a glass of tea on a tray and stood by the stairs, "*Befarmayid*—Afsaneh *Khanom*."

"*Mamnoon*—I'll drink it right here."

She sat on the stairs, searching for the right words, for some conversation to share, to form a bond with her old lady once again.

"Today I completed a substantial part of my work. That's why I'm so relaxed."

The old lady laughed but her laughter was strangely distant. *Really*, the woman asked herself, *what have I done?*

Now she had to talk, perhaps ask about the house or say something about the tea. She had to say the tea was good, or that the colonel had become himself again.

"Where does the colonel buy those seeds?"

The old lady said that she did not know, and at the sound of the doorbell she got up to leave. Standing by the door, she began to laugh happily.

"Come—come in. There's no one here, just our tenant."

Then she heard the sound of the whispers of a girl who refused to enter. Nahid.

⁂ ⁂ ⁂ ⁂

The woman flew upstairs. She had escaped from something formless, and she yearned to hide herself. It was fortunate that she did not get a chance to ask the colonel's wife anything, or else she would have understood ... But what is it that she would have understood? *No, there is nothing. You just have to sit and work. If you pace like this in your room, they will hear your steps downstairs and they will understand. They need to know that you are not bothered by anything, not bothered by anything at all. The sound of the typewriter has a soothing effect ... you become comfortable and then you don't feel the need to hide yourself anymore.*

؉ ؉ ؉ ؉

When the colonel's wife came upstairs, she had a bowl of *ash* in her hands. "*Ash-e Posht-e Pa*—time for *ash* since the dear traveler has gone. Nahid made it."

The woman rose from behind her desk, indicating to the old lady that she had worked extremely hard but was not exhausted. The colonel's wife feared, however, that she was imposing upon the writer's work, and turned to leave the room. Too suddenly, it seemed, the old lady was gone and the bowl of *ash* was left on the table. Why had the colonel's wife left so abruptly? Aha! Because the woman let her know that she was working. Tomorrow there will certainly be news of the young man. He could not just leave them without any news. He could not.

She reached for his letter; she read it and laughed. He had written that he would call her. The telephone lines were probably out of service. Perhaps they attacked the city where he was living. They were pounding everywhere, and Urmia could certainly be a target. What if they were to strike the area that makes *seh-tar* instruments? What if they had already hit that place? The newspapers ... she had not been reading the newspapers ... But no, if anything serious had happened, the old lady would not have looked at her with such indifference. She would have grabbed her by the collar and screamed, "You killed him—you!"

In the morning the woman scanned the newspapers from the past few days. She even called the telephone company. There were no reported attacks. All the telephones were working. At the publisher's, she could not put her heart into her work and sat vacantly until at last it was time to leave. She had listened to the secretary who answered the phones, and a thousand times she jumped up at the ring; but nothing—no news.

In the evening, the streets were dark and depressing. People moved list-lessly, with no apparent plans for what would happen from one day to the next. She could tell by the way that they walked that they knew where they were going. *And what about you, do you know?*

-178-

When she arrived home, she asked the colonel's wife, "Did I receive a letter from Shiraz?" She felt compelled to explain, "I'm waiting for a package. My father will send it."

The colonel's wife quickly gave her dinner. The woman slipped on her *chador* and went out; she laughed gaily as if she knew where she was going.

Inside, she was hollow. A choking grief pressed against her throat, and she could not even smoke a cigarette and walk at the same time, her restlessness was so great. When she returned to her room, she fell onto the bed, exhausted. She pressed the pillow hard against her mouth so that the sound of her weeping would not reach downstairs.

— 35 —

The large city had become small and suffocating, cutting off her air supply and closing in around her. She ran frantically down narrow streets and up broad thoroughfares. She pounded on the city walls. There was no path for escape. She could not talk to anyone, not even the secretary. Several times, she passed by the girl's desk and just stood there. Tears choked her voice. All she could ask were banal questions about things that no longer mattered.

"What was the last book that you read?" Or, "What's the news of the book's sales?"

Strangely, the secretary herself was so distracted that she hardly seemed to recognize the woman. She mumbled short replies to questions and hung her head on her chest. The woman would go back into the room and find that she could not sit patiently. She was incapable of doing any work at all. She only came into work to try to pass time more quickly.

Mr. Mohajerani said, "You're exhausted. Perhaps a vacation isn't a bad idea."

She laughed. Nothing made a difference to her anymore. Now that Mr. Mohajerani had mentioned it, maybe a break was not such a bad idea—she might take the suggestion.

"I don't know ... Maybe if for one week I could just focus on the story about the Horseman."

"That's right—it's better that you just finish the story once and for all."

"But you know that having a place to write is very important to me. I'm accustomed to writing at home."

"So stay home."

"I couldn't possibly. Nothing would get done here without me ... But I suppose a one week trial period to finish my story couldn't hurt."

One week at home, ears constantly waiting for the sound of the doorbell and the mail that would not come. The colonel's wife should not suspect this, and no one should know anything of her vigil.

She locked the door from inside and flicked on the lights. The young girl writer was confused and had lost her interest in the typewriter, so often the woman had to force her to focus on work. The sound of the keys striking the sheet prevented anyone downstairs from guessing her true state, but on the days the girl came, the woman could hear the sound of her cries. One day, as the young girl writer ascended the stairs, the colonel's wife followed her and said to the woman, "He has probably given you his news."

She was taken aback. The woman struggled to maintain her dignity, but she saw the hostility in the old lady's eyes. This was impossible. No one should treat her as worthless! It became evident to the old lady that the woman had not received any news and she scoffed. If a conflict arose, the woman would scream and demand her rights—but it was not clear what those rights were. If only Mr. Mohajerani or Father would hear of this ... Ah.

"*Khanom.* Believe me, none of this has anything to do with me at all."

The colonel's wife was happy. The woman stood in such a way that suggested she would like the old lady to leave—she had work. The old lady and the girl left her alone. How slowly the days and nights were passing.

꒰ ꒰ ꒰ ꒰

Let me go and look for Nargess Khanom. Perhaps she will recognize me—but then what? Perhaps she will say something. She claims to know everyone and that she has the ability to tell the future.

From a distance, Nargess *Khanom* caught sight of her and yelled, "It's time for you to go to Shiraz!"

To Shiraz! How would she go and what would she say? Wasn't it better for her to stay where she was and lose herself among strangers? She took her ration cards from the colonel's wife.

"I'll go and fetch the food myself, Mrs. Hamidi."

The owner of the store looked at her with surprise and said, "One person?"

"Yes."

She stuttered, "But you're still young."

"It's not for me—it's for the old lady who lives up there."

She returned to the house and gave the ration cards back to the colonel's wife.

"The line is very long—I wasn't able to wait there any longer."

꒰ ꒰ ꒰ ꒰

When she finally fell asleep, she had a nightmare: the two spinsters with their stained yellow wedding dresses were chasing after her. She was in a desert filled with dry carnations, and an aggressive whirlwind was moving toward her. It crept closer, slowly attempting to devour her and the spinsters. It circled around and around them.

Wet with sweat, she sat up—what if her screams had awoken those sleeping downstairs? Nothing stirred in the dark night, only drops of water being poured into a cup, and a glowing cigarette butt ... ghostly sounds that she knew from before. She yearned for human contact.

⁂ ⁂ ⁂ ⁂

She wandered through the streets, past flower shops and fabric stores. Finally, she stood still. She did not know what she wanted, except that she wanted to buy something. But for whom? There was no one. She had no one. What about the colonel's wife? Perhaps it was Mother's Day? No, it had already passed. But she bought some flowers anyway and told the colonel's wife, "I bought these for you."

Her hands trembled. The words jumped from her mouth in a whisper, "Do you have any news of your son?"

The colonel's wife touched her hands through the cloth flowers. She pretended not to hear the woman's desperate plea, so that she would not have to answer. She merely turned away and mumbled to herself under her breath, "No. He told me that he'd return in six months."

"But he promised to call me."

Her voice was feverish. The old lady understood, but was happy. Why? She laughed heartily, "So he hasn't called? He has probably forgotten."

The color drained so quickly from the woman's face that the old lady grew worried. She glared at the woman and said, "You were right when you said he was a liar."

That was it. The old lady had offered her words to the woman so that she would be spared saying anything else. The woman went upstairs. She collapsed on the bed, and the words of Nargess *Khanom* echoed through the city.

"Leave for Shiraz ..."

— 36 —

For sixteen hours, she was on the road. She took the bus on purpose. Sixteen hours is plenty of time to think, if the spinsters would stop their machines from clacking long enough to allow it. Both of them ran after the bus with their stained yellowed dresses and hands punctured with needle marks. The hems of their shirts were soiled. They yelled for the woman to get off the bus, to purchase the dresses, to bring their mother's soul back to life, and to put it into a glass so that they could sew a wedding dress for her and for all the widows in the world.

They reached Esfahan. The woman screamed into the air that no dead person could come back to life. A whirlwind carried her and Nargess *Khanom* to the top, where they searched for a *Zar* cigarette. The whirlwind also lifted up the two spinsters. Nargess *Khanom* ran alongside the bus until it reached Abadeh. She stretched out her arms to give the woman a cigarette, but instead denied her, throwing it under the bus's tires. A layer of half-smoked *Zar* cigarettes covered all of Shiraz, and Nargess *Khanom* stayed behind to pick them up. The young girl writer pointed out the window to the tower.

"The Hero and his army are over there ..."

She had no energy, but she turned her head around to please the young girl writer. She thought of Shiraz and the woman who was fleeing on the rooftops. Why was she fleeing?

She turned around and faced the young girl writer, "That man that you spoke of ... the one with silver eyes ... and that woman ... can you talk about her again?"

"I don't really remember, it was so long ago."

"Perhaps you have intentionally forgotten."

"No, it has nothing to do with consciousness or sub consciousness, being or non-being. Your sense of time is distorted. It makes you lose direction, and lost in the labyrinth of the past it can become difficult to judge reality."

"But you remember some things, don't you?"

"Some. There was a man who always made his wife sleep first so that she could not see him secretly remove something, and we're not talking about fake teeth. The man was young. He could not tolerate the glow of a cigarette in the dark. He wanted to hide his eyes, to hide his empty eye sockets. His eyes were made of glass. Every night before he slept, he put them under his head and close at hand, so that in the morning he could put them in their place again. I'm not completely sure of the details. But this is what I still remember."

"I believe that his eyes were made of glass because he couldn't see, not even the light of day. I saw his empty eye sockets with my own eyes. I saw his hands searching under the pillow for his eyes. It was at that same time that I escaped. But I think you said something else. You said that a long time ago, someone had blinded him."

The young girl writer was sweating. She was cold, and a hill of gouged-out eyes came to life behind the bus window, trailing and scattering along the road. Suddenly she screamed. The woman covered her mouth so that the sleepy travelers would not hear her, but the driver's aid noticed and came toward her with a glass of water. He splashed some on the face of the young girl writer, who had passed out.

"You know, in those days it was as if they were throwing stones at Moshtagh, and Khan Qajar wanted two *mans* of eyes, two *mans*, no more no less ..."

¿¥ ¿¥ ¿¥ ¿¥

Blue Quran Gates. A city as it had always been. The frightened woman, who was still fleeing on the rooftops, remained the same. She ran, turning her head around in fear. The young girl writer said, "You must write that she didn't flee. And it would be better if you confirmed the facts with your father. He knows history."

When she got off the bus, the woman stood still, hesitating. Could she speak without her voice catching in her throat? She needed to ask Father about those things that the young girl writer had forgotten or did not want to say. Did these narrow threads of doubt fill history? What was Father doing now? Perhaps he was sitting in some corner of a room, or perhaps he was lying down and reading *The Hero of Zand*. And how wise that she brought part of the book and ... her first book ... Certainly it was odd that Father had not said anything yet not even in a letter, a note, a message ...

¿¥ ¿¥ ¿¥ ¿¥

Someone rang the doorbell.

One of the pregnant weaving girls looked out and said, "Perhaps it's that beggar again ..."

She rang the doorbell and announced that it was indeed she. Slowly, the door opened. It was Father, holding *The Memoirs of General Ironsides*. Father always coughed as he spoke of history. The woman smiled, stood on her toes, and kissed him. This woman, no longer dressed in orange and no longer fleeing on the rooftops, held him in an embrace.

A long time ago, Father had said something that she remembered: "Time gives all understanding its own color. According to time's own wishes."

Now she could finally tell Father the truth. She could look straight into his eyes without trembling. He had read her book—it was clear as day. They could sit down and talk frankly, something for which she had longed with all her being. Then she would tell him she was writing about the Hero of Zand and show him some chapters. But Father only asked, "How much did you make with this book?"

She stood still.

"Nothing to speak of. I was working under a contract."

"Useless … How about the other book?"

All the weaving girls, pregnant or not pregnant, gathered and spoke with her. They laughed and planned. *People can find a dozen ways to make money. In Sweden, they sell books at double the price … You know, I bought some and distributed them to my friends. You have to sign a few others but the cover is a mess. If only it were lined with gold ink!*

❧ ❧ ❧ ❧

Something was in flames. There was a scream in the depths of her throat that wanted to explode and shatter the world. What had she done in her life to be called Afsaneh, 'legend'? People had once called her this! What had happened to her?

She smelled her own solitude, bare and lonely in a dry and frozen desert. The attackers had stolen everything. How positively she had once thought of the voice of Father, of the pregnant, virgin girls' greetings.

Father said, "If a revolutionary Horseman comes and takes control of this country, like Khan Qajar … Someone who is willing to cut the throats of everyone nine years and older to bring about change, this is the person we need."

Her mouth gaped, her ice-cold hands trembled, she replied, "Don't search for a clear and pure Horseman. You won't find him."

Now how could you ever speak of that night? All of those events were merely part of the tragicomedy of history. She did not utter a word. All the pregnant weaving sisters were sitting down with their husbands and Father. The young girl writer said, "I'll speak of that night if you don't."

The young girl writer told the story of the woman who fled on the rooftops one night and she explained why. Father roared with laughter, "You're crazy! Why should she flee after seeing someone's eyes?"

Father put his hands on his own pupils and brought out the black stones in front of all the pregnant weaving sisters and their mothers. The woman saw his empty eye sockets, and the young girl writer put her hands on the woman's mouth so that she would not scream. Then she asked, "But why?"

Father dissolved into laughter, and with his empty eye sockets, sifted through the travel memoirs of General Ironsides. He said, "That same day that they stoned Moshtagh, I faintly recall them throwing him down from the rooftop. We were also there and, as you know, Khan Qajar wanted two *mans* of eyes. No more, no less. We witnessed this, all of us. We all witnessed the blinding and murder of the musician Moshtagh. We shouldn't have looked, but we did. It took years until everyone found their own pupils in that hill of eyes. And see, I still have my scar. Still."

Her head spun, she could not see anyone, and she did not know how much time all these eyes needed to heal.

"We will throw a party in your honor."

Who will dance in honor of a life of constant wandering? Her voice cracked in the back of her throat, "I have work I must get back to."

Father said, "Perhaps another story. Do you already have a contract?"

All the pregnant weaving sisters were screaming and applauding with support: "From the beginning, we knew …"

Yet no one knew the musician, Moshtagh, and no one had seen a woman escaping across the rooftops in an orange dress.

"Would you like a cigarette? You used to smoke Winstons."

That is what I was addicted to back then … Until the end of time, everything must be done according to habit … She had refused to become accustomed to anything, even to begging, but in the end, she became accustomed even to that. All these years, she had been a beggar. She had begged, and now beggars surrounded her.

The original sin started with the Horseman who had once yelled, "Let's settle camp right here."

⁂ ⁂ ⁂ ⁂

She stood and left the house. So many years had passed. She knew that no dictators wore stars on their shoulders any longer, but even without decorations they could force you to obey. *But why did you obey? Why didn't you scream?* … She stepped along freely, unfettered by the calculations of those people who sit in their window frames measuring everyone's movements. How fragrant the air was in the month of *Bahman*. Blooming flowers surrounded her, and she no longer felt cold. It was as if she had stolen into Shiraz. In the morning, she arrived, and in the evening she would leave; before she left though, she needed to find a small, lost garden alley. She had to find it so that she could make everything clear. Clear—but for whom? Perhaps for herself. Perhaps, but time had passed.

She found that same small garden alley. There was no escaping the smell of dead memories ... *You yourself did not believe it. You were scared, but of what? Perhaps you were frightened of your habits and of all the people who are sitting in window frames. So it was the old lady who monitored Nasrin who had dried up all the bitter oranges. If they are dry, would you like to look? Yes, just look ...*

The woman reached the small street. That same dead end and that same propped door. She had forgotten that the street was a dead end. She pushed open the blue door, the half-open gray door. She entered and saw that the old lady who monitored Nasrin had dried up. Her wilted body replaced the bitter orange tree. The tree that was no longer there.

In the yard, children's underwear hung on the line. A young child was crying and a woman with a pot was leaving the room.

"What do you want, *Khanom*!"

"There used to be a bitter orange tree here, didn't there?"

The woman laughed. "Are you Afsaneh?"

"Yes, and you?"

"Me? Well, isn't it clear?"

She showed her the pot.

She paced back and forth through the dry grass of the yard before turning around and walking toward the door. She passed by the small room near the hallway, and she saw a man sitting down in the middle of a group of colored telephones. He had placed his glass eyes in a cup half-filled with water, and he was waiting for the telephone to ring. His empty eye sockets were scarred. Bloody pus poured from them.

As he coughed and searched for the cup, the frightened woman ran out into the street. The pain in her stomach was sharp, and she began to vomit. The Dictator struggled to get out of her way. He screamed and called for help, and she started to laugh aloud. All the windows opened. Young, vibrant hands stretched a branch of *narenj* blossoms out toward her.

The young girl writer said, "I think he's dead. Let's bury him."

"No! No, let him stay where he is."

She quickened her pace. Next to the walls of the houses the bitter orange trees grew taller and the branches of ripe fruit bent down toward her. It was winter. The winter of 1986.

— 37 —

Tehran's exhilarating climate enticed her. Cries and moans permeated the city. Mr. Mohajerani said, "When the telegraph arrived saying you had left for Shiraz, I was shocked."

She laughed out loud.

"Perhaps you went because of the story," he said.

"No. I went because of myself. I wanted to go," she answered.

The secretary was excited.

"What are you weaving?" the woman asked.

"A jacket, for Reza."

"Has he returned?"

"No. He's a prisoner. But he'll return, when the war has ended."

"When will it end?"

"I don't know."

"And you will weave until he comes?"

"Yes."

"Teach me too."

The secretary was startled.

"You want to learn to weave, Ms. Sar-Boland?"

"Yes, I do."

"But who, may I ask, do you want to weave for?"

The woman answered frankly, "Why should it matter?"

"Well—would it be for a woman or a man?"

"A man."

The secretary laughed and the woman pinched her cheeks with two fingers, "You little devil!"

She went with Nasrin and bought yarn.

"You've gone mad."

"No, I have to learn."

"God forbid that you ever want anything!"

She laughed. It was very difficult. Admirers are never satisfied … Who would agree to change the course of a river that runs in only one direction? Such a project would be a massive undertaking. This full-length mirror … One can live forever in this full-length mirror. She bought it: one full-length mirror and ten boxes of yarn. Nasrin burst into laughter. She did not believe it. She could not believe it ...

"Let's go to the beauty parlor."

"Don't tell me something's going on, Afsaneh."

"A thousand things are happening. Now leave me alone."

This time, she surrendered herself to the hands of the beautician without a tear.

"Remove all of the extra hair from my eyebrows and my face."

⅔ ⅔ ⅔ ⅔

The old lady fled from her; it was as if she were afraid of something, and she stumbled over her words. "I told Nahid that Afsaneh *Khanom* is an intelligent university graduate ... All Afsaneh wanted was for Siya to recover from his illness."

The woman wanted to remind the old lady of what she had once said and not allow her to take back her words. The colonel looked at the woman and was frightened. He did not want to lose anything. Now he and his wife were uncertain and both of them sat at the window frame. Ms. Sar-Boland was a widow, and there was a five year difference in their ages. The colonel's wife said, "But Siyavash is four years older than Nahid."

The woman laughed. The colonel's wife became upset. Why did everyone just want her to be Ms. Sar-Boland?

The young girl writer said, "Well, you are ... Aren't you, Ms. Sar-Boland?

"No. Didn't you see there, in Shiraz, in that street? He was struggling and calling for help. He was drowning in all of that vomit."

The eyes of the young girl writer grew round and she began to splinter, eroding at the seams. Her particles broke into pieces and scattered in the air.

The woman took off her watch and placed it on the table.

"Come—sit down and let's work. You're hurting yourself for no reason."

She realized that the young man had not been responsible for the stolen earrings. The others understood this before she did. The colonel's wife would say, "God help me. If I'm lying, may He take my life."

Nasrin giggled, "You can't be serious."

The woman put all the yarn on the table in front of the secretary. "It's for you."

The girl's eyes sparkled with happiness. "I'll sew a man's jacket. A large one will fit him just right."

Suddenly her face changed and she was upset. Her lips trembled and her hands shook.

"In your opinion, whose fault is it?"

"What?"

"The war and all these prisoners."

"It's the fault of the Medes and all the people who saw Moshtagh's murder. Even Moshtagh himself is responsible!"

The secretary did not understand and glanced at the woman, who smiled.

"You know, you, I, and everyone else shouldn't have allowed them to kill the musician Moshtagh, or at least we should not have looked. A show without an audience has no purpose. When someone believes in something, they do not need an audience—but a mere actor never completely puts his heart into the role. His voice trembles, his movements become slow."

The secretary looked at her without comprehending. The woman tried to make the girl understand. "Look at the small things: You can sew while I cannot; I can write and you cannot. What we are and what we are not can all be traced back to our ancestors. It's all because of the Medes."

꙳ ꙳ ꙳ ꙳

The young girl writer asked, "Why are you mixing things up?"

The woman laughed, "This is unlike you! You shouldn't doubt me. You know I'm right."

"So it's because of this that you didn't yell at him—at that man—in Shiraz?"

"No, he wasn't a sinner. No one is a sinner. Not him or the pregnant weaving girls. Not even the gambler. Everyone gambles—but when one wins, another loses."

"But what if someone gambles off someone else?"

She chuckled, "Everyone gambles over someone else's head. Have you ever seen anyone in a situation of simply winning or losing? In the end even the winner will lose."

The young girl writer said, "The gambling man was the Dictator's story, not mine!"

The poor soul continued to talk nonsense. All dictators imagine that they are eternally winners. Then you see that the destiny of them all is exactly the same. It does not matter whether they bear a general's stars on their uniforms. In the end, they will fall. If they want to continue in their role, they must accept their fate.

It was winter and there was a dry cold in Tehran. It was snowing as she walked through the crusted streets. She wanted to raise her face so that the flakes would land on her lashes and melt. She spun in circles and bumped into people. She laughed at them. One frowned but another understood that she was laughing out of pure joy. Some of them understood and smiled knowingly.

She arrived at the beet market.

"*Agha*, I'd like one beet."

How big this beet is! It is only the color of the beet that will make you yell joyfully, "Snow. Snow!"

She asked the salesman, "Do you like the color of beets?"

The salesman was covered in snow. His hair and eyebrows were buried in white flakes.

The woman did not wait for him to respond, "I like it because of its color. Like a mulberry. The snow's falling … Look at how they walk under the snow—and that one—that woman—let me call over to her."

The salesman said, "But you haven't paid yet."

She laughed. She pressed one hundred *tomans* into his hands and said, "Put one more in the bag."

The salesman stuffed another beet in her bag and exclaimed, "Ah, the color of mulberry!"

She pulled out a beet and walked all the way to the colonel's house, savoring its sweet juice.

❧ ❧ ❧ ❧

The colonel's wife was frightened and pushed the woman aside. She took the bag of beets and did not invite the woman to sit by the furnace. It seemed as if the colonel and his wife wanted to get rid of her, such a familiar sensation. The colonel coughed and the old lady left the room. She frowned often these days. It seemed like the old lady did not want to the woman to rent the second floor any longer. She was making a plan. It takes strength to rid yourself of someone. It takes time.

"Give Afsaneh *Khanom* some sweets, lady!"

The colonel's wife gave her some.

"The neighbor's daughter is getting married!"

The colonel said, "God willing, you'll move on with your life."

Strange! There must be something going on. They are worried that she will scream and demand her rights. She stopped herself from laughing. They were talking like the beet salesman who said: "You haven't paid for it, *Khanom*."

All the beets were the color of mulberry. Mulberry! She went upstairs. It was still snowing. She still loved the color of beets, the wonderful color of mulberry. The young girl writer said, "Will you work?"

"Certainly."

❦ ❦ ❦ ❦

The Horseman returned from his long, faraway trip. The horse's hooves resonated through the city … Distant sounds in the sky! Khan Qajar had died and the Horseman planned to rid the city of the sound of clashing swords. He would stay in the town. He surrounded himself with music, the music of Moshtagh. The bitter orange blossoms that floated in the blue sky were like pieces of scattered light.

❦ ❦ ❦ ❦

In the morning she woke up to the colonel's screams. A thousand pigeons were pecking at him and trying to carry off the bag of seeds. Snow was resting on the rooftops. The woman recognized the two rebellious pigeons flapping their wings in the air with the bag of seeds in their beaks. The colonel was spinning around in circles, and she tittered.

She was happy to sit in the house and work. The young girl writer said, "Don't you want to call the publishing house?"

"No!"

Her eyes fell on the windows in the bathroom and the hallway, which had once again turned black. She was starting to clean them when the colonel's wife became fearful that the woman would once again entangle herself in their affairs.

"We'll take care of the cleaning ourselves."

We! The old lady was setting her apart. The woman tried to set everyone's minds at ease.

"I'm not doing this cleaning for your sake. I'm doing it for myself."

She was just finishing up when the mail arrived. The colonel's wife took the letter, but this time she did not have a chance to hide it anywhere ... She had to lose, lose.

"Is it a letter?"

"Yes!"

"From where?"

"I don't know ..."

"Let me see."

The woman grabbed the letter from the old lady's grip and immediately recognized the handwriting. She tore it open. He was well, and he hoped that she was in good health—but he did not understand why she had not responded to any of his letters, and why she had not called him at the number he had given. He was coming soon.

The letter remained in her hands as she stared angrily at the old lady, who looked at her and said, "I did it for your own sake."

The woman breathed heavily and then forced herself to laugh. She saw her own curious smirk in the mirror and asked, "So where are the rest of the letters?"

"The colonel burned them all."

The woman hesitated as she struggled to control her emotions. When the colonel's wife regained her own composure, she said, "You were right, you know. There's really nothing worse than living with a lie."

— 39 —

He returned twenty days later with a blond beard and brown manly eyes. She observed him closely and noticed he was wounded. His eyes were scarred, but they were not glass eyes that he would put into a cup half-filled with water. They were his own. He could still see and listen.

٭ ٭ ٭ ٭

Time had passed, and now from downstairs came the sound of singing while she packed her books into boxes upstairs. She locked the door from the inside so that even she could not open it. The door drew attention like a magnet: No one could come in without being noticed. Tomorrow she was turning in her work and leaving ... *What will you do? ... I will write ... But before any of this happened, you were writing already ... Not like before. This time, I don't write for the sake of anyone ... Everyone has died, that old lady who was sitting at the window frame and Father with his empty eye sockets; those virgin girls and that man ...*

There was a tapping on the door and she rose to open it. The eyes and cheeks of the young girl writer were wet.

He took out a cigarette, lit it, and sat down. He looked at the boxes, bewildered. His hands were trembling. How often she had seen him these days in the yard with his eyes staring upward.

He said, "Are you really going to abandon us?"

Was she really leaving? Why was she leaving—was it his long absence? She did not utter a word. She just laughed and crammed another book into the carton. He rose and tried to help her pack the box, but he could not. She helped him. The young man grinned, "Do you always pack these up all alone?"

"Yes, always alone."

The colonel's wife was calling from downstairs. She was still scared.

"Siyavash, Nahid's here."

He grinned and yelled down to her, "I'm coming, Mother."

He stood next to the door, "You didn't believe that story—or did you?"

"Which one?"

"The one of the prisoners and the Iraqi hospital and that Iranian nurse. The nurse looked like you ... like you ... I had gone to fight for my country."

"I believe it."

Again the anxious voice of the colonel's wife: "Siyavash, Nahid's here!"

He left. The woman closed all of the boxes and just one thick book remained on the table. She chuckled. Her new house did not have an old lady. Just her and the young girl writer and a thousand windows that faced the sky.

The young girl writer asked her, "How many pages are left until you finish?"

"Two."

She sat down behind her desk.

The city was calm, and there were no longer any surrounding walls or gates. Instead, carnations fluttered in all the girls' hair. The sound of Moshtagh's music floated on a breeze. A magnificent horse without a rider trotted into the middle of the city. The young girl writer held a golden rose in her hand and walked toward the horse. The horse recognized her. He neighed three times in the direction of the sun, and the young girl writer seated herself on his back. He circled two or three times until the young girl writer grabbed the reins and pointed the red-maned horse toward the horizon. Perhaps he had heard the terrifying news that Khan Qajar was still alive.

— Translator's Afterword —

Moniru Ravanipur, a female novelist and short story writer, is one of the most radical and stylistically revolutionary voices in Persian literature today. The Iranian government has reacted against her controversial work by banning reproductions since 2006. Her boldness, subversiveness, and anti-orthodoxy emanates not from her political views but from her narrative experimentation, her unsentimental exploration of mental instability, and her unrelenting fascination with spirits, ogres, and demons. Like most of her fiction, *Del-e Fulad* (Heart of Steel)—in this translation re-titled *Afsaneh* after the protagonist's forename—is populated with imaginary characters and the personifications of inner forces. Most notably these include the Dictator and the Horseman, who, respectively, represent cruelty and love. Ravanipur's talent for blending history with fantasy and weaving autobiographical details with grotesque illusions exemplifies "magical realism," or the departure from reality and traditional narrative forms. Her daring, unconventional style flouts the strict values of authority and obedience that often define her society. However, the weight of her work and its haunting beauty transcends social and political critique beyond the indictment of patriarchy. *Afsaneh's* protagonist, a female writer, portrays a world of omnipresent personal pain with the lingering sense of opening wounds. Ravanipur's work attempts to answer the question: *How does one feel fertile, create and breathe life, and love, into her characters in the midst of murder, ignorance, and destruction?* Under such circumstances, sanity is madness, and so the splintered, delusional quality of her narrative is the clearest, most truthful way of expressing the damage done to a nation's psyche. *Afsaneh* is the offspring of the marriage between destructive trauma and creative genius.

※ ※ ※ ※

Moniru Ravanipur was born in 1952 into a large family in Jofreh, a small village in Southern Iran. During her childhood, she developed a deep love for story telling that continues to influence her work today. Many of her earliest memories have been woven into her semi-autobiographical works. The history of Ravanipur's family itself seems almost like fiction, fantastical and influential. Her maternal grandparents married when they were just sixteen years old and they faced many hardships throughout their young lives. Her grandfather's sister, Tavoos, fell in love with a man outside the family, which was considered a crime among her relatives. When the family plotted to kill Tavoos to cleanse the lineage of her shameful act, Ravanipur's grandparents escaped with her great-aunt and founded their own small village by the sea near Bushehr. Her grandfather, still just sixteen years old, secured a job in a British hospital and became fluent in English. He worked his way up the chain, eventually opening his own medical office in the small village where his family had taken refuge. Despite his professional status, he remained illiterate in Persian and stressed the importance of giving his own children and grandchildren the best education possible.[1]

By the time Ravanipur was born, Iran had entered a state of political turmoil. She was born one year before the 1953 CIA led coup that removed the nationalist leader Mossadeq from power and reinstated the Shah. Her family was devastated by the change in regime, and the resulting conversations surrounding politics colored her childhood. They frequently gathered to discuss politics and love, and to engage in captivating poetry readings in drunken revelry. As a young girl, Ravanipur absorbed everything, and these early experiences instilled the importance of intellectualism and the arts. Her father was a revolutionary, a member of the National Front, and her cousin and uncle were also intensely political. Her father had a truck filled with

---

[1]Miranda Mellis, "An Interview with Miranda Mellis," *Paul Revere's Horse* (San Francisco: Sawkill Press, 2011) no.5: 27-32. Information in the following four paragraphs is gleaned from this interview as well as the translator's personal correspondence with Ravanipur.

pamphlets written by the Nationalist Party, and would drive out to the countryside to distribute them. In exchange for these pamphlets some Nationalists gave him poems, which he brought back as souvenirs for his daughter. In addition to the aforementioned exposure, she grew up with her grandmother's stories of genies and other Persian legends. This mix of political idealism and traditional fables countered the harshly restrictive society in which she lived. The stories of her erudite family and the tumultuous political environment encompassed and inspired her, and remain her primary sources for literary material today.

Her family's home housed multiple generations. As a young child, she read books by the Tudeh Party that her communist cousin brought home. Her first foreign book was *Gorki*. At ten years old, she completed her elementary education and began to keep a diary. She participated in the poetic and theatrical societies that flourished in her hometown of Bushehr. By sixteen, she had immersed herself in literature. Her stories infused the sights, smells, and sounds of her surroundings with the images from her vivid imagination. She was interested in Tolstoy and Dostoevsky, and befriended their characters. Their novels motivated her to write more seriously. Her compositions were consistently ranked best in her class, and paved the early miles of the road to success. She attended college in Shiraz, not far from her birthplace, joined the Shiraz Theater Group, and acted in several plays. The stories of these dramas seemed to meld with her life, and she consistently drew parallels between her family and the archetypes present in fiction. She identified Ursula from *One Hundred Years of Solitude* with her grandmother. During her college years, she invested in a typewriter to type and print her stories, and finally began to attend poetry society meetings and readings to share her work.

From the tranquility of her college life sprang chaos. At the beginning of the 1979 Islamic Revolution in Iran, her brother, a communist, was murdered. Her sister and brother-in-law were also assassinated. Two of her sisters and a brother-in-law were imprisoned and her eleven and sixteen year old siblings were dragged out of school by the police. Everything her family owned in Bushehr was confiscated. After this upheaval, the remaining members of her family moved to Shiraz, and Ravanipur moved to Tehran with a disguised name and worked in the Daroupakhsh Factory. Whenever her true identity was discovered, she would move on to another factory, until she found a job as a nurse in a private hospital using yet another alias. When she visited her parents in Shiraz, she was arrested on the street as part of the government's campaign of mass incarceration. While imprisoned, she realized that she, like many men and women of her generation, could be killed namelessly; however, she could prevent her anonymous despair if she created a public and respected identity for herself as a writer.

Ravanipur's literary career, however, did not commence until after the Iranian Revolution, and thus it is important to understand the literary context. While pre-revolutionary women often discussed socio-political issues in their texts, it was not until after the 1979 revolution that the private experiences of women became public.[2] Noted Iranian Studies scholar Kamran Talatoff argues that Ravanipur is one of the most significant representations of the post-revolutionary literary movement. Her assertive themes have given her a prominent position among post-revolutionary literary activists. According to Talatoff, Ravanipur's emphasis on the importance of women in literary endeavors explicitly addresses issues related to women's social conditions and gender relations.[3] Though not explicitly a feminist writer, Ravanipur has made great strides in exposing the details of the diurnal lives of post-revolution Iranian women in a machismo society.

Ravanipur's exploration of socio-political issues is manifested in her prolific bibliography. Her tremendous productivity after the Iranian Islamic Revolution makes her one of the leading figures of the contemporary literary scene in Iran. Her career as an author officially began in 1988, almost ten years after the revolution, with the publication of her first book, *Kanizu*, a collection of short stories. It was not until the publication of her first novel, *Ahl-e Gharq* (The Drowned), in 1989, however, that she broke into the traditionally male dominated literary scene and established herself as an important Iranian writer. In *Ahl-e Gharq*, she mystified readers with magical realism and innovative stylistic technique inspired by her childhood. The novel recounts a day when the sky turns black, seawater inundates the homes of the townspeople, and men and women are forced to flee their homes, leaving the townspeople to rely on dance, music, and the prayers of females to stop the disaster. The story is a testament to and celebration of women's unusual and exceptional bravery in the face of destruction.[4] The imagistic novel served as inspiration to Iranian artist Shireen Neshat's piece *Rapture*

[2]Kamran Talatoff, "Iranian Women's Literature: From Pre-Revolutionary Social Discourse to Post-Revolutionary Feminism," *International Journal of Middle East Studies*, Vol. 29, No. 4 (Nov., 1997): 531-52.
[3]Kamran Talatoff, "The Politics of Writing in Iran: A History of Modern Persian Literature (New York: Syracuse University Press, 2000), 148-158.
[4]Nasrin Rahimieh, "Magical Realism in Moniru Ravanipur's Ahl-e Gharq." *Iranian Studies* 23, No. 1/4 (1990): 61-75; M.R. Ghanoonparvar, "Introduction to Satan's Stones (Austin, Texas: University of Austin Press, 1996), vii-viii.

(1999), which is comprised of two black and white screens, one populated by 100 women, and the other by 100 men. The men engage in trivial actions, while the women perform important acts such as prayer, ululation, transporting a boat to sea, and then sailing off.[5] This interplay between text and the visual arts is representative of Ravanipur's lifelong passion for all artistic disciplines.

After the publication of *Ahl-e Gharq*, Ravanipur completed two more novels, *Del-e Fulad* (Heart of Steel, 1990), and *Kowli Kenar-e Atesh* (Gypsy by the Fire, 1999). Ravanipur published *Sang-e Shaytan* (Satan's Stones), a collection of short stories, in 1991, but it was quickly banned for inappropriate content. In 1993, she published her third short story collection, *Siriya, Siriya,* and a fourth collection, *Zan-e Ferankfort* (Frankfurt Airport's Women), in 2001. In addition to her novels and short story collections, she has written a compilation of southern Iranian legends and beliefs, including *Afsaneha va bavarha-ye Jonub* (The Fairy Tales and Beliefs of Southern Iran's Region), which was published in 1989. She has also compiled children's stories based off her grandmother's stories from her youth.[6]

Afsaneh (first edition 1990)—a forename, which means "legend" in Persian—is not based on Ravanipur's childhood, although autobiographic elements are interspersed through the novel. The author's experiences as a graveyard shift nurse in the early 1980s and her work on the Iran–Iraqi war

---

[5]Negar Mottahedeh, "After-Images of a Revolution, "*Radical History Review*, Issue 86 (Spring 2003): 183-92.

[6] M.R. Ghanoonparvar, vii-xiii. Also see *www.moniruravanipur.com*.

front serve as creative inspiration. Magical realism intertwined with the bitter realities of contemporary Iran characterize this novel, in which Ravanipur pushes the boundaries of temporal space, disrupting the notion of traditional textual layouts within the novel. The postmodern narrative tells the story of a single, thirty-year old female writer whose last name is Sar-Boland, a name

which can be translated literally to "holding one's head up with pride, dignity, and conceit." Ms. Sar-Boland struggles to carve a space for herself in a chaotic society that has been ravaged by the scars of war. Childhood tragedies combined with the devastations of the Iran–Iraq war and an abusive marriage drove her mad. One night, she escapes her husband, alone, in a thin orange dress, and creates a new life. Tainted by the shame of being alone in the night and accused by her father and society of illicit behavior on the

night she cannot remember, she begins to unravel, mixing the present with memories of the past. She protects herself by creating an imaginary world full of invented characters. The Dictator (an oppressor) and the Horseman (a man searching for love, adventure, and freedom) travel along with her, pulling her in different directions, similar to the metaphorical devil and angel riding on her shoulders. These characters oftentimes become as real to the reader as they are to Ms. Sar-Boland.

The plot tosses between dream state and reality, as fantasies and flashbacks juxtapose tangible, present circumstances. By continually shifting between what was and what is now, Afsaneh finds herself adrift in time as well as space. The very act of writing her own version of history empowers Afsaneh to recreate her own reality, allowing her to imagine new and fluid spaces of discourse. She bases the subjects of her story through her own creative process; in doing so, her once absent voice becomes strikingly present. Indeed, she often evokes Shahrazad from *One Thousand and One Nights* because of the central role of writing and storytelling in the narrative.[7] Ravanipur finds herself on solid ground as she leans on the richness of the Eastern tradition to instill hope in a narrative dealing with the severe historical and cultural dislocations existing in contemporary Iran. The central themes woven throughout this novel include: gender issues, drug abuse,

---

[7] Rebecca Joubin, translation and introduction to Heart of Steel, an excerpt from a novel by Moniru Ravanipur, in *Radical Society* (Vol. 30, Issue 3-4, 2003):95-102.

madness and schizophrenia, the Iran–Iraq war, the impact of the Iranian Revolution on today's youth, generational dislocations, the concept of historical truth, and the act of writing and literary creation.

According to Ravanipur, this is the first novel in contemporary Iranian literature that depicts an intellectual single woman, with all of the psychological components of her struggle to find her way. Yet Ravanipur, despite her heroine, insists that this is not a feminist novel, though there are elements of female oppression woven throughout the text. In this story we see a solitary, scholarly woman imbued with interior monologues. As the forces of the horseman and the dictator tear her in different directions, she struggles with both external oppression and internal repression. As Ravanipur says, "She is like many others who, on the one hand, oppose dictators, but also unconsciously mimic autocratic behavior of dictators when in positions of power."[8] Her harsh critique of other writers' works and her cruel, condescending behavior toward her young secretary, who dreams of becoming a writer, expose her internal struggle with a dictatorial mindset. It is easy to oppose a dictator but hard to acknowledge the despotic elements of one's own personality. And so we see that the novel is about the human condition, the impact of war, oppression, violence, the essence of dictatorship and its impact on human society, and the breakdown of social relations. Indeed, the legacy of violence shapes its future perpetuators.

Ravanipur was one of the seventeen activists to face trial in Iran for her participation in the 2000 Berlin Conference on politics, where they discussed the country's reform movement and consequently were accused of participating in anti-Iran propaganda. In 2006, police removed copies of her current works from bookstore shelves as part of a countrywide government initiative. From January to June 2007, she served as the fourth International Writers Project Fellow at Brown University's Watson Institute.[9] For three years, from 2007 to 2010, Moniru Ravanipur was a writer in residence at the Las Vegas City of Asylum, which gives refuge to writers who are forced to escape persecution in their home countries.[10]

---

[8] Translator's interview with Moniru Ravanipur, 14 April 2012.

[9] Motoko Rich, "For Writers, a Voice Beyond the Page," April 24, 2007, *http://www.nytimes.com/2007/04/24/books/24pen.html?_r=0*;

Taylor Brown, "Iranian Author Ravanipour Takes Refuge at Brown," March 9, 2007, *http://www.browndailyherald.com/2007/03/09/iranian-author-ravanipour-takes-refuge-at-brown/.*

[10] Megan Edwards, "Vegas Unexpected: City of Asylum," January 9, 2010, *http://living-las-vegas.com/?p=13123.*

My translation is based on the third edition of *Del-e Fulad* published in 2000. It is an honor for me to acknowledge my former professor of Persian, Manouchehr Kasheff, who met with me on a weekly basis during the 2001–2002 academic year while I was a doctoral student at Columbia University to answer my questions regarding historical and linguistic issues in the original Persian novel. He found for me the exact page references to the book *Tarikh-e Zandiyya* written by Ebn al-Karim Alia Reza Shirazi to which Moniru Ravanipur often refers in the first few chapters. There is no way I can thank him enough for his patience, dedication, and giving spirit. Many years later, during the spring of 2012, he was willing to confirm my English transliteration of Persian words and phrases. It is hard to imagine where I would be

today without the guidance and support of Hamid Dabashi, my mentor at Columbia University. His extraordinary passion for teaching and research is the source of my daily inspiration. Moniru Ravanipur gave me freedom to transform and change certain phrases in order to keep the melody in translation. I am grateful for her willingness to answer my questions, and then to ultimately give me freedom to make my own decisions with respect to interpretation. With her consultation, the title was changed from *Heart of Steel* to *Afsaneh*. Her responses to my questions about her life and work have also contributed to the content of this introduction.

I thank Clark Ross, Dean of Faculty, for his unwavering support for my teaching and research at Davidson College. My Malcolm O. Partin Professorship awarded in the spring of 2011, provided the funds for research assistants I needed to follow through on this project I had begun as a doctoral student at Columbia University. In particular, I would like to thank Kelly Granger and Christine Noah for their incisive critique and meticulous attention to detail on the final draft of this translation. I am grateful to my parents, Behnaz and Jahan, for their continual support. Finally, I thank my daughter Jana, whose sweet and patient personality, created the atmosphere that allowed me to carry this translation through to completion. It is an honor for me to dedicate this translation to her. This novel has been an important part of my life for years, and I am thankful to finally present it in translation to an English-speaking audience.

— Glossary —

Afrasiyab .... A character from Shahnameh(The Epic of the Kings), the national epic of Persia. Written by the tenth century poet Ferdowsi, the Shahnameh is a compilation of episodes beginning with the creation of the world and ending with the Arab invasion of Iran. Afrasiyab, the king of Turan king, was the father of Farangis. He would later kill Siyavash, Farangis' husband.

Afsaneh .... Legend, Tale.

Agha .... Sir.

Ash .... a thick soup made of various greens such as mint, parsley, and herbs. It is often served with yogurt.

Ash-e Poshte Pa .... A kind of ash (commonly *ash-e reshteh*) prepared three days after a family member has left on a trip, and taken to friends and also given to the poor.

Azar......................... The month in the Iranian calendar from approximately November 20 through December 22. The exact calendar date changes from year to year.

Bahman .... The month in the Iranian calendar from approximately January 21 through February 21.

Bani Sadr .... Bani Sadr Abolhasan was born in 1933 or 1934 into a family of Ayatollahs from Hamadan. After studying theology and then sociology at the university, he became an opponent of the Shah's regime. Throughout the 1950s, he was an active supporter of Mossadeq and the National Front. Forced into exile in France, he pursued his studies in economics and sociology and became the leader of students abroad opposed to the Shah's regime. Early in 1980, Bani Sadr was elected the first president of the Islamic Republic with seventy-five percent of the vote. He was soon caught in a power struggle with the clerics and dismissed from office in 1981.

Befarmayid .... A polite expression used as an introductory part or the replacement of an imperative phrase or a request.

Bozorg .... Big.

Chador .... A large veil worn by a woman to cover her body and dress.

Dah Shahi .... Persian currency, equivalent to the penny.

Dakhil .... A piece of ribbon or cloth that is tied around a shrine in the hopes that a particular wish will be granted. (The shrine may even be a venerated tree).

Dervish .... An ascetic religious adherent who shuns material possessions and wealth, taking pride in his own poverty.

Enghilab .... Revolution.

Farangis .... A character in the *Shahnameh*. She was married to Siyavash, who was later killed by her father, Afrasiyab.

Genghis Khan .... Mongol warrior known for his cruelty and atrocities in Iran and other conquered territories.

Hajj/Hajji .... A title of respect given to an old man or to a man who has made the pilgrimage to Mecca.

Hammam .... Public bath.

Hero of Zand .... Refers to Lotf-Ali Khan Zand, the last ruler of the Zand Dynasty. His six-year reign was filled with bloody fighting until, in 1795, he was captured, blinded, and killed by the Eunuch Agha Mohammad Khan. Indeed, he was blinded in the presence of his own servants, and Mohammad Agha Khan even ordered his servants to sodomize Lotf-Ali Khan. The italicized passages describing the history of the Hero of Zand are taken from the text

Tarikh-e Zandiyya written by Ebn al-Karim Ali
Reza Shirazi, ed. Ernst Beer, Leiden, 1888.

Inshahallah .... "God willing."

Ironsides .... General Ironsides, the British chief of military
mission stationed in Iran at the turn of the century.
He helped bring Reza Shah to power.

Jamadi-al-aval .... The fifth month of the Islamic calendar which
begin with the migration of the Prophet
Mohammad from Mecca to Medina in 622 A.D.
Islamic months, which are lunar, are approximately
29–30 days long.

Jan .... Literally, "dear soul." The expression is often used
after someone's first name and means "sweet, dar-
ling."

Jinn .... Genie.

Karbala .... Karbala is a holy city in Iraq. The martyrdom of the
Prophet Mohammad's grandson, Husayn, at Kar-
bala has had an enormous impact on Shi'is
throughout the ages. In addition to the Shrine of
Husayn, Karbala holds the Shrine of 'Abbas as well
as the shrines of other members of Ali's family.
Through the years, Karbala has developed into an
important religious center and site of pilgrimage.

Kashkool .... A cup suspended by a chain and carried by a
Dervish.

Key Kavus .... A Kayanid king in the *Shahnameh*. During Kavus'
reign, the war between Iran and Turan intensified,
due in part to a dispute between Kavus and his son,
Siyavash, who escaped to the court of the Turanian
king, Afrasiyab. Later, however, Siyavash would be
killed by Afrasiyab, who had become his father-in-
law.

Khajeh .... A title originally used in the sense of the "director
of…, chief, vizier." Later it was used to refer to a

eunuch, a castrated male, who guarded the harem. The eunuch was the master of the house.

Khan .... Title of respect placed before or after the first name of a man when addressing him. It can mean vizier, gentleman, or master.

Khanom .... Title of respect placed before or after the first name of a woman when addressing her.

Khodat Bedeh Madar May God take care of your needs.

Khodaya .... Oh, my God.

Kiseh .... A small rigid cloth bag into which the hand is placed. It is used in the public bath or shower to rub the skin and clean off the dead skin.

Koofti .... Despicable, miserable. Literally translates to 'syphilitic.'

Kowkab .... Dahlia.

Loobiya Pollo .... A popular Persian dish consisting of beans, meat, and rice.

Man .... A unit of weight, about 3 kilos.

Mantow .... From the French *manteau*. An outer garment.

Marg Bar Bad Hejab . A revolutionary slogan that means "death to the woman who is not wearing her headscarf and *manteau* properly."

Medes .... An ancient Iranian people who established the first Iranian empire in the first millennium. BC.

Mehr .... The Persian month of kindness. The period on the Persian calendar extends from approximately September 20 to October 20.

Melamin .... Enameled metal used to make various kitchen accessories in Iran such as tea kettles, cups, and plates.

Moshtagh .... Moshtagh Ali Shah, an early 18th century Sufi who prayed and played the *seh-tar* at the same time. He added a fourth string to the *seh-tar*. This was a period of great resentment against the Sufis. Moshtagh was killed and cut into pieces by a mob in a mosque.

Nahid........................ A goddess of the Zoroastrian religion, the religion of Iran before Islam. The word 'Nahid' literally means immaculate.' She lives in water and is the deity of running streams and purity.

Narenj........................ Bitter orange.

Qajar .... A monarchical dynasty which ruled Iran from 1779–1925. Like its Safavid predecessors, it was a weakly centralized regime that faced strong provincial tribal forces as well as an increasingly autonomous religious establishment.

Rostam .... is the greatest of all the heroes of the *Shahnameh*. The majority of his heroic deeds take place during the reign of King Kavus. Rostam's appearance in the *Shahnameh* spans three centuries, and in the end he would be killed in vengeance for having caused the death of the Shah Esfandiyar.

Salam........................ Greetings. Hello.

Salavat...................... A special formula of praise and greeting to God, Mohammad, and his descendents. Sometimes said when asking God for forgiveness because of a bad thought, or said when asking for luck. Often used on solemn occasions.

Samovar .... A Russian tea urn in which the water is heated by charcoal burning slowly in an inner container.

Sar-Boland .... Holding one's head up high with pride and dignity; conceit.

Seh-Tar...................... A plucked instrument with four strings, which is smaller than the tar *and lower in pitch.*

Shahrazad .... The narrator of One Thousand and One Nights, who marries the Monarch Shahriyar in order to liberate the world of his tyranny.

Sham'dani .... Geraniums.

Tabbal .... Drummer. *Khajeh Tabbal* literally means "Mr. Drummer," and it indicates that this person is from a family of drummers. The drum is beat historically in Iran on many occasions, such as to make an announcement, to honor someone or something, at the time of an execution, on special occasions, at dusk and dawn, and at shrines and the occurrence of miracles.

Tar .... A plucked instrument with six strings.

Toman .... Persian currency. In early 2002, there were approximately 800 *tomans* to the American dollar.

Turan Zamin .... In the *Shahnameh*, this is a land at the northeast border of Iran and is known as the land of the Turanians, who were the enemies of Iran.

Urmia .... A city in northwest Azerbaijan.

Zand Dynasty .... An Iranian dynasty, begun in Shiraz and Esfahan, which lasted less than 50 years, from 1749–1795.

Zar .... The brand name of a local cigarette, literally translates to 'gold.'

CPSIA information can be obtained at www.ICGtesting.com
Printed in the USA
LVOW08s2207250214

375200LV00005B/346/P